C. F. Raymund Palmer

The Life of Philip Thomas Howard, O.P. Cardinal of Norfolk

C. F. Raymund Palmer

The Life of Philip Thomas Howard, O.P. Cardinal of Norfolk

ISBN/EAN: 9783744657334

Printed in Europe, USA, Canada, Australia, Japan

Cover: Foto ©Raphael Reischuk / pixelio.de

More available books at **www.hansebooks.com**

THE LIFE

OF

PHILIP THOMAS HOWARD, O.P.,

CARDINAL OF NORFOLK,

GRAND ALMONER TO CATHERINE OF BRAGANZA

QUEEN-CONSORT OF KING CHARLES II.,

AND

RESTORER OF THE ENGLISH PROVINCE OF FRIAR-PREACHERS
OR DOMINICANS.

COMPILED FROM ORIGINAL MANUSCRIPTS.

WITH A SKETCH OF THE

RISE, MISSIONS, AND INFLUENCE OF THE
DOMINICAN ORDER,

AND OF ITS EARLY HISTORY IN ENGLAND.

BY
FR. C. F. RAYMUND PALMER, O.P.

LONDON:
THOMAS RICHARDSON AND SON;
DUBLIN; AND DERBY.
MDCCCLXVII.

TO

HENRY, DUKE OF NORFOLK,

THIS LIFE

OF

PHILIP THOMAS HOWARD, O.P.,

CARDINAL OF NORFOLK,

IS

AFFECTIONATELY DEDICATED

IN MEMORY OF THE

FAITH AND VIRTUES OF HIS FATHER.

Dominican Priory,
Woodchester, Gloucestershire.

PREFACE.

The following Life has been compiled mainly from original records and documents still preserved in the Archives of the English Province of Friar-Preachers. The work has at least this recommendation, that the matter is entirely new, as the MSS. from which it is taken have hitherto lain in complete obscurity. It is hoped that it will form an interesting addition to the Ecclesiastical History of England. In the acknowledging of great assistance from several friends, especial thanks are due to Philip H. Howard, Esq., of Corby Castle, who kindly supplied or directed attention to much valuable matter, and contributed a short but graphic sketch of the Life of the Cardinal of Norfolk taken by his father the late Henry Howard, Esq., from a MS. in the Library of the Minerva at Rome.

C. F. R. P.

Vidimus et Approbavimus :

F. Vincentius King, Prior, Sac. Theol. Lect. ;
F. V. H. Ferreri, Sacræ Theol. Lect.

Attentâ relatione duorum Revisorum Ordinis nostri à nobis designatorum super opus R. P. Fr. C. F. Raymundi Palmer, cui titulus: *The Life of Philip Thomas Howard, &c.* illud typis mandari permittimus.

Fr. J. D. Aylward,
S. Theol. Lect., Præd. Gen.,
Prior Prov. Ord. Præd. in Anglia.

Die 18° Aprilis, 1867.

CONTENTS.

INTRODUCTION.

CHAPTER I.

CHAPTER II.

CHAPTER V.

CHAPTER VI.

CHAPTER VII.

PAGE

returns into England. — Marriage of Charles II. and Catherine of Braganza. — F. Thomas Howard is made first chaplain to the queen.—He attempts to found a second convent near Dieppe; F. Vincent Torre; F. Lawrence Thwaits.—F. Peter Atwood alias Pitts; Henry Errington. —F. Thomas Howard visits his convent.—Brother Herman makes good the cellars.—Defence of theses by FF. John Canning and Lawrence Thwaits. — Profession of FF. Edward Bing and George Mildmay. — F. Thomas Howard returns to England.—Death of F. John Jenkin. — Brother Hyacinth Coomans 123

CHAPTER VIII.

Zeal of F. Thomas Howard as the royal chaplain.—The queen's and master-general's satisfaction.—He is continued prior of Bornhem.—Official appointments made by him.—F. Vincent Torre, sub-prior.—F. William Collins, confessor to the nuns at Vilvorde.—The sub-prior's injudicious government.—The secular college put down, and the scholars sent to Vilvorde. —John and Esme Howard.—Ill-arrangement of the schools. —F. Antoninus Wichart.—F. Albert de Groet.—Disquietude about the French observance.—The greater part of the Religious sent away to various houses.—Fruitless attempt to get fresh members.—Brother Henry Packe.—F. Peter Atwood.—F. Thomas Howard visits the convent.—Obtains ecclesiastical and civil leave to found the convent of nuns at Vilvorde.—Sister Barbara Boyle.—Sister Magdalen Sheldon. —Sister Catherine Mildmay.—Their house put under F. John Baptist Verjuyse prior of Antwerp.—F. William Collins sent to the English mission.—F. Joseph Vere.—F. Martin Russel: convent of Tangier passed over to the English province 130

CHAPTER IX.

CHAPTER X.

CHAPTER XII.

CHAPTER XIII.

CHAPTER XIV.

CHAPTER XV.

THE LIFE

OF

PHILIP THOMAS HOWARD, O.P.,

CARDINAL OF NORFOLK.

INTRODUCTION.

The work which we have here taken in hand is the simple narrative of the Life of an English nobleman, who laid his rank and riches aside, and became a poor Mendicant Friar. To a Religious who keeps strictly bound to his holy duties, those varied incidents and changing fortunes can seldom happen, which charm the imagination and teach so much in the biographies of great men in the world. Still, the history of Philip Howard of Norfolk is interesting and useful, because he played a great part in civil and ecclesiastical affairs during the times of the last two English kings of the house of Stuart, and did honour to his Order by giving fresh life to the Dominican Province of England.

I.

The Order of Friar-Preachers sprang up early in the thirteenth century. The founder of it, St. Dominic,* was born in the year 1170 at Calareuga in the diocese of Osma and kingdom of Old Castile. His father Felix Gusman was one of the grandees of Spain, and his mother Jane de Aza came of a noble family. The virtue of the Gusmans was greater than their rank. Dominic's mother is now among the Blessed of the Church, as well as his second brother Mannez who joined the Order, whilst his eldest brother Anthony, a secular priest, was famed for his holy life. The

---

* We refer our readers to Lacordaire's "Life of St. Dominic," translated by W. G. Abraham, Dublin, 1851; and to "The Life of St. Dominic, with a Sketch of the Dominican Order," London, 1857.

legends tell us that wonders went with the birth of Dominic. Shortly before he came into the world, his mother dreamed that she bore a spotted dog which carried a lighted torch in its mouth and set the world on fire; and at his baptism his godmother saw a bright star upon his brow: foretokens of the zeal and success of his Order, and of the holiness which has placed him on the Altar. From his childhood he led an austere life, although he passed ten years amidst the allurements of a student's life in the university of Palencia. Even then in his great charity he sold all the little he had, in order to help the needy, and did not shrink from offering himself to Moorish slavery that he might ransom a poor captive.

When he was twenty-four years old Dominic became a priest. About the same time canons-regular of St. Augustine were placed at the cathedral of Osma; Dominic was called into their number, and put on the canon's habit. In 1203 he went with Diego de Azevedo, bishop of Osma, on an embassy that took him twice to the royal court of Denmark. On his way towards the north he passed through Toulouse, and deeply was he moved on seeing how frightfully the Albigenses had overrun Languedoc with their false teaching and laid the Church waste with fire and sword. He longed to rid that fair province of its heresies and bring it back to the Catholic faith. In returning from Denmark the second time, in 1205, the bishop and Dominic made a pilgrimage to Rome, when Diego in vain begged the pope to let him lay aside his bishopric to go and preach among the Cuman Tartars, who were plundering the eastern parts of Europe. They then turned their steps towards Spain. In the neighbourhood of Montpellier they met with three papal legates and several other Cistercian abbots, whom the pope had charged to put down the Albigensian heresy, as the bishops and pastors neglected to guard their flocks from the wolves. There Diego found his true Tartar mission, and

Dominic full scope for his pent-up zeal. The bishop had leave from the pope to preach for two years in Languedoc. The Cistercian legates and abbots had set about their work in all the pomp of their high estate, and had failed of success. But now following the advice and example of the bishop, on whom, says the historian, the Spirit of God came, they sent away their followers, horses, and carriages. Then as purseless, scripless, and shoeless as the seventy-two disciples of Christ, they went forth with power and signs.

Dominic was one of the few ecclesiastics whom the bishop kept with him out of his retinue. The little band of missioners preached throughout all the country, to the Catholics in churches, and to the Albigenses in public places and private houses. Such were the good effects of Dominic's toils, that all the successes in Languedoc have been set down to him, though the bishop was the real head of the mission. Dominic, indeed, was the very soul of it, and drew down upon himself the wrath of the baffled Albigenses, so that he often ran the risk of his life. But his dauntless courage and child-like trust in Providence carried him through every difficulty and snare. He found that many Catholic children, especially females of noble but reduced families, fell through poverty into the hands of the Albigenses, or being badly brought up became an easy prey to error. With the aid of Fulk, bishop of Toulouse, in 1206, he founded a convent* adjoining the church of Notre Dame, at Prouille, a small village near Montreal at the foot of the Pyrenees. In this house, many ladies found a safe shelter from the moral corruption around them, and numbers were

* We have used the word *convent* for the Religious of both sexes, though in England the houses of men are popularly called *monasteries*. In strict language the Latin *conventus* is applied to men, and *monasterium* to women; but the English meaning of the words is now reversed.

educated in a Christian manner. Dominic put this convent under the Rule of St. Augustine, and added certain Constitutions: it was governed by a prioress, but he kept it under his own control, so that it afterwards became the mother-house of the nuns of the Order.

When the bishop went back to his diocese in 1207 he gave up the mission of Languedoc to Dominic, who soon found himself almost alone, for the Cistercians withdrew to their monasteries and the Spaniards into their own country. This was a heavy trial to Dominic, for almost overwhelming difficulties were gathering around him. In 1208 the Albigenses crowned their crimes with the open murder of the Papal Legate: all Christendom was aroused, and a crusade was proclaimed against them which lasted for many years. Dominic's energies rose with every occasion. Seven or eight French and Spanish priests soon joined him and amongst them his own brother Mannez: he drew up a rule of life for them, but they were not bound to him by any other tie than their own choice. Still this was the foreshadow of the coming Order. Dominic dwelt chiefly at Fanjeaux in the neighbourhood of Notre Dame de Prouille, and at Carcassonne, one of the head-quarters of the Albigenses. He took no part in the terrible warfare between the Catholics and the heretics. His great weapon was the Most Holy Rosary of the Blessed Virgin, revealed to him by Mary herself, it is said, in her sanctuary of Drache which was one of his favourite resorts. He went among the crusaders and found disorders, vice, and ignorance as great as those of the Albigenses; for most of the mercenaries joined the Catholic army only for the sake of bloodshed and plunder: and them too he strove to recall to morality and virtue. His work was blessed with many miracles. In 1211 he was praying in a church on the banks of the Garonne near Toulouse which the crusaders were besieging, when he was disturbed by the cries of the people outside. A band of forty English pilgrims wending their way to the shrine of St. James of Compostella had been upset in a boat whilst crossing the Garonne. When he reached the river the pilgrims had sunk beneath the water, and not one was to be seen. He threw himself on the ground in silent prayer, and then rising cried, "I command you all in the name of Christ to come to the bank." The pilgrims immediately rose to the surface, and all landed safely with the help of some soldiers, who flung their shields and reached their lances to them.

Dominic laboured for ten years in Languedoc. In 1213 he was for a short time vicar of the bishop of Carcassonne. He had long dwelt on the idea of forming an Order which should follow the highest counsels of the Gospel and preach its morality to the world. In 1215 he began his foundation at Toulouse. He was joined there by two wealthy citizens, and one of them gave up his house to him for the use of his brethren. There were only seven altogether: they wore the habit of canons-regular of St. Augustine which Dominic had always kept, and betook themselves to a life of poverty and prayer under a conventual rule.

The new Order was powerfully aided by Fulk, bishop of Toulouse, who gave a sixth part of the tithes of his diocese to support the brethren. As it was necessary for the Roman See to approve the Order, Dominic in the fall of the year went to Rome with the bishop, who had to attend the great Lateran council. Innocent III. confirmed the foundation at Prouille and took it under the protection of the Holy See, but he hesitated in respect to the Order as the general council had just forbidden new Orders to be formed. It is said that a dream, in which he saw the Lateran basilica tottering and upheld by Dominic, settled his doubts. He sent for Dominic, approved his plan, and bade him go back to his companions, and according to the decree of the council choose the rule of some old Order for his own.

Dominic's brotherhood had not yet any name but that of *Preachers.* About this time Innocent had to write to them. When the secretary asked how the letters were to be directed, he replied, "*To Brother Dominic and his companions.*" Then hesitating he said, "No let it be *To Brother Dominic and those who preach with him in the country of Toulouse.*" Again stopping he said, "Write *To Master Dominic and the Brother-Preachers.*" And thus the title of Friar-Preachers was taken for the Order.

Early in the following spring Dominic went back to Toulouse. Whilst he was away his little company had increased from seven to sixteen: eight were Frenchmen, seven were Spaniards, and one was an Englishman named Lawrence who is *said* to have been one of the pilgrims saved from drowning in the Garonne. In April Dominic and his sixteen *Freres* (or Friars) met at Prouille and chose the Rule of St. Augustine, which being very simple could be moulded into almost any form; and to it were added particular Constitutions from the Premonstratentians, so as to form an admirable code of laws for the new Order. To the three great religious vows of chastity, poverty, and obedience, were joined, the divine office (with midnight matins) in choir, perpetual abstinence, fasting from Holy Cross day (Sept. 14th) to Easter and on all Fridays and certain vigils, cloistral silence, and the close study of the divine and human sciences; with preaching to the faithful and to infidels and giving the Sacraments of Penance and the Holy Eucharist.* Thus the contemplative life of the cœnobite

* The Order inherits the peculiar spirit of its Founder in his devotion towards the Blessed Sacrament, towards the Blessed Virgin particularly in the Most Holy Rosary, and towards the dead. The feast and octave of Corpus Christi are kept by the Dominicans with extraordinary solemnities equal to those of Easter and Christmas. The full office of the dead said chorally every

and the active life of the missionary were united: the duties of Mary and Martha were blended into one harmonious service.

When Dominic got back to Toulouse the bishop and chapter gave him three churches in the diocese; close to that of St. Romanus in the city he built a convent and removed from the private house. In September he took a copy of the rule to Rome, but met with some delay in having it approved, as Innocent III. had died and his successor was at Perugia. At last he obtained two bulls, December 22nd, from Honorius III. sanctioning and confirming the Order. For some months he was kept by the pope to preach in Rome, which he did with wonderful success. He often saw the servants and followers of the cardinals idling about the antechambers of the sacred palace and wasting their time in gambling, whilst their masters were taken up with the affairs of the Church. He was pained at such sad conduct and suggested to the pope how useful it would be to have some one for instructing and reforming them. The pope thereupon created the office of Master of the Sacred Palace and appointed Dominic to it. Many important duties have been added to this office, as the Master is now the pope's theologian, and censor of all works published in Rome, assists in consistories, grants the degree of doctor of divinity at court after the examination, and names the pope's preachers: the charge has always been held by a Dominican. In May 1217 Dominic was again at St. Romanus bent on the spread of his Order. On the feast of the Assumption (Aug. 15th) the sixteen friars met at Prouille and made the profession of the

---

week (except at Easter and Pentecost) was imposed, in 1551, in place of the vigil of three lessons, which before was used daily. The Order of St. Dominic still keeps its first liturgy and rites.

three solemn vows in his hands, and the nuns added to theirs a fourth vow of enclosure. The *Dogs of the Lord* were now let loose to cast that fire on the earth which He longed so much to kindle. Two of the friars were to remain at Prouille for directing the nuns and two at Toulouse; seven and among them Lawrence the Englishman were sent to establish the Order in Paris, and four into Spain and Portugal, whilst one was to go into the East with Dominic, whose day-dream was to gain infidels to Christ or to win the palm of martyrdom. They chose one to govern the Order in their founder's absence and styled him abbot: a title never used again, for since 1220 the head of the Order has been called simply the master-general.

After taking several fresh subjects into the Order Dominic started out a fourth time for Rome, and arrived there about the close of the year, on his way to those eastern countries, which he was never to reach. Pope Honorius treated him very kindly and gave him the church of St. Sixtus for a convent. Whilst the half-built house next the church was being finished Dominic gave theological lectures in the sacred palace and in the city and preached in many of the churches. He had been divinely guided to the great and crying want of the age: evangelical poverty against worldliness, and zeal against lukewarmness; and by ministering to the keenest spiritual yearnings of the heart, he reached the feelings of the people. His winning speech and holy manners, with his fame as the Thaumaturgus or great wonder-worker of the time, drew immense crowds around him, and he soon numbered a hundred disciples in his new cloister. His frequent miracles, even to bringing the dead back to life, were the talk of Rome and all the neighbouring country.

"While the brethren were still living at St. Sixtus and were a hundred in number, on a certain day blessed Dominic ordered Friar John of Calabria and Friar Albert the Roman to go about the city and quest for alms. But they employed themselves to no purpose from morning till the third hour of the day. They were going home again and had already reached the church of St. Anastasia, when a woman met them who was very devout towards the Order: seeing that they were carrying nothing back she gave them a loaf, saying, 'I will not have you return quite empty.' A little farther on a man came up and earnestly begged charity. They excused themselves from giving because they had nothing for themselves; but as the man only went on to press them all the more they said to each other, 'What shall we do with one loaf? Let us give it him for the love of God.' Then they gave him the bread; and forthwith they lost sight of him. Now as they were going into the convent the pious Father, to whom the Holy Ghost had already shown what had passed, went to meet them, and said with a cheerful voice, 'Children, have you nothing?' 'No, Father,' they answered; and they told him what had happened, and how they had given the loaf to a poor man. He said to them, 'It was an angel of the Lord. The Lord will know how to feed His own. Let us go and pray.' Thereupon he went into the church, and coming out in a short time he told the brethren to call the community into the refectory. 'But, holy Father,' they said, 'how can you have us call them, as there is nothing for them?' And they purposely delayed to do what he told them. On this the blessed Father sent for Friar Roger the cellarer and commanded him to assemble the brethren for dinner, for the Lord would see to their wants. Then the cloths were laid and the cups were set out, and at the signal the whole community went into the refectory. The holy Father gave the blessing, and when all were seated Friar Henry the Roman began the reading. Meanwhile blessed Dominic was praying with his hands clasped upon the table: when lo! all at once, just as he had promised by the inspiration of the Holy Ghost, two beautiful young men ministers of Divine Providence appeared in the midst of the refectory carrying loaves in two white napkins, which hung from their shoulders before and behind. They began to give out the bread from the lowest rows one on the right and the other on the left, and set a whole wonderfully-beautiful loaf before each brother. And when they had come to blessed Dominic and had likewise put a whole loaf before him they bowed their heads and vanished, without any one knowing to this day whither they went or whence they came. Blessed Dominic said, 'My brethren, eat the bread the Lord hath sent you.' Then he told the serving brothers to pour out the wine; but they answered, 'Holy Father, there is none.' Then the blessed Father full of the prophetic spirit said to them, 'Go to the cask and pour out for the brethren the wine the Lord hath sent them.' So they went and found the cask brimful of excellent wine, which they hastened to carry. And blessed Dominic said, 'Drink, my brethren, of the wine the Lord hath sent you.' Then they eat and drank as much as they would, that day and the next and the day after. But after the meal on the third day he had all of the bread and wine over given to the poor, and would not have any of it kept longer in the house." Friar Lawrence of England, who had been called from Paris to Rome, was present; and he and others who were there told all about it to the nuns of St. Mary beyond Tiber and even gave them some of the bread and wine, which they long kept as relics. Hence in the Order came the custom of serving from the lowest tables upwards and of gathering up the crumbs after meals.

In summer 1218 Dominic went to Bologna, where the year before a house had been formed; thence to Toulouse and before Christmas he was at Segovia in Old Castile, where he gathered many disciples together in a convent. Then he went to Madrid and changed the house raised there into a convent for sisters. Many other houses were founded in Spain; but what share Dominic himself had in them is not certain. He established his great Confraternity of the Rosary everywhere he went. In April 1219 he was again at Toulouse, and about June went to Paris, where the friars after suffering the greatest want for two months had settled in a convent and had the church of St. James. At first some of them had trembled to go to Paris and perhaps would have given it up altogether had it not been for Friar Lawrence the Englishman. "For as they drew nigh to that large city they went along in much doubt and sorrow, because in their humility they greatly feared to preach in such a renowned university, where there were so many famous doctors and masters skilful in sacred science. But to give them courage, God let His servant Lawrence know all that would afterwards happen to this mission and all the favours He and the Blessed Virgin would show them in their house of St. James and all the bright stars both of holiness and learning that would rise thence and enlighten not only the Order but the whole Church. Which revelation as it greatly comforted the soul of Friar Lawrence, he likewise told to his companions, to enliven them also. And they believed it for the opinion they all had of the holiness of that servant of God and they had a lively faith. Wherefore they went joyfully into the city; and all things happened there as he had foretold."

Dominic found thirty Religious at Paris. After he had settled their discipline he sent out some to establish houses in various cities of France, as at Limoges, Lyons, Rheims, Poitiers and Orleans. At Paris too he met Alexander II. of Scotland, who pressed him to send some of the brethren into his kingdom and promised them his royal countenance. On his way back to Bologna he founded convents at Avignon, Asti, Bergamo, and Milan. In the course of eight months he had spread his Order throughout all Spain and France.

At midsummer 1219 Dominic was again at Bologna and sent some of his brethren to preach in all the north of Italy. Towards the end of the year he made his fifth visit to Rome. At that time nuns were not generally required to keep strictly enclosed and they spent their leisure-hours in entertaining relatives and friends at home and in visiting them abroad. The evils of such a lax discipline made Innocent III. anxious to gather all the nuns of Rome into one house of enclosure to be added to the church of St. Sixtus. Even his authority quailed in the storm of tongues which the encroachment on ancient rights and privileges stirred up. Innocent died before the building of the convent was finished. Honorius III. tasked Dominic with the reform, and joined with him the cardinals Ugolino bishop of Ostia, Stephen of Fossa Nuova, and Nicholas bishop of Frascati.* Dominic strove to follow out the plan of Innocent III. and offered to give up the convent of St. Sixtus to the nuns. For some time he did no good, but at last the nuns of St. Mary beyond Tiber, who had stood out most of all, yielded to his holy words and even vowed obedience to him. On Ashwednesday, which that year (1220) fell on February 11th, the three cardinals and Dominic met in the chapter-room of St. Sixtus where the abbess gave up her authority to Dominic and his brethren. "Whilst blessed Dominic was seated with the cardinals," says an eye-witness, "the abbess and all her nuns being present, lo! a

---

* Many later authors say that this happened in 1218. Such a date does not at all tally with what took place about that time, and moreover it clashes with pontifical grants to the friars and the nuns. We have followed the learned editor of the *Bullarium Ordinis Prædicatorum*, as he has the best ancient historians on his side and is guiltless of any anachronisms.

Nicholas cardinal-bishop of Frascati was not raised to his high rank in the Church till 1219, so that the reform of the nuns could not have been earlier than that year.

man rushed in tearing his hair and uttering loud cries. When he was asked the cause he said, 'The nephew of my lord Stephen has just fallen from his horse and is killed.' Now the young man's name was Napoleon. His uncle hearing it fell fainting on the breast of blessed Dominic. They supported him, and Blessed Dominic rose and threw holy water on him and then leaving him in the arms of others ran to the spot where the young man's body was lying bruised and horribly mangled. He ordered them to remove it directly into another room and to keep it there. Then he desired brother Tancred and the rest to get everything ready for Mass. Blessed Dominic, the cardinals, friars, the abbess and her nuns all went to the place where the altar stood, and blessed Dominic offered up the Holy Sacrifice with many tears. And when he came to elevate the Body of the Lord and held it up between his hands as usual, he was himself raised a palm from the ground in the sight of all and to their great wonder. When Mass was over he went back to the body of the dead man, along with the cardinals, abbess, nuns and the others. And when he was there he straightened the limbs one by one with his holy hands. Then he prostrated himself on the ground praying and weeping. Thrice he touched the face and limbs of the dead man to put them in their place, and thrice he prostrated himself. When he had risen the third time he stood by the head and made the sign of the Cross; and then with his hands stretched out towards heaven and his body raised more than a palm from the ground he cried out with a loud voice, 'O young man, Napoleon, in the name of our Lord Jesus Christ, I say to thee, arise.' And immediately before all those who had been drawn together by such a wonderful sight the young man arose unhurt and said to the blessed Dominic, 'Father, give me to eat.' And blessed Dominic gave him to eat and drink and restored him joyful and scarless to his uncle the cardinal." In grateful thanks to Heaven for his nephew being thus wonderfully brought back to life cardinal Stephen gave to the convent of St. Sixtus the yearly rent of fifty marks (£33. 6*s*. 8*d*.) out of the revenues of the parish-church of Bamborough in Northumberland. This church then belonged to the monastery of St. Oswald of Nostel in Yorkshire: the sub-prior and cellarer who happened to be at the Roman court agreed to the gift, which was confirmed by Honorius III. and in 1244 by Innocent IV. The nuns enjoyed the rent for two hundred years, when it was disputed and fell into arrears, till in 1428 land in Italy and 3086 florins of gold were given in place of it.

On the first Sunday in Lent following (Feb. 15th) the nuns, about forty in number, settled at St. Sixtus.* The first of them who begged of Dominic the habit of his Order was Sister Cecily, and she was followed by all the rest; and thus the third house of women was formed in the Order. Sister Cecily who was of the family of the Cesarini was then young. She afterwards became prioress of the convent of St. Agnes at Bologna, and about 1240 dictated to Sister Angelica what she had heard or seen of St. Dominic: we have taken her narratives of the two miracles at St. Sixtus.

From St. Sixtus, the friars removed to St. Sabina which the pope gave them. Among those who witnessed the raising of Napoleon Orsini were Ivo bishop of Cracow, and his two nephews Hyacinth and Ceslaus canons of his cathedral. The last two, with Henry of Moravia and Herman a German noble, entered the Order, and in a few months were sent out as missionaries. The apostolate of Hyacinth extended over the northern and eastern nations of Europe and into Asia even to China; while Ceslaus planted the Order in Bohemia. The first is now a canonized Saint, the second a Blessed in the Church. Henry went into Styria

* The nuns left St. Sixtus in 1572; and in 1602 it was given back to the friars.

and Austria and founded many convents particularly that of Vienna. Herman governed a convent at Friesach. One of the greatest who gave his name to the Order at St. Sabina was Reginald of Orleans, doctor of canon law in the university of Paris. Twice he had a vision of the Blessed Virgin bearing a white scapular as the habit of the new Order, in consequence of which Dominic had the linen surplice of the canons-regular laid aside.*

Honorius III. made Dominic, in a formal manner, master-general of the Order. Dominic called a general chapter of his brethren to meet at Pentecost (May 27th) in the convent of St. Nicholas at Bologna. In this chapter the laws of the abstinence and fasting and the authority of superiors were passed; and it was decreed that the brethren were not to have any property but to live solely on the alms of the faithful, and that the chapter should meet every year. Both these decrees had to be changed in after-ages. When charity grew cold and the desolation of the great Revolt stood in holy places, it was needful for the convents to have fixed revenues. And as the Order spread the fathers could not meet every year, nor was it so much called for when its government was firmly settled.†

---

* The full habit of the Friar-Preachers is, a tunic (with a girdle), a scapular hanging loose, and a capuce, all white. In public and during winter in choir a black cappa or cloak and capuce are worn; whence in England the Dominicans were formerly called *Black Friars.* In tropical climates where the cappa is less worn they became known as the *White Robes* or *White Priests.* Woollen only is used, all other materials being strictly forbidden.

† The Order is governed by a master-general with his council of definitors, elected by the general chapter, formerly for life, now for twelve years; each Province, by a prior-provincial and his definitors, chosen by the provincial chapter, usually every four years;

Dominic never quitted Italy again; he went about preaching from the Alps to the Apennines and particularly in Lombardy. The north of Italy was overrun like Languedoc with false doctrines, and the Church was oppressed and stripped by its foes. To defend it he set on foot the *Militia of Jesus Christ.* This was an association of persons of both sexes in the world, who without vows took upon themselves as far as possible a religious life in their own houses, keeping certain fasts, vigils, and abstinences, and saying a number of Paters and Aves every day instead of the divine office. The men were bound to uphold the Church and its rights by all due means within their power. Some writers say that this Militia was formed about twelve years earlier under the same circumstances in Languedoc; but this is very doubtful. In course of time the association ceased to be military, and became wholly religious as a Third Order called *The Brothers and Sisters of Penance of St. Dominic.* Though in the main it is secular, a conventual branch has sprung up in it. It has been very fruitful in the Saints and holy persons it has given to the Church and to the Order.*

---

and each convent by a prior elected by the qualified fathers usually every three years, with his conventual council.

* The Third Order of Penance of St. Dominic flourishes under the most solemn sanctions of the Church. Besides the strict conventual branch, there are two other classes of Tertiaries (as the members are called), one in which the Tertiaries in the world profess the Rule openly, have an elected prior, and hold regular chapters; the other in which they wear the habit in secret and practise the rule in the bosom of their families or in the secular college. The first of these classes is numerously spread throughout Ireland, the second chiefly prevails in England. Tertiaries gain immense spiritual privileges and blessings, as they fully share in the merits of the whole Order, and by saying their office are joined with the prayer of the Church. In its threefold spirit of prayer, penance,

In December 1220 Dominic paid his sixth and last visit to the city of the great Apostles. Honorius III. granted him many graces for his Order. In about four months, as the time for the second general chapter was drawing nigh, he went back to Bologna, and there presided over the assembly at Pentecost (May 30th) 1221. The Order was now spread over Spain, France, Italy, and Germany: it had sixty convents, and more were being built. A simple legend says, that two of the brethren going to Bologna for the chapter were joined by a man, who began to talk with them. When they told him it was likely that friars would be sent into Hungary, England, and Greece, he cried out in anguish, "Your Order is my confusion." Then he leaped up into the air and vanished, and they knew him to be the great enemy of man. It was settled by the chapter to carry the torch of

---

and works of mercy, the Third Order has been looked on even by the greatest Saints as one of the most powerful means to forward holiness of life in the world. The late Dr. Faber, in his work "The Blessed Sacrament: or, The Works and Ways of God," says that the Third Order of St. Dominic "rivals Carmel as a mystical garden of delights to the Heavenly Spouse." And then he speaks of it in a still higher strain of admiration. "It is not one of the least blessings for which English Catholics have to thank the infinite compassion of their Lord during the last few years, that we possess now the Third Order of St. Dominic in England. Those who are conversant, indeed who find the strength and consolation of their lives, in the Acts of the Saints, well know that there is not a nook of the mystical paradise of our Heavenly Spouse where the flowers grow thicker or smell more fragrantly than this Order of multitudinous child-like Saints. Nowhere in the Church does the Incarnate Word show His 'delight at being with the children of men' in more touching simplicity, with more unearthly sweetness, or more spouselike familiarity, than in this the youngest family of St. Dominic."

Dominic into Hungary and England. The whole Order was divided into eight provinces, Spain, Provence, France, Lombardy, Rome, Germany, Hungary, and England; and a prior-provincial was set over each of them, while for the last two kingdoms a number of friars were chosen and sent straight into those countries.

The work of Dominic was now almost over; and God forewarned him that his time of rest was at hand. From Bologna he went to Venice, and founded the house of SS. John and Paul. On his way back he stopped at Milan, and he preached as usual in places as he passed along. But he was worn out with his austerities and toils, although he was only in the 51st year of his age. As he drew nigh to Bologna, at the close of July, he felt unusually overcome by the summer-heat. When he reached St. Nicholas a dysenteric fever seized him, and he began to sink rapidly. As change of air was thought good for him he was taken to St. Mary-on-the-Mount outside the city, where he received Extreme Unction and made his last bequest to his children in God: "Have charity, keep humility, and uphold voluntary poverty." He desired to be buried in his own church "at the feet of his brethren;" so he was carried back to his convent though it was feared he would have died on the way. He had no cell of his own, for he spent all his nights in prayer within the church and only snatched short repose upon the altar-step or floor. He was taken into the cell of one of the brethren. They began the service for the dying, and when they came to the words, *Subvenite, sancti Dei; occurrite, angeli Domini, Suscipientes animam ejus offerentes eam in conspectu Altissimi*, he raised his hands to heaven and calmly fell asleep in Christ.

Saint Dominic died about noon Friday Aug. 6th 1221. He was solemnly canonised July 3rd 1234 by Gregory IX., and as the Transfiguration of our Lord was kept on the day of his death his feast was fixed for the 5th. But when the

Dedication of the basilica of St. Mary ad Nives was ordered for Aug. 5th, Clement VIII. changed his festival to the 4th. The body of St. Dominic rests under a beautiful tomb in the church of St. Nicholas, yet not so fair and lasting as the love and reverence for him in the hearts of his children who follow in the path he trod.

II.

When St. Dominic was called to rest from his labours the work which Divine Providence had fixed for him to begin was carried on by his chosen sons. Far and wide have they spread their apostolate through every region of the world. Within ten years after his death the whole of Europe divided into eleven provinces was colonized with Friar-Preachers; for in 1228 were formed the provinces of Poland with Russia, Denmark with Sweden and Norway, and Greece. In after-ages as convents increased in number or otherwise were called for, these eleven provinces were again parcelled out, and down to the beginning of last century twenty-four were added to the European list. The province of the Two Sicilies was formed in 1294, Arragon, Bohemia, in 1301; Provence, Saxony, in 1303; Dalmatia in 1308; Island of Sicily in 1395; Portugal in 1417; Scotland in 1481; Ireland in 1484; Andalusia in 1514; Belgium in 1515; Apulia, Calabria, in 1530; Languedoc in 1569; St. Dominic of the Venetians in 1580; St. Peter Martyr in Lombardy, Teremo, in 1601; Russia in 1612; Paris, Lithunia, in 1647; St. Louis in France in 1670; St. Rose in Belgium in 1686; and Sardinia in 1706.

The third general chapter was held at Paris in 1222, when Blessed Jordan of Saxony was chosen master-general. The apostolical spirit of the Order was there shown in a degree worthy of notice. The new master-general proposed the heathen missions to the friars, when all except a few old men broken with years and infirmities offered themselves for the service. In 1253 numberless Dominicans were preaching in the lands of the Saracens, Greeks, Bulgarians, Cumans, Ethiopians, Syrians, Iberians, Alans, Goths, Jacobites, Nubians, Georgians, Armenians, Indians, Tartars, Hungarians and other infidel nations of the East. Such was the missionary zeal of the Dominicans that in 1235 a congregation had been established in their body called, "The Friar-travellers for the love of Jesus Christ among the Infidels." Pope John XXII. in 1325 gave a general leave for the brethren to join it, but he was soon obliged to set bounds to the grant, as the convents of Europe were in danger of being left empty. The Eastern languages were very freely studied in the Order. In the general chapter of 1333 two convents in particular were appointed for that branch of learning, one at Pera close to Constantinople and the other at Caffa in the Crimea. For the same purpose St. Raymund of Pennafort in 1250 founded a college at Toledo, also one in Murcia and one in Tunis, both in the midst of the Moors.

St. Hyacinth after joining the Order in 1220 preached in Poland, then in Russia, Pomerania and other countries bordering the Baltic sea, the Island of Rugen, Denmark, Sweden, Gothland, Norway, and in Lesser or Red Russia. He passed down to the Black Sea, into the islands of the Greek Archipelago, and into Great or Black Russia. Then turning eastward he worked his way quite through the Steppes of Tartary and through Thibet to the northern parts of China Proper or Kathay as it was then called. He returned into Poland, went again into Red Russia, and after travelling about 12,000 miles arrived at Cracow in 1257, when he died in the 73rd year of his age. As he went along he marked his way by the many convents he founded, and countless were the souls he brought into the Church from the ranks of the Greek schismatics and infidels.

Henry of Cologne (or Albert as Matthew of Westminster

calls him) was provincial of the English Dominicans, when in 1240 he was made archbishop of Armagh in Ireland. About four years after, he went into the more eastern parts of Europe, for which perhaps his mother-tongue best fitted him, as archbishop of Russia, Livonia, and Esthonia. In 1246 Innocent IV. sent him to the Russian court to strive and put an end to the schism of the East in Russia, giving him power to appoint bishops in that country. The labours of the archbishop were very successful; for in the following year he brought the king and the whole nation over to the orthodox faith of the Roman Church, and shortly before his death which happened July 1st 1254 he converted from idolatry the king of Litland or Litten in Livonia. About 1248 Thomas, an English Dominican, was bishop of Abo in Finland.

Asia became the great battle-field of the Dominicans with error. The province of the Holy Land formed in 1228 extended over Egypt and Ethiopia and the whole of Asia. The master-general, Blessed Jordan of Saxony, sailed with many of his brethren for Palestine in 1237, but just as he was in sight of shore a storm arose and all perished by shipwreck off the city of Acre. The province of the Holy Land was governed for some time by Friar Ivo, a very holy English Dominican who lived about 1234. Friar Geoffry also an English Dominican was bishop of Ebron in Palestine and vicar of the patriarch of Jerusalem: in October 1281 he wrote to his special lord Edward I. and gave an account of the wretched conditions of the Christians in the East, perhaps with the hope of stirring up the royal zeal for another crusade against the Saracens.*

* A little before this time another Englishman of the Order seems to have been labouring in the East. This was Friar William de Fraxinent or Freney, often called William (or Geffrey) of Edessa,

The Dominicans and Franciscans divided Asia between them: to the latter were given China and the eastern parts.* The Dominicans spread over the land from the Black Sea to Coromandel and Malacca and from the confines of Egypt to Siberia. As they went eastward from the Holy Land they rested amidst the ruins of mighty Babylon or crossed the mounded site of unremembered Nineve: types of the evil power they sped to overthrow. Their voice was heard by the Brahmins and Pariahs on the banks of the Ganges, and the Tartar chiefs and their slaves by the streams of northern and central Asia, by the Arabs in their tents and the Persians in their cities and vast treeless plains and deserts. Worshippers of Buddha and of Brahma, followers of Zoroaster, of Confucius, and of Mahomet, and schismatical Christians alike listened to their words and yielded to their wondrous teaching. Countless multitudes were converted to the faith, and in Armenia the Greek schism was almost rooted out. The mission of Armenia became one of the

---

whom pope Urban VI. in 1263 consecrated archbishop and then wrote to the patriarch of Antioch to give him a title. He became Archbishop of Rages; and was much favoured by Henry III., who gave him in 1265 and 1266 the deanery of Wimbourne, the rent of fifty marks a-year out of the manor of Havering and his dwelling there, until he was otherwise provided for, or returned to his own province. He was at the dedication of Norwich Cathedral in 1278, and was still living in 1286. It is probable that he was buried at the Dominican convent of Rhyddlan in Flintshire, as his tombstone is now found built into the wall of a barn near the site of that house. The stone bears the figure of an archbishop in full pontificals, with the inscription around:

✠ . . . . PVR LALME FRERE WILLAM FRENEY ERCHEVESKE DE RAGES.

* See "Missions Dominicaines dans l'extrême Orient, par le R. P. Fr. André-Marie." Lyon: Paris: 1864, 2 vols. 8vo.

most flourishing in the east. In 1318 an archbishopric with six suffragan bishoprics was set up all in the hands of the Dominicans, taking in the whole of the countries from Coulan in the south of Hindoostan to Caffa in the Crimea. The metropolitan see was fixed at Soultaniye or Sultania in Persia, near the Caspian Sea, because that city was on the route of the caravans for central Tartary and Kara-Koroum in the country of the Kerites; had on the N. and N.W. Armenia and Asia-Minor, and the cities of Tauris, Erivan, Teflis and Mosul. In all these cities the Dominicans had convents and large missions. In Sultania alone there were twenty-five Catholic churches, and that of the Dominicans was remarkable for its beauty.

One of the suffragans was Friar Bartholomew of Bologna surnamed the Little, who was bishop of Maragha near the lake of Urumeah. Through his unwearied zeal the Armenian monks of St. Basil who were very numerous abandoned their schism in a body in 1330, joined the Dominican Order, and formed the congregation called "The United Brethren of St. Gregory the Illuminator," which was approved in 1356 by Innocent VI. A fellow-labourer of Friar Bartholomew was Friar John an English Dominican, who helped him to translate the Bible and many theological works into the Armenian language, some of which were still in the convents of the country in the middle of the seventeenth century. The archbishopric of Nakichevan at the foot of Mount Ararat was created about 1333: Friar Bartholomew was the first to fill it and soon received a crown of martyrdom. In 1403 Friar William Belets, an English Dominican, was raised to the archiepiscopal see of Sultania. Although this city has long been in ruins and depopulated through the inroads of Mahomedans, the metropolitan see of Nakichevan sprinkled with the martyr's blood has been passed over by the destroying angel and still exists. The Armenian Church too has continued faithful to the Roman See.

In 1321 three Dominicans left England to preach among the Saracens. Friar Richard an Englishman in or before 1328 went with Friar Francis de Camerino an Italian into the Levant and then along the borders of the Black Sea. They underwent great calamities and toils, but gathered a vast harvest and built many churches. Through them the princes and chief men of several countries were brought back into the Church from the schisms which had been handed down to them from their forefathers. Thus they converted Milleni prince of the Alans, and Versacht king of the Zicci an Asiatic tribe on the N. shores of the Black Sea; and the greater part of the people followed the example of their rulers. In 1332 these two princes sent the missionaries to the Roman Court, both to carry their submission to the Holy See and to beg more labourers for their countries. On their way to Rome the missionaries passed through Constantinople and had many conferences with the emperor Andronicus III. and the Greek patriarch and part of the clergy of the imperial city, whom they sought to win over to Catholic unity. The emperor showed himself eager to put an end to the Greek schism, and the clergy too seemed favourably disposed. Pope John XXII. made Friar Francis archbishop of Vospero on the shores of the Cimmerian Bosphorus, and Friar Richard bishop of Cherson, and sent them as legates to Constantinople. But the Greek clergy despite their former fair words obstinately refused even to treat on union, and the two prelates turned to the more hopeful Saracens and Tartars of Asia. Friar Richard dedicated his cathedral in honour of St. Clement pope who was martyred in Chersonesus. What became of the English bishop of Cherson, whether he died in peace or fell in the persecution which after a time overtook his flock, will probably be known only at the great day of doom.

Till the end of the fifteenth century scarcely anything was

known of Africa except the countries bordering on the Mediterranean and Red Seas, beyond which the vast deserts of sand seemed to set bounds to the habitable world. But even that small portion of the African continent was quickly colonized by Dominicans. St. Raymund of Pennafort, when he had converted, by 1256, ten thousand Moors in Spain, sent his brethren into Barbary and founded convents as far as Tunis and Tripoli. In 1316 there were very many Dominicans in Abyssinia and Ethiopia, where they had given the habit to several natives and even to a prince of the royal blood.

In East-Greenland the Friar-Preachers had a convent which existed long before 1380, and which the Dutch were amazed to find at the beginning of the seventeenth century.

Thus were the children of St. Dominic spread over every known region of the world.

The Catholic missions of the East were paralyzed and for the greatest part destroyed at the beginning of the fifteenth century by the fearful plague which had desolated the convents of Europe, by the still more dreadful lukewarmness that hag-rode the sluggard orders, and by the great schism most terrible of all that for thirty-nine years rent the Western Church. The threefold scourge of God came on the people, then the Spirit breathed on the dry bones and they lived again. The work of the missions had to be begun afresh.

Towards the end of the fifteenth century and during the sixteenth, the inroads of the Greek schism and of Mahomedanism and the outburst of Protestantism desolated six of the Dominican provinces and scattered innumerable communities of religious. But in place of these, fourteen provinces with countless convents and churches sprang up in the East and in the two Americas.

The Dominican province of Armenia was organised in 1583.

In the wake of Portuguese enterprise the Dominicans, before 1463, settled at Ceuta in Morocco, in Madeira, and in the Canary Islands, also in the Azores. The province of the Canaries was formed in 1650. The Dominicans went from Cape Verde along the coast of Guinea and southward to Congo, where in 1484 they began the glorious missions which stretched far and wide into the neighbouring countries of Loango, Angola, and Benguela, and went on till almost the close of last century. At Congo a Dominican bishopric was fixed.

In 1503 five Dominicans went out with Alphonso Albuquerque, founder of the Portuguese empire in the East, when he seized the island of Ormuz in the Persian Gulf, took Goa, conquered the whole coast of Malabar, and made Sumatra and various other islands in the Indian Archipelago tributary to the Portuguese Crown. At Cochin in Malabar they built their first church and dedicated it to St. Bartholomew, whom they chose for patron of their apostolate in India. In that country where a Dominican bishop had toiled in the fourteenth century they found more than twelve thousand Christian families. In 1505 numerous Dominicans went out of Portugal into India and settled in Ormuz and at Goa. As Albuquerque went eastward so the fathers penetrated into Ceylon, along the coast of Coromandel, into the isles of Sunda, into Malacca, and along the coasts of Siam, Cambogia, Cochin-China and Tonquin into China. They prepared the way for the great Apostle of the East, St. Francis Xavier, whose confessor and companion for some time was Friar Denis of the Cross, a Chinese Dominican.

In 1548 Paul III. nominated a Dominican bishop and vicar apostolic of the Indies with residence in the island of St. Thomas in the gulf of Guinea; the Congregation of the Holy Cross of the East Indies was formed; and the Dominicans settled at Mosambique on the east coast of Africa.

The fathers had numerous convents and churches and very flourishing missions, and chiefly spent their strength not only in bringing over the natives of the various countries but also in opposing or softening the oppressions they suffered from their Portuguese conquerors. Ormuz became the centre of the gospel for Arabia and Persia and even for Abyssinia. The Dominican missions on the west side of Hindoostan extended from the gulf of Cambay to Cape Comorin. Goa soon became entirely Christian, one Dominican alone baptizing seven thousand persons in three years, while another baptized seven hundred in one day. In the peninsula of Malacca and neighbouring islands there were eighteen convents or churches with 60,000 Christians under the care of the Dominicans. In 1557 Paul IV. founded three sees, the metropolitan or primitial at Goa, one at Malacca, and another at Cochin. The mission of Mosambique, after long struggles and many martyrdoms, extended southward into Soffala and northward to Melinde in Zinguebar, from Sena to central Africa and into Madagascar. The Dominican fathers baptized innumerable natives and built churches on the ruins of the deserted pagodas.

In the middle of the seventeenth century the Dutch step by step drove the Portuguese from their possessions in the East, and at last only Goa and Diu at the entrance to the gulf of Cambay remained in their hands. The Portuguese Dominicans shared the same fate and their splendid missions were blasted by the intolerance of the Dutch Protestants. The convent of Macao was given up to the Spanish Dominicans in 1640. The Congregation of the Holy Cross held their latest chapter in 1814; and now it is perhaps totally wrecked by the political oppression of the Church in Portugal.

Magellan a Portuguese in the service of Spain in 1525 discovered in the eastern seas a group of islands which he named the Archipelago of St. Lazarus; but these islands were afterwards called the Philippines in honour of Philip II. of Spain when prince of Asturias. The islands lay very convenient for commerce, being within some few days' sail of Japan, Corea, China, Tonquin, Cochin-China, Cambogia, Siam, Malacca, and the numerous islands of the Indian ocean. In 1571 the Spaniards took possession of these islands, and at Manilla on the west coast of Luzon the largest of them established a flourishing colony. The bishopric (afterwards archbishopric) of Manilla was erected and a Dominican was the first who held it. Great numbers of his brethren followed him, and in 1580 formed themselves into the "Congregation of our Lady of the Most Holy Rosary of the Philippines," which in twelve years became a regular Dominican province rich in Christian enterprise, fruitful in saints and martyrs, and distinguished by austerity of conventual observance. They founded the university of the Manillas in 1616.

In less than two hundred years the Dominicans rescued nearly four millions of souls from paganism in the Philippines. Their labours extended beyond these islands into China, Japan, and Tonquin. In 1587 they settled at Macao and founded a convent and mission there, and three years after they went to Hai-Teng but were soon driven out. After many vain attempts to get into the centre of the Celestial Empire they succeeded to some extent in 1611, but could not make a firm footing for themselves. They fixed themselves in the island of Formosa in 1625 where they built a church and convent and a seminary for Chinese and Japanese priests. Both there and in Manilla they converted multitudes of Chinese, many of whom entered the Order. The Dutch captured Formosa in 1643 and ruined the mission which formed the key to China. The Dominicans often strove to gain back their position in the island but it was not till 1860 that they were again established in that "Garden of flowing waters."

From Formosa the Dominicans passed in 1635 into the province of Fo-Kien on the coast of China and settled them at Fou-Gan, whence they spread themselves over the country. In course of time they had eleven residences, twenty churches, and many oratories in towns and villages; they occupied five cities, three towns, and five villages in the provinces of Fo-Kien, Tche-Kiang, and Kouang-Tong. Out of all these they were forcibly driven in 1666, and the charge of the Christians fell on a single Chinese Dominican, who in the course of thirty months consoled the weak, reconciled apostates, and baptized more than three thousand persons in ten great provinces. When the persecution was lulled the Dominicans again flocked into the country from Manilla. In 1679 a Dominican vicar apostolic was appointed over many provinces. The vicariate of Fo-Kien, one of the most flourishing in China, was given up to the Order in 1726, and from that time the Fathers have held it and laboured with unceasing zeal.

St. Francis Xavier first carried the faith into Japan. He was followed by the Fathers of the Society of Jesus and by the Franciscans till 1597, when the martyrdom of twenty-three Franciscans and three Jesuits, whose canonization has lately gladdened the Church, checked for a time the progress of the faith. In 1601 the Dominicans from Manilla went into the island of Cogiqui a dependent of Satzuma at the southern extremity of Japan, where they built a church dedicated to our Lady of the Rosary. Afterwards they had churches and convents in the imperial city Meaco and many other important places and evangelized in particular the kingdom of Figen. About twelve years passed when the English captain of a Dutch vessel, in his hatred of Spaniards and of the Catholic faith, so prejudiced the mind of the king against the missionaries, that Christianity was forbidden and the fathers were all driven out or massacred. The Dominicans again ventured into the island in 1618, but down to the present time they have gained little more than the crown of martyrdom.

Since the beginning of this century Tonquin, with Cochin-China and the Annamite Laos and Camboge, forms the Empire of Annam. After the Portuguese Dominicans the Jesuits in 1615 and 1627 entered Cochin-China and Tonquin, and in 1659 Alexander VII. divided those countries into two vicariates. In the midst of a fierce persecution the Dominicans of Manilla were called in, in 1676, and fourteen years after they had in the southern province alone sixty churches and 18,000 Christians in their charge. That same year (1690) they baptized 725 infants, 486 adults among whom were twenty-five bonzes or Buddhist priests, heard the confessions of 14,200 persons, blessed 112 marriages, and gave Extreme Unction 141 times. In 1692 the eastern vicariate of Tonquin was given entirely to them, and they had 140 churches, and preached in 500 cities, towns or villages. This vicariate was divided in 1848 and the central formed out of it. Both have always continued in the hands of the Dominicans and have each its bishop and his coadjutor. Seventeen Dominicans six of whom became martyrs have governed these districts. At the present time the Eastern district, out of about six million inhabitants has 55,000 Christians, and the Central district out of about four million inhabitants has 155,435 Christians. These two Dominican vicariates in 1857, 1858, had 41 priests of the Order two-thirds being natives, 30 native secular priests, 163 students some in holy orders in seven seminaries, 275 admirably organised catechists, 1141 pupil catechists, 26 convents of Dominican Tertiary nuns, 3 convents of nuns "Lovers of the Cross," in all 624 Annamite nuns, of whom 550 belonged to the Third Order: and there were 770 churches.

The history of the Dominican missions in China and Tonquin from the beginning to the present time shows a regular and oft-repeated series of heroic labours, vast success, and then deadly persecution, imprisonment, exile, sufferings unspeakable, and martyrdom. The land is well watered with the blood of the saints, the seed is sown, but the time of the harvest has not yet come.

The discovery of America was due in some manner to a Dominican. F. Diego Deza, preceptor of the Infanta Don Juan of Castile and confessor of Ferdinand the Catholic, encouraged Columbus in his great enterprise, and after that intrepid Genoese had been repulsed as a visionary adventurer by the courts of Portugal, England, and Castile, obtained for him of Queen Isabel in 1492 three ships, aboard which a Dominican friar was one of those who first hailed the land that opened a new world to European enterprise and to Christian heroism. Columbus discovered the islands of Guanahani, Cuba and Hayti; in his second voyage, Jamaica; and in his third, Trinidad and the coasts of Paria and Cumana in South America. Little more than half a century passed when Spain possessed the western countries of the two Americas from the north of Mexico to the boundaries of Patagonia, and the Portuguese discovered and took Brasil.

No sooner was the existence of vast nations of barbarians made known than the Church hastened to carry Christian truth and civilization to them: and it was her task too, in which the Dominicans took the leading part, to raise her voice and use her authority against the oppression and wrongs which the Indians suffered from the rapacity of the Spanish colonists and adventurers. In 1510 the Dominicans entered the island of Hayti which took the name of San Domingo, where in 1522 the famous "Protector-General of the Indians," Bartholomew de Las-Casas, who spent his life in seeking justice for them, joined the Order, as he found in it the greatest supports of his righteous cause. The Dominicans soon outstripped the limits of the colonies and went into Mexico, where they underwent immense troubles and persecutions and gained many a martyr for the Order.

When the intrepid Cortez took Mexico for the Spanish crown, Charles V. in 1519 had a bishopric erected at Telascala or Texcalan, now called Peubla de los Angeles, and Julian Garces, a Dominican, was the first to fill it. He went out from Spain to his see with a number of his religious brethren and founded a convent at Texcalan, whilst they scattered themselves over the country and raised more than a hundred houses and convents. The Dominican province of the Holy Cross in the West Indies was formed in 1530 for the whole of the western world. Las Casas in 1544 was made bishop of Chiapa, but wearied out at length with his fruitless struggles in favour of the Indians he quitted the scenes of so much misery in 1551, and died after five years of cloistral retirement near Madrid. For a long time the tide of Indian conversions ebbed and flowed, but at last it set in favourably for the Church. As the Order spread and grew in strength the provinces were founded, of St. James in Mexico, and St. Vincent the Martyr in Chiapa and Guattemala, in 1551; of St. Hippolytus in Oaxaca in 1592, and of the Holy Angels in Texcalan in 1656. The early history of the first three Provinces is unrivalled by any missionary records in adventures and interest. Friar Lewis Canceri evangelized the Floridas. The West Indian islands were soon occupied by Spanish Dominicans. About 1633 many French fathers were sent from Paris into the islands of Martinico, Gaudaloupe, St. Christopher, Santa Cruz, and Dominica, and into the island of St. Vincent then unsubdued and inhabited only by Caribbean savages. Hence was formed the congregation of the Most Holy Name of Jesus in the Antilles, which spread into all the French colonies from St. Domingo to Trinidad.

Friar Vincent Valverdo had been named bishop of Panama,

when he went out with six other Dominicans in 1530 in the expedition of Francis Pizarro against Peru. The fathers immediately scattered themselves over the country. The bishop was so much shocked at the cruelty of Pizarro against the natives that he returned and denounced him at the Spanish court. He was declared "Patron and Protector of the Indians" and made bishop of Cuzco in 1533, returned into Peru and preached with great fruit among the savages. At length he was martyred and torn to pieces while he was celebrating Mass, by the cannibals of Puna near the lake of Titicaca. New Granada was colonized by Spain in 1536. In the following year Friar Jerome de Loaysa was made first bishop of Cartagena, after which he left Spain with a company of his brethren whom he scattered among the aborigines of his diocese. They soon gained over innumerable Indian families to the Church. Afterwards, in 1538 he became first archbishop of Lima, where he founded the university. It is reckoned that he converted as many as were lost to the Church in Europe by the Protestant revolt. In 1562 St. Lewis Bertrand, the great Dominican Apostle of the West, landed in New Granada. In three years he converted more than ten thousand Indians in the isthmus of Panama, island of Tobago, and province of Cartagena. He baptized all the inhabitants of Tabara and places adjacent, and with the same effects preached in the territories of Cipacoa and Paluato; among the wild inhabitants of Santa Marta, he baptized 15,000 persons. He penetrated the forests and ranged the mountains of the cannibal Caribbees. In the country of Monpaia and island of St. Thomas he won over whole races to Christianity.

The Dominican provinces of St. John Baptist in Peru and of St. Antoninus in New Granada were established in 1551: out of the latter that of St. Catherine the martyr in Quito was formed in 1589. There were forty convents and houses in Chili in 1541, and as they increased, the province of St.

Lawrence the martyr sprang up in 1589. The Order also spread into La Plata, colonised in 1553 by Spain, and the province of St. Augustine in Buenos Ayres was formed in consequence, at the beginning of the 17th century.

Father Francis of the Cross laboured with great fruit among the Indians who had withdrawn from the Spaniards into the Andes of Acobamba in Peru. In 1658 he was made bishop of Santa Marta. In fact the Dominicans worked amongst the Indians with the same zeal as the Jesuit Fathers among those of Paraguay in Brazil, and with the same success. The glory of their apostolate has been kept for the Great Day. The Dominicans drew the Indians from the forests and mountain fastnesses, settled them in the plains near the Spaniards, and gave them the blessings of civilization. These Indians have now disappeared, not by being exterminated, but by becoming blended with the settlers. The present inhabitants of those countries are as much the representatives of the first owners of the soil as of the Spanish conquerors and colonists.

Most of the Dominican missions throughout the world flourished till near the close of last century. Then came the French Revolution, and after it the wars, tumults, and political strifes, which have overthrown dynasties, removed the landmarks of nations, formed new empires and kingdoms, and remoulded the whole of society. Amidst all these mighty disturbances the Church has suffered persecutions and trials in every form. The Religious Orders would have been destroyed if they had not been rooted in the deepest foundations of Christianity. The Dominican Order had to struggle for its very life. It was driven out of France, and has been desolated in Spain and Portugal, the convents were destroyed in Germany and Belgium, and are now broken up in Poland and the greatest part of Italy. But in some of those countries whither peace has returned the Order is once more springing up, especially in France, England, and

Belgium, and again puts forth its missionary strength. Even in times of the greatest affliction four Dominicans went out from England in 1804, 1805, and formed the Province of St. Joseph in the United States. The Order has now missions in North and South America; at the Cape of Good Hope; in Ytuy, Paniqui, and Batan, in the Philippines; and in China, Tonquin, Russia, Constantinople, Mesopotamia, Mosul, and Kurdistan. In these place there were in 1844 1002, and in 1860 1276 Dominican missionaries, and of late the number has greatly increased. California has now a Dominican bishop and his brethren are again in that country. An archbishop of the Order rules the Church of Trinidad, and the old inhabitants are again gladdened with the "White Robes," the loss of whom they had long mourned with many a regretful sigh.

An Order of Apostles is an Order of martyrs. When complaints were made to the Apostolic See that the severities of the Friar-Preachers' rule were far too great for missionary undertakings, the general chapter of 1335 replied, that within the century from 1234 there had been 13,370 martyrs in the Order; and this simple answer at once put an end to the charge. For the most part the palms of martyrdom had been gathered in the East, on the confines of Europe and in Asia, and in Egypt and the neighbouring countries. Blessed Sadoc and his forty-eight companions, while they were chanting the *Salve Regina* after Complin, were martyred in 1261 by the Cuman Tartars in the convent of Sandomir, in Poland. Two hundred Dominicans were slain that same year at Damietta in Egypt and in the parts around; and in 1268 the Dominican patriarch of Antioch and more than a hundred religious fell by the hands of the Saracens in Palestine. Asia was the vast arena where the heroes fell unconquered in defeat.

As the Catholic missions of the east faded away in the fourteenth and fifteenth centuries, so the numbers lessened of those who laid down their lives for the sake of the faith. Yet during all that dreary hundred years of zealless faith the blood of the martyrs kept trickling from the Dominican altars and made the world fruitful for coming harvests. As the Portuguese gained their power in Africa and India, so the blood of the Order drenched the land from Cape Verde to Congo, from Soffala to Zinguebar, in Madagascar, Ormuz, Abyssinia, Arabia, and Persia, and all along the coasts from the gulf of Cambay to China. Between 1565 and 1638 there was an almost unbroken chain of Dominican martyrdoms, by the hands of infidels, Mussulmen, and even of the Dutch, in the Sunda islands, Sumatra, Java, Pagna, Flores, Solor, Timor, Maquera, Duan, in the Moluccas, in Malacca, and in Corea. From 1500 to 1600 the Dominican Order had 26,000 martyrs.

The Province of the Most Holy Rosary has brought forth long generations of martyrs. Numbers of Dominicans fell in the Philippines from 1625 to 1684 under the Nigrellos Zambales, Mandayas, Foulots, Igorrotes, and many other savage races; in Formosa from 1633 to 1636 under the barbarous inhabitants; and in Japan in the general persecution from 1614 to 1617, in the great martyrdom of 1622, and in 1633, when many were beheaded or burnt alive, or perished in the terrible fire, smoke, and sulphureous waters of the volcanic Mont-Ungen fitly called the Mouth of Hell. Dominican blood was first shed in China in 1648, and its measure has still to be filled up. Two Dominican bishops, vicars apostolic of Fo-Kien, fell in the cause of Christianity: Peter Martyr Sanz in 1747, and Francis Serrano in 1748. Tonquin is now the crown of the Order jewelled with martyrdoms even down to our own days. Within the last thirty years six Dominican bishops have sacrificed themselves in blood to their missionary zeal: Clement Ignatius Delgado and Dominic Henares in 1838, and Jerome Hermosilla in 1861, vicars apostolic of the Eastern District; and Joseph Mary

Diaz Sanjurjo in 1857, Melchior Garcia San Pedro in 1858, and Valentine Berrio-Ochoa in 1861, vicars apostolic of the Central District.

Both the Americas and the West Indies had their hosts of Dominican martyrs, the numbers of whom will be known only when some diligent historian has ransacked the unedited records, which the carelessness of the Order as to its own fame has left to moulder in the dark.

The Order has always abounded in heroes of confessorship as well as heroes of martyrdom. There were, St. Dominic (1221) the great patriarch of the Friar-Preachers; St. Peter Martyr (1252) who was assassinated by heretics and wrote the first words of the Creed in his life-blood whilst it was welling from his wounds; St. Hyacinth (1257) apostle of the East; St. Thomas Aquinas (1274) the angelic Doctor, who made theology a science, and the philosophy of Aristotle Christian; St. Raymund of Pennafort (1275) the great canonist, and founder, with St. Peter Nolasco, of the Order of our Lady of Mercy;* St. Agnes of Montepulciano (1317) on whose virgin-form a snow-white manna fell; St. Catherine of Sienna (1380) the Seraphic Tertiary who bore the Wounds of Christ, brought back the sovereign pontiffs from Avignon to Rome, and saw in prophetic vision the great schism of the West and its miseries, and after it the coming glories of the Church; St. Vincent Ferrer (1419) who preached throughout Spain, France, Italy, Germany, England, Scotland, and Ireland, and is likened to the great angel of the Apocalypse; St. Antoninus (1459) the zealous archbishop of Florence; St. Pius fifth pope of that name (1572) who at Lepanto broke the power of the Turks, wherefore was established the festival of

---

* Two Friar-Preachers were charged to correct and mitigate the rule of the Order of Our Lady of Mount Carmel, and Innocent IV. in 1247 confirmed and established the result of their labours.

the Most Holy Rosary; St. Lewis Bertrand (1581) apostle of the West, who spoke only one language yet every one heard his own tongue; St. Catherine of Ricci (1589) the Wound-stricken bride of Christ; and St. Rose of Lima (1617) the Seraphic Tertiary, who was the first fruits of holiness in the New World. Many hundreds of all three branches of the Order are now styled Blessed or Venerable, some of whom are formally beatified, while the process of canonization or beatification is still in hand for others. Among those not yet canonized, but whose feasts are kept with Mass and Office, may be marked out, B. Jordan of Saxony (1237) second master-general of the Order; B. Bartholomew of Braganza (1270) bishop of Nemesia in Cyprus, and about 1258 papal legate in England; B. Albert the Great (1280) "great in natural science, greater in philosophy, and greatest in theology," who was the master of St. Thomas Aquinas; Pope Benedict XI. (1304); B. Henry Suso (1365) the sweet mystic writer; BB. Peter de Rodulphia (1365), Anthony Pavone (1374), Anthony Neyrot (1459), and Bartholomew de Cerveriis (1466), four martyrs, who fell by the hands of unbelievers; B. Margaret daughter of the king of Hungary (1470); B. Jane daughter of the king of Portugal (1490); B. Catherine of Raconigi (1547) another Wounded bride of Christ; B. John (1572) one of the nineteen martyrs of Gorcum whose canonization is now going on; B. Bartholomew de Martyribus (1590) archbishop of Braga in Portugal, who aided in the council of Trent, and was the friend and adviser of St. Charles Borromeo; and B. Martin Porres (1639) lay-brother the Indian half-caste of Lima.

Down to the year 1825 the Order has given to the Church, four popes (Innocent V. B. Benedict XI. St. Pius V. and Benedict XIII.), 70 cardinals, 29 patriarchs, 460 archbishops, 2136 bishops, 4 presidents of general councils, 25 legates-a-latere, and 80 apostolic nuncios. The Dominicans have been great and most learned writers in every branch of knowledge,* and long led the way in the fine arts.† For three hundred years they swayed the most famous universities of the world. The art of printing has in a great measure removed the college to the private study. For the Dominican, whose Order possesses in itself all the rights and privileges of an university, his cell is now his professor's chair whence he teaches with his pen: from the press and the pulpit he must wage the battles of his Lord.

III.

Thirteen Friar-Preachers, of whom Father Gilbert de Fresnoy was head, set out for England soon after they had been chosen for that mission by St. Dominic in the general chapter of 1221. It so happened that Peter de Rupibus, bishop of Winchester, was then at Bologna on his way back from the Holy Land, and they travelled in his company. At Canterbury they immediately waited on the archbishop Stephen Langton. He made F. Gilbert the same day preach before him in the Church, and he was so well pleased with the sermon and with the religious bearing of the whole company that he took the brethren into his good graces and became their friend and protector. They reached London August 10th, and thence went on to Oxford, which they entered on the feast of the Assumption. There they built a little Oratory dedicated to our Lady. They soon spread over the country and began their holy work of preaching to the people. Everywhere they were received with favour, by

---

* See Echard's "Scriptores Ordinis Prædicatorum," 2 vols. fol. 1719-21.

† See Marchese's "Lives of the most Eminent Painters, Sculptors and Architects of the Order of St. Dominic," translated by Meehan. 2 vols. 8vo: Dublin, 1852.

Henry III., by the most powerful of the clergy and by the people, so that the Order rapidly increased, and convents were soon built in the chief towns of the kingdom.

From England the Order passed into Ireland, whither it was carried in 1224 by F. Reginald an Irishman, one of the thirteen founders, who was afterwards archbishop of Armagh. Ireland long formed a part of the English province, though its dependence seems to have been quite nominal; for the Irish Dominicans had their own provincial chapters and were governed by their own vicars-general. In the general chapter of 1314, it was decreed that the English provincial should have power in Ireland, only when he was himself there; and in 1484 Ireland was made into a province of itself.* In 1230 the Dominicans first went into Scotland, and that kingdom too formed part of the English province till 1481.

---

* Though the Irish Province was thus separated from the English, the Irish Dominicans have unceasingly shown the greatest friendship towards their English brethren, and in times of the deepest need have stretched out to them that helping hand, without which the English Province might have fallen amidst its sufferings. That aid was given in the spirit of heaven-born charity, when the oppression of Ireland had reached a pitch almost unequalled in the annals of persecution, and the Irish Dominicans were undergoing trials which few could possibly have withstood. In spite of the halter, sword, and penal laws, that fair Province has flourished and is now becoming one of the brightest gems in the crown of St. Dominic. In the Irish heart so keenly sensible of truth and beauty, the Order has found a cherished home. Dominican Tertiaries are now scattered over all the country, and the members of the Confraternity of the Holy Rosary, called "Rosarians," wearing according to an ancient custom the little white scapular of our Lady everywhere *hail* Her, through whose hands those graces flow which make the Isle still the land of Saints.

Within fifty-six years more than forty convents were built in England and Wales; in the next twenty-five years above twelve more were added; and in after times they became still more numerous. We give here a short notice of each foundation.*

Arundel, Sussex. Built soon after the Order came into England. To this convent, St. Richard, bishop of Chichester, bequeathed in 1253, his book of Sentences and 20*s*. Edmund Fitz Alan, earl of Arundel, in 1324, gave 2 *a*. of land for enlarging. After the suppression, granted Nov. 1540, to Edw. Myllet of Westminster, yeoman. No trace left: it is supposed that the site is taken up with the custom-house.

Bamborough, Northumberland. At the prayer of F. John de Derlington, Hen. III. Nov. 20th 1265 gave leave for the convent to be founded. The king in the following year gave 7 *a*. of land for the purpose, and in 1267 he added 10 *a*. for the oratory &c. Granted 2 Eliz. to Tho. Reeve and Nich. Pinder.

Bangor, Caernarvonshire. As early as 1250, and probably rebuilt or enlarged by Tudor ap Gronow, lord of Penmynydd, who was called founder. Anian, bishop of Bangor, in 1301, gave 1 *a*. of land. Leland, in his Itinerary, about 1542, says this convent was dedicated to Jesus, but by mistake he gives it to the White Friars. Granted 7 Edw. VI. to Tho. Brown and Will. Breton: Dr. Jeffrey Glynn, brother of William bishop of Bangor, bequeathed it, in 1557, for a free school, and it is still called "the Friars' Grammar School."

Beverley, Yorkshire. Before 1263. Leland says that it was of one Goldsmith's foundation, and so the town; but the

* We have not thought it necessary to load our present pages with references to the documents in the Public Record Office we have used in these notices. We hope soon to complete a Monasticon Dominicanum.

Lord Darcy had of late strove for the patronage with the town. Granted 36 Hen. VIII. to John Pope and Anthony Foster.

Boston, Lincolnshire. During a fair, July 26th 1288, a squire named Rob. Chamberlain, with a lot of followers, set fire to the merchants' booths, and a great part of the town, with the Church of the Friar-Preachers, was burnt down. Granted 32 Hen. VIII. to Charles duke of Suffolk.

Brecknock. Before the end of the 13th century. Henry VIII. by letters patent of Jan. 19th 1541-2 transferred to it the college of Abergwili, in Caermarthenshire, named it Christ College, and made it into a school for educating youth, and particularly for teaching Welsh the English tongue. The ruins of the church by the west gate of the town are still to be seen.

Bristol, Somersetshire. Founded in 1228 by Sir Maurice Gaunt. Trivet says that, in 1249, a friar of the Order brought into England a footprint of our Lord, and it was here till the brethren gave it to Henry III. who had it placed in Westminster Abbey, where it was long held in veneration. Granted in 1540 to Will. Chester, has passed through countless hands, and is now used in part as a school for the Society of Friends.

Cambridge. Before 1240, when the friars had royal license to exchange some land for enlarging their churchyard. Dedicated to St. Dominic. Alice widow of Robert de Vere, earl of Oxford, about 1280, enlarged or rebuilt, so as to earn the title of foundress. Surrendered in 1538, by the prior, sub-prior and fourteen friars. One Mr. Sherwood turned it into his dwelling-house. Sir Walter Mildmay, chancellor of the exchequer, purchased it, and in 1584 founded Emanuel College, which now stands on the site.

Canterbury, Kent. Built soon after the friars came into England by Archbishop Langton, and dedicated to St. Nicholas. Henry III. was also a founder; in 1236 he gave a river-island, and in 1258, at a cost of £32, erected buildings in honour of St. Edward his patron. Granted to Tho. Wiseman and 2 Eliz. to John Harrington. The churchyard was made into an artillery ground, and on parts of the site are the Anabaptists' and Methodists' meeting-houses. Some ruins are still to be seen in Blackfriars, between Best-lane and the river Stour.

Cardiff, Glamorganshire. Probably as early as Henry III. Leland says, "The Black Freres house was withoute Meskin (or West) gate, and by side this is litle building there."

Carlisle, Cumberland. Founded before 1233; in 1237 the friars had to remove some buildings which encroached on the public street. Noticed by Leland.

Chelmsford, Essex. Said to have been founded by Malcolm king of Scotland, but he died more than half a century before the Order came into England. Still the house was built at an early date, and stood in the adjoining hamlet of Fulsham. Dedicated to St. Dominic. Yearly rental in 1535 £9. 6*s*. 5*d*. Granted 34 Hen. VIII. to Anthony Bonvisso.

Chester, Cheshire. Founded before 1235 by a bishop of Coventry and Lichfield, in the S. W. suburbs of the city near Water-gate. Granted 36 Hen. VIII. to John Cokke.

Chichester, Sussex. Built in the time of Henry III. Eleanor queen of Edward I. was a great benefactress. Granted 32 Hen. VIII. to the mayor and citizens; the church was formed into the guildhall.

Dartford, Kent. Eleanor first consort of Edward I. was deeply attached to the Order, and was planning the erection of a nunnery in 1290 when she died. Edward II. made a vow to carry out his mother's intention, and wrote to Pope John XXII. in 1318 upon the subject, desiring to turn the convent of Guildford into a house of the second order. Then he determined to erect a house at Kings-Langley, and requested the master-general to send over seven sisters. The king died before he could carry out his intention. Edward

III. took the same vow upon himself, and in 1344 commissioned Tho. de Wake to bring into England four or six nuns of the Order of Preachers from Brabant,* and then he founded the convent of Dartford for forty Religious. To it he gave the yearly rent of £100 out of the exchequer, which he afterwards changed for landed and other property. Richard II. by his liberality earned the title of second founder. This became a very famous house of education; many ladies of the highest rank entered the convent, and amongst them Bridget fourth daughter of Edward IV. This only Dominican nunnery in England, valued in 1535 at £408 a year, was suppressed in 1538, when the prioress and twenty-five religious in all were pensioned off. Henry VIII. changed the house into a hunting seat, and 1 Edw. VI. it was given to Lady Ann of Cleves, Henry's fourth wife. Mary restored it in 1558 to the surviving nuns, and Elizabeth turned them out again. Granted 4 Jac. I. to Robert Cecil earl of Salisbury, who conveyed it six years after to Sir Robert Darcy knight, with whose descendants it remained. The house was made into a farm-dwelling, and little now remains except the ancient gateway.

Derby. Founded before 1257, and dedicated to the Blessed

---

* Some few years later the king granted special pensions to the prioress and sisters who had come into England from abroad.

Antiquarians are puzzled to say to what order this house belonged, and make it Augustinian or Dominican again and again in an extraordinary manner. The fact is, the sisters here, like all others of the Order, were "Ordinis sancti Augustini, secundum instituta et sub curâ Fratrum Ordinis Prædicatorum." Martin V. July 16th 1418 confirmed their obedience to the Dominican prior of Kings-Langley: and the prioress in a letter to secretary Cromwell, about 1535, says, "We be of that profession and habit that none other be within this realm."

Virgin. Surrendered Jan. 3rd 1538-9 by the prior and five friars. Granted 35 Hen. VIII. to John Hynde.

Doncaster, Yorkshire. Founded in the reign of Hen. III. Cardinal Wolsey being arrested Nov. 1st 1529 at Cawood, when he was led towards London, lodged the second night with the Black friars here.

Dunstable, Bedfordshire. At the request of Henry III. the Augustinian lords of Dunstable in 1259 allowed the Friar-Preachers to settle in the town, and under the protection of cardinal Hugh and with the help of the charitable they increased from time to time. Yearly rental in 1535 £4. 18*s*. 4*d*. Granted 1 Edw. VI. to Sir Will. Herbert.

Dunwich, Suffolk. Founded before 1255, by Sir Roger Holishe knight. When the sea had washed away the shore almost up to the walls, it was arranged in 1384 to remove to Blythburgh in the same county, on condition that the house here should be destroyed. But the exchange was not made, and the friars remained here till the dissolution. Granted 36 Hen. VIII. (1544) to John Eyer. The whole has long been swallowed up by the sea.

Exeter, Devonshire. The Friar-Preachers were settled here by a bishop of Exeter, as the bishops of that see were styled their only patrons and founders. The Church was being built in 1232, when Henry III. granted stone out of the quarry near the castle ditch; and was dedicated Nov. 26th 1259. Suppressed Sept. 12th 1538, and granted July 4th 1541 to John lord Russel, who changed the convent into a large mansion and called it Bedford-house; it was demolished in 1780 to make room for a crescent.

Gloucester. Founded about 1239, by Henry III. and Sir Stephen de Herneshull knight, near the castle-yard by the South Gate. Granted 31 Henry VIII. to Tho. Bell, who made it into a draper's house, and since his time it has often changed hands. The buildings of this fine convent still stand on all four sides of the cloister-quadrangle, on the

N. a cruciform Church now a dwelling-house, on the south the dormitory very perfect now used as a warehouse, on the E. the chapter-house now almost hidden by modern buildings, and on the W. the refectory changed partly into a stable and hay-loft and partly into small dwellings.

Guildford, Surrey. Founded by Queen Eleanor wife of Henry III., and dedicated to St. Dominic. Here reposed the heart of Henry second son of Edward I. who died young, and his body was buried Nov. 20th 1272 in Westminster Abbey: the heart was solemnly exposed Oct. 21st every year. The building stood on the E. bank of the river Wey, a little to the north of the High-street. On the site Henry VIII. erected a mansion, which in the time of James I. passed into private hands, and so to the Onslow family. In the war at the beginning of the present century it was used for barracks, and then it was made to accommodate the judges during the assizes.

Haverfordwest, Pembrokeshire. Before 1256, in which year Henry III. gave the friars, who had diligently preached the crusade, 15 marks (£10) towards removing to a better spot. Granted 38 Hen. VIII. to Rog. and Tho. Barlow. There are some ruins.

Hereford. Begun about 1270, in which year (May 10th) the friars had royal letters of protection for their place in Portfeld.* Leland says, "Ther cam in the tyme of Ser Thomas Cantelope, 3 Friers Prechars to Hereford, and by the Favour of William Cantelope, Brothar to Bysshope Cantelupe, they set up a litle Oratorie at Portfelde; but Byshope Thomas toke that Place from the Friers. Then one Syr John Daniell, havynge a litle Place in the Northe Suburbe, let them have the use of it. Then the Bysshope of Hereforde gave them a

---

* The friars "qui commorari debent" in Hereford had royal license July 13th 1246 to acquire a certain plot of land, for enlarging the place given them by Agnes Byset.

Plot of Ground hard by Daniel's Place, and ther they began to builde, and make a solempne Pece of Worke, Daniell helpynge them." The Portfield is in the Ive Gate suburbs of the city: the convent was without the north or Widemarshgate. This house suffered much from fires, for before 1414 it had been three times burnt down. Granted 5 Eliz. to Elizabeth Wynne; and out of the ruins Sir Thomas Coningsby of Hampton-Court erected the buildings which in 1614 he made into a hospital for worn-out soldiers and superannuated faithful servants. There still remain the ruins of some offices and of a beautiful hexagonal cross, or rather stone pulpit, which stood probably in the preaching-yard.

Hull, or *Kingston-on-Hull*, Yorkshire. Stood between the present Queen Street and the landing place, where the Hull falls into the Humber. Site granted 36 Henry VIII. to John Broxholme, and 5 Edw. VI. to John duke of Northumberland.

Ilchester, Somersetshire. Before 1283, when the friars had royal license to add two and a half acres of land given them by Will. Whytbred. Granted 37 Hen. VIII. to William Hodges.

Ipswich, Suffolk. Dedicated to St. Dominic, and stood near the river-quay. Founded in 1263 by the king, Hen. de Manesby, Hen. Redred, and Hen. de Loudham; John Hares afterwards gave land to enlarge it. The site, which was very large, was granted 33 Hen. VIII. (1541) to Will. Sabyn, and Mr. Southwell sold it in part to the corporation and in part to John Tooley. The corporation made their share into Christ's hospital, a free grammar school, a public library, a bridewell, &c.: Tooley's executors according to his will established an almshouse for poor men and women which was confirmed in 1556 by a charter of queen Mary. The cloisters and other conventual buildings are still entire, but the refectory (or school) has been recently pulled down.

The new Catholic church stands on part of the ground not far from the house.

Kings-Langley, Hertfordshire. Dedicated to St. Dominic and first established at the sole labour and expense of the friars of Oxford probably in the reign of Hen. III. It became the house of studies for all the four "Visitations" into which the houses of the Order in England were divided. Edward II. in 1308 removed it to a better site, close to the king's palace at Langley. When Sir Piers Gaveston was summarily beheaded June 19th 1312 near Warwick, a Dominican friar who was passing took up the head of the royal favourite and bore it in his capuce to the king; the body was taken to the convent of Oxford, where it rested for more than a year. Edward had the remains removed to Langley and interred in the friars' church, which he built; and for the repose of Sir Piers' soul he supported the students out of the treasury. Edward III. enlarged and endowed the house for sixty friars. Richard II. had the bones of his brother Edward buried here, and himself also lay here till his body was removed by Henry V. to Westminster Abbey. At the dissolution this convent had the clear yearly rent of £122. 4s. Queen Mary placed the nuns of Dartford here in 1556, but they left two years after for their former cloister. Granted 16 Eliz. to Edward Grimston.

Lancaster, Lancashire. Founded in 1260 by Sir Hugh Harrington knt., the royal license to the provincial being dated May 27th. Granted 32 Hen. VIII. to John Holcroft.

Leicester. Founded by Simon de Montfort earl of Leicester in the reign of Henry III. "Le Blake Freares in le Ashes" as it was called was surrendered November 10th 1538, by the prior, sub-prior, and eight friars. Granted 38 Hen. VIII. to Hen. Marquis of Dorset.

Lincoln. Founded about 1237 when Henry III. made them a grant of building timber; and stood on the east of the city, just outside Potters' Gate. Granted 37 Hen. VIII. to John Bellew and John Broxholm.

London, Middlesex. When the Friar-Preachers came into England in 1221 they formed a house in Holborn just outside the city walls near the Old Temple. In 1235 Henry III. and Gilbert earl of Pembroke gave them much building timber. Hubert de Burgh was a great benefactor, and bestowed on them his place in Westminster: they never lived there, but sold it to Walter archbishop of York, and it formed the palace of the archbishops called York Place till 1529, when Henry VIII. took it from Cardinal Wolsey and named it Whitehall. Two general chapters of the Order were held in Holborn; May 18th 1250 and May 20th 1263. "In the yeere 1250," says Stowe, "the Fryers of this Order of Preachers, throughout Christendom, and from Jerusalem, were by Convocation assembled together, at this their house by Oldboorne, to entreat of their estate, to the number of 400, hauing meate and drinke found them of Almes, because they had no possessions of their owne. The first day, the king came to their Chapter, found them meate and drinke, and dined with them. Another day, the Queene found them meat and drink; afterward the Bishop of London, then the Abbot of Westminster, of St. Albons, Waltham, and others." At the chapter of 1263, the great Angelic Doctor St. Thomas Aquinas was present.

F. Robert de Kilwardby, after he became archbishop of Canterbury removed his brethren of London to a better place. In 1275 Sir Robert Fitz Walter sold or gave him Baynard Castle with the tower of Montfitchett, and in the next year the mayor and barons of London granted him two lanes next the castle. On this site and partly out of the stones of the tower, the Archbishop with royal aid raised a church and convent for the brethren of his Order, who left Holborn after they had been there for more than fifty-five years. The old house in Holborn was confirmed by Edward

I. in 1287 to Henry Lacy earl of Lincoln, who built his inn there. This inn afterwards passed to the bishops of Chichester, whose palace adjoined and became at last an Inn of Court for law-students; and now as a residence of lawyers it still keeps the name Lincolns-Inn.

The second convent stood in the city between Ludgate and the Thames, where Printing-house Square now lies. It had a very large extent of ground shut in with four walls and gates, and in it numerous artizans lived and plied their trades. All who dwelt there were subject only to the king, to the superiors, and to the justices within the precincts. The inhabitants kept these liberties for some time after the dissolution. This was a very famous house. In the church were buried many great personages: here reposed the hearts of the foundress Eleanor, Edward the First's "chere reine," and of Alphonsus her son. Here were held, the general chapters of May 26th 1314, and June 14th 1335; the court of queen Isabell in 1327, when the furious fray occurred between the Heinhaulters and the English archers; and the provincial synod of 1382, in which the opinions of Wycliffe were condemned. In 1450 the parliament begun at Westminster was adjourned to this house and hence to Leicester. In 1522 the Emperor Charles V. lodged here. In 1524 the "black parliament" was opened here and adjourned to Westminster abbey. And in 1529 cardinals Campeggio and Wolsey sat in the "parliament-chamber" as judges in the cause of Henry VIII. when queen Catherine made her touching appeal to her faithless husband. John Hilsley bishop of Rochester commendatory prior and fifteen friars surrendered it November 12th 1538; the temporalities were then valued at £104. 15s. 5d. a-year. The site and buildings were granted to Sir Tho. Cawarden knt., who after the death of Henry VIII. unroofed the church of St. Anne which served the inhabitants of the precincts for a parish church, and let part of it for stables. Afterwards he pulled down the church walls and built a tennis-court "to the mayntenance of vice and great hurte and corrupcion of the youthe of the citie of London," and let part of the churchyard as a carpenter's yard. The precincts became a place of fashionable residence, and many of the nobility built houses for themselves. Here queen Elizabeth when sixty years old danced at a wedding. Close by the convent-church on the spot still known as Playhouse Yard was erected in 1575 the Blackfriars' theatre, to which Shakespere has given an everlasting fame. The Blackfriars was desolated in 1666 by the great fire of London: the ground is now built over, yet among the back houses some remains of the ancient walls may still be seen.

Lynn, Norfolk. Dedicated to St. Dominic, being founded in 1272 by Thomas Gedney. Temporalities in 1535 valued at 18s. a-year. The prior and eleven brethren signed the surrender in 1538. John Eyre esq. bought the site in 1544 of the king, and through many hands it is now held by the corporation of Lynn and others. Few traces of the buildings are to be seen.

Melcombe-Regis, Dorsetshire. Founded about 1417 by Hugh Deverell and John Roger, who gave two houses and land, and began to build the convent and church, for encouraging the town, which had been often attacked and nearly ruined by invaders. Pope Martin V. August 17th 1418 granted license for the foundation and also for a convent at Wendover,* which other benefactors had begun. This convent made no progress till 1431 when the royal license

---

* Wendover was probably soon abandoned.

In 1267, the Friar-Preachers had a royal grant of twelve oaks, for the fabric of their church at Gillingham in Dorsetshire. And in 1279 John de London gave them a site in Windsor, and they had the royal license to establish themselves there. These foundations were soon either given up or removed.

was given for it; meanwhile the Religious dwelt and carried on their services in the two houses. In Feb. 1445-6 Henry VI. granted them land in the sea and £10. a-year for twelve years to build a tower and jettee for defending the town and port against the flowing of the sea; which they did at "grete charge and costes" to themselves. Granted 35 Hen. VIII. (1543) to Sir John Roger of Brianston, of the family of the founder. The convent became changed into small dwellings, and the church into a malthouse.

Newcastle-on-Tyne, Northumberland. Near the West Gate, founded about 1260 by Sir Peter Scot first mayor and Sir Nich. Scot his son. In the church John Baliol king of Scotland did homage in 1344 to Edward III. and yielded up to him the five southern counties of his kingdom. Yearly rental in 1535 £2. 19s. 4d. Surrendered January 10th 1538-9 by the prior and twelve friars. Sold 35 Hen. VIII. (1544) to the mayor and burgesses of the town. In 1553 the corporation demised the friary to nine of the mysteries or ancient trades of the town, and thus the buildings though greatly altered have been well preserved to the present time.

Newcastle-under-Lyne, Staffordshire. Founded before 1281. Leland says it stood on the south side of the town.

Newport, Monmouthshire. On the banks of the Usk below the bridge. Granted 35 Hen. VIII. to Sir Edw. Carn. There are still remains: some years ago the small but elegant chapel was taken up with a cider mill.

Northampton. Built about 1235, when the king gave fifteen oaks for building-timber. Dedicated to St. Dominic. John de Dabington was either founder or a considerable benefactor. Eleanor queen of Edward I. in 1279 gave the friars a spring called Floxewell. Yearly rental in 1535 £5. 7s. 10d. Surrendered October 20th 1538 by eight friars. Granted 38 Hen. VIII. to Will. Ramsden.

Norwich, Norfolk. The Friar-Preachers entered Norwich

in 1226. Sir Thomas Gelham knt. was their patron. They had the old parish church of St. John Baptist in the Colegate now called Black Boys Street; and made it conventual. When the Order of Sacked Friars was put down in 1307 their house in Norwich on the opposite side of the river was given (Oct. 28th) to the Friar-Preachers, who quitted their old house in 1309, but left one of their brethren in it for serving the church. In 1413 a great part of the city with this convent was burnt down, and the friars went back to their old house. They had not been very long settled there when they were again burnt out in 1449 and driven back to their new house which they restored, the church dedicated to St. John Baptist being finished about 1462. Here Elizabeth queen of Edward IV. lodged with her daughters and suite in 1470, when she visited Norwich. All the possessions of the Friar-Preachers in this city were granted by Henry VIII. in 1540 for £81. and 9s. a-year rent to the mayor and corporation, and have been variously used. The ground of the first house was parcelled out to several persons: the Unitarian chapel stands in the churchyard and the Independents' meeting house is within the precincts near the orchard. In 1804 a great part of the buildings of the second house was made into a workhouse and the choir (which had long served as a place of worship for the Dutch Protestants) was used as a chapel for the paupers: the fine nave has always been used by the corporation as a corn-market and guild-hall, called from the parish St. Andrew's Hall.

Oxford. F. Gilbert de Fresnoy and his brethren found their little oratory of our Lady too distant from the city, so they obtained a more suitable place within the Jewry, hoping at the same time to bring over the inhabitants of it to Christianity. Isabel countess of Oxford and Stephen Malclerk bishop of Carlisle, who afterwards gave up his see and joined the Order, bestowed on them two pieces of land, and the canons of St. Frideswide let them have several lands at a very low rent. Here they built a house, while the countess of Oxford erected an oratory with a burial-ground attached. They were soon joined by four of the greatest theologians, philosophers, and writers of the age: F. John of St. Giles, F. Robert Bacon, F. Richard Fishacre, and F. Robert de Kilwardby, for whose schools they built a separate house. In this convent was held in 1230 the first chapter of the English province, and in 1258 the "Mad Parliament" sat here.

The convent became too small to hold the scholars from all parts of Europe who crowded to this school, which was taught by Dominican professors who had a world-wide renown. About 1259 Henry III. granted the friars in the south suburbs, outside Little Gate and close to the river Isis, a piece of land which was formed into an island by the brook called Trill Mill stream. They sold their place in the Jewry and with the money and benefactions built a larger house. The church dedicated to St. Nicholas was consecrated June 15th 1262 by the bishop of Lincoln. Here they had distinct schools for theology and philosophy, and performed all their solemn acts of divinity in the church and chapter-house and those of philosophy in the cloister. The house was made a general college open to all the Order and to the whole world, where for nearly three hundred years many men of eminence were educated.

Henry VIII. destroyed this house, and in 1540 sold it with the Greyfriars, for £1094. to Richard Andrews and John How, who some time after parted with it to Will. Frere of Oxford and Agnes his wife. Frere pulled down the church and most of the convent, and sold the stone, lead, glass, bells, &c. at the lowest rate; and thus the seat of the Friar-Preachers at Oxford vanished. "But," says Wood, "their memory has a right to be eternally preserved, who lived with us to the immense benefit of the university;

whilst the very prelates of the Church, attracted both by their learning and unspotted course of life, laid down their honours and preferments, and often repaired to Oxford to take that rule upon them."

Pontefract, Yorkshire. Founded before 1266. Surrendered November 26th 1538 by seven friars and one unprofessed novice. Granted 36 Hen. VIII. to Will. Clifford and Mich. Wildbore.

Rhuddlan, Flintshire.. Anian de Shonaw called Y Brawd du o Nanneu or the Blackfriar of Nanneu was prior of Rhuddlan in 1268, when he was made bishop of St. Asaph. It suffered greatly in the Welsh wars of Edward I., but kept up till the dissolution. Granted 32 Hen. VIII. to Henry ap Harry.

Salisbury, Wiltshire. Begun in 1277 by Rob. de Kilwardby, archbishop of Canterbury, at Fisherton close to Salisbury. To it a community of friars removed from the adjoining parish of Wilton where they had been established much earlier.* Edward I. in 1281 and Eleanor his queen in 1289 were benefactors. Granted 36 Hen. VIII. to John Pollard and Will. Byrte.

Scarborough, Yorkshire. Founded about 1245 by Sir Adam Sage knt. At the request of the burgesses the friars in 1285 removed to a better spot.

Shrewsbury, Shropshire. The Friar-Preachers settled here in 1232 (not in 6 Hen. III. as the historians of the town state) when the king granted them stone and timber for their church. Lady Matilda de Lasci wife of Geoffry de Genevile was so great a benefactress that she was styled foundress. Stood a little without the wall on Severn side at the end of Marwell St. Suppressed in 1538, and sold by

---

* The friars seem to have kept the site at Wilton; Tanner says it was granted 1 Edw. VI. to Sir Will. Herbert.

Henry VIII. in 1543 to Rich. Andrewes and Nich. Temple; and since that time it has passed though many hands. The buildings have long disappeared; but in 1823 when the site was levelled for a wharf, the foundations of three chambers were laid bare and many fragments of fine stonework found.

Stamford, Lincolnshire. Founded before 1240 it is supposed by Will. earl of Albemarle. Surrendered October 7th 1538 by the prior and eight friars. Granted 33 Hen. VIII. to Rob. Bocher and David Vincent.

Sudbury, Suffolk. The friars settled here about 1242, through the aid of Baldwin de Simperling and Mabilla his wife, together with John de Chertsey. Granted in 1539 to Tho. Eden esq. clerk of the Star Chamber; and after being sold many times the buildings were pulled down about 1819.

Thetford, Norfolk. Thetford was an episcopal see from 1075 to 1094. The church was for a short time in the hands of the Cluniacs who gave it up soon after 1114, and it fell into decay. At length Sir Edmund Gonvile (founder of the Gonvile Hall now Caius College Cambridge) induced Henry earl of Lancaster lord of Thetford, to whom he was steward, to repair this old church and house and to settle Friar-Preachers there. This was about 1336. John earl of Warren by royal license of April 28th 1338 gave them land; he was esteemed a founder with Gonvile and the earl of Lancaster. Dedicated to Holy Trinity, St. Mary, and All Saints. The prior and five brethren signed the surrender in 1538; but Blomefield thinks that there were many others who would not join in it. Granted in 1540 to Sir Rich. Fulmerston, who by will in 1566 founded a grammar school and a hospital for two poor men and two poor women, which were built on the ruins of the old cathedral. There are still considerable remains.

Truro, Cornwall. Founded by the Reskiner family and dedicated to St. Dominic. Henry III. was also reputed a founder. Walter bishop of Exeter consecrated the church September 29th 1258. Leland says it was in Kenwyn Street. Granted 7 Edw. VI. to Edward Aglionby.

Warwick. Founded by John Plessets earl of Warwick who died in 1263. Stood in the west suburbs of the city. Yearly rental in 1535 £4. 18s. 6d. The prior, sub-prior, and *four* brethren surrendered it October 20th 1538. Granted January 5th 1552 to John duke of Northumberland; "and that it was soon after demolished," says Dugdale, "we need not doubt; so that what became of the ground whereon it stood, after it was escheated to Queen Mary by his attainder, is not worth while to enquire."

Wincheleca, Sussex. Founded by Edward II. who March 19th 1317-8 gave twelve acres of land for the convent and church. As they were too far from the town the friars had royal license Apr. 10th 1339 to receive six acres of land from Will. Batan which was nearer. Granted 38 Hen. VIII. to Will. Clifford and Mich. Wildbore.

Winchester, Hants. Founded about 1230 by Peter de Rupibus bishop of Winchester, with whom the friars first came into England. Hen. III. in 1235 gave forty oaks for the building. Granted 35 Hen. III. to the warden and scholars of Winchester college.

Worcester. Founded about the end of Henry III. reign by Will. de Beauchamp of Powick. Stood in the north part on the highest ground of the city. Granted 31 Hen. VIII. to the bailiffs and citizens.

Yarm, Yorkshire. Peter de Brus the second who died in 1271 was founder. John de Aslacby and Petronilla his wife in 1301 gave five acres of land for enlarging. Surrendered in December 1538 by the prior five friars and six novices. A gentleman's residence stands on the site.

Yarmouth (*Great*), Norfolk. At the south end of the town, founded about 1270 by Thomas Falstolf and Geoffrey de Pykgrin or Pykering. William Charles and in 1271

Henry III. gave land for building on and enlarging. The church rebuilt in 1380 and dedicated to St. Dominic was burnt down in 1525. Granted 34 Hen. VIII. (1542) to Rich. Andrews and Leonard Chamberleyn; occasionally used as one of the defences of the town, particularly in 1588 at the Spanish invasion. Site now possessed by several owners.

York. The Friar-Preachers were settled here by Sir Brian Stapleton, and Henry III. March 8th 1227-8 gave them the chapel of St. Mary Magdalen in the Kingstofts. Surrendered Nov. 27th 1538 by seven friars and four novices. Granted 32 Hen. VIII. to Will. Blythman. On the site was afterwards built in Tanner's Row by lady Hewley, a Presbyterian, relict of Sir John Hewley of Bell hall, a hospital for ten old women of her own religious persuasion. Rest of the site turned into spacious gardens called the Friars' Gardens, all private property.

This short account of the convents in England and Wales shows how rapidly the Friar-Preachers spread over the country. An Order given up to study as well as piety is more select than those religious bodies in which piety alone opens the cloister-door to the untalented but holy ascetic. What the Dominicans wanted in numbers they made up for in learning, and by learning in moral power, so that they secured the confidence of royal and noble personages, and won the esteem of the middle classes and the reverence of the humblest ranks of the people. Their convents were generally built in the suburbs of towns and cities amidst the dwellings of the lower orders to whom they mostly gave their ministry. Henry III. showed them great favour and had some of them always with him, for whom he had the pope's leave April 30th 1250 enabling them to ride on horseback, when he took the cross and intended them to go with him into the Holy Land. They were employed in preaching the crusade: the provincial chapter of 1255 chose out those who were to stir up the people in the various dioceses against the encroaching Saracens. They also laboured to convert the Jews: it is pleasing to mark that when the child Hugh of Lincoln, in 1255, was crucified in scorn of Christianity, the Dominicans successfully pleaded for the lives of innocent Jews, on all whom as a body the bitter hatred of the age charged the crime. The Londoners were so angry with the Dominicans for this really just and charitable act that they withheld the usual alms, and for several days the friars of Holborn had not even bread to eat. The Dominicans were constantly engaged in the affairs of state, from the time when one of them persuaded Henry III. to send away from his council the obnoxious Poitevins. They were sent as ambassadors to Sweden and other kingdoms, and to the courts of France and Rome, particularly in the matter of the crusades and in the quarrel about Guienne. Henry III. Edward I. Edward II. and Edward III. chose Dominicans for their confessors; Edward II. once when his life was in great peril made a vow in favour of the friars of Kings-Langley, and he faithfully kept his promise in 1312. And after that unhappy king was dethroned, the Friar-Preachers took up his cause vigorously among the people, seeking to restore him; for they did not know that he had met with a miserable and cruel death. Edward III. granted many favours, and established in the provincial chapters of the body, a solemn anniversary for the soul of his consort queen Philippa, which Richard II. and many succeeding kings confirmed. Richard II. used the divine office according to the Dominican rite; and in 1395 Boniface IX. granted leave to all clerics saying it with him to continue it for two months when absent for a time. There were some of the Order always in his council. Henry VI. had a Dominican confessor. Even Edward IV. was attached to the friars, and in their house at Shrewsbury his two sons, Richard and George were born. And the first confessor of Catherine of Arragon, the injured queen of Henry VIII. was a Dominican.

To the Church the English Dominicans rendered their full measure of service. St. Edmund archbishop of Canterbury, whose relics now repose at the college of the archdiocese of Westminster which bears his name, always kept Dominicans with him in his household, and his schoolfellow at Oxford, F. Robert Bacon, aided in making those formal enquiries into his holiness which in 1246 led to the canonization of that great servant of God. F. Ralph Bocking was the confessor and biographer of St. Richard of Chichester, and F. John of St. Giles was the friend of Robert Grosseteste, while F. Thomas Jortz took in hand, but unsuccessfully the canonization of that stern but good bishop of Lincoln. The office of penitentiary in the various dioceses which requires deep knowledge of theology and of canon law was often given to a Dominican. Many Dominicans of the English province have filled the sees of England and Ireland or held titular bishoprics *in partibus infidelium*, and have been coadjutors of the bishops, and some have been raised to the dignity of princes of the Church.

DOMINICAN CARDINALS OF ENGLAND.

Robert de Kilwardby,* *tit. S. Rufinæ* and bishop of Porto, 1278—1279.

William de Macclesfield, *tit. S. Sabinæ*, 1303; but he had died before his promotion.

---

* Parker by his loose use of the word Friar-Minor which he applied both to Dominicans and Franciscans has led Godwin, Collier, and some others to fancy that Kilwardby was a Franciscan, though in his list of English cardinals he says directly that he was a Dominican. Older authors agree on the point, and the State Records of England place the matter beyond all dispute.

William de Winterbourne, *tit. S. Sabinæ*, 1304—1305.
Thomas Jortz, *tit. S. Sabinæ*, 1305—1310.

DOMINICAN ARCHBISHOP IN ENGLAND.

Robert de Kilwardby, archbishop of Canterbury, 1272—1278.

DOMINICAN BISHOPS IN ENGLAND.

St. Asaph. Hugh, 1234—1242. Anian de Schonaw, 1268—1292. Alexander Bache, 1389-90—1394. Thomas Bud, 1450—1462-3.

Bangor. Thomas de Ringstead, 1357—1365. Gervase de Castro, 1366—1370. John Gilbert, 1371-2; translated to Hereford, 1375. Thomas Cheriton, 1436—1447. James Blakeden, 1452—1464.

Carlisle. Robert Reade, 1396; translated to Chichester.

Chichester. Thomas Rushook, 1385; translated to Kilmore in Ireland, 1389. Robert Reade, 1396—1415.

Coventry and *Lichfield.* John Burghill, 1398—1414.

St. David. John Gilbert, 1389—1397.

Ely. Thomas de Lisle, 1345—1361.

Hereford. John Gilbert, 1375; translated to St. David, 1389.

Llandaff. John Egglescliffe, 1323—1346. Thomas Rushook, 1383; translated to Chichester, 1385. William de Bottlesham, 1386; translated to Rochester, 1389. John Burghill, 1396; translated to Coventry and Lichfield, 1398. John Hunden, 1458—1478. George Athequa, 1516-7—1536-7.

Norwich. John Hopton, 1554—1558.

Rochester. William de Bottlesham, 1389—1399. John Hilsley, 1535—1538.

Sodor. John Sproton, 1392 (1400 ?) John Howden, 1523 (1532 ?)

ENGLISH DOMINICAN ARCHBISHOPS AND BISHOPS IN IRELAND.

Armagh (Archb.) Walter Jortz, 1307. Roland Jortz, 1313—1321.

Meath. William Andrew, 1374—1385. John Payn, 1483—1507.

Down and *Connor*. John de Egglescliffe, 1322; translated to Llandaff, 1323. Robert de Rochfort, 1451—1456.

Kilmore. Thomas Rushook, 1390.

Dublin (Archb.) John de Derlington, 1279—1284; John de Hotham, 1297—1298.

Ossory. Richard Winchelsea, 1479—(1486 ?)

Lismore and *Waterford*. Robert Reade, 1394; translated to Carlisle, 1396.

Tuam (Archb.) John Baterley, 1427—1437.

Achonry. William Andrew, 1374; translated to Meath, 1380. James Blakeden, 1442; translated to Bangor, 1452.

As writers, the English Dominicans were not excelled by any others in the country, and shone, as Leland says of F. Henry Escheburn, like the evening star among the lesser lights, and though they lived in the ages of chattering sophists many of their works were worthy of later times. They wrote on every subject: commentaries on Scripture, Theology, Canon Law, Metaphysics, Logic, and all branches of Philosophy, Physics, History, Biographies, Philology, and even Medicine and Magic: nor did they despise the pleasing art of poetry; and their quodlibets and sermons are unnumbered.* As preachers they taught the people in market-

* A French Dominican first began the Concordance of the Bible by making an index of the bare words; but three English Dominicans, F. Rich. de Stavensby, F. Hugh de Croyndon, and F. John de Derlington about 1250 and 1252 gave us the concordance as it now stands by quoting the passage with each word.

places, in portable pulpits, and in public crosses, they aided the parochial clergy, particularly at certain seasons, with missions and retreats and in the confessional; they spread

---

The first English-Latin Dictionary was compiled by Richard Fraunois, called F. Geoffrey the Grammarian. The following is the number of English Dominican works or treatises as far as we have yet collected them.

Rob. Bacon 5, Rich. de Fishacre 9, Rob. de Kilwardby 45, John of St. Giles 18, John de Derlington 3, including the "Concordantiæ magnæ Bibliorum Sacrorum Anglicanæ dictæ," Will. de Boderisham 3, Will. de Kingsham 3, Will. de Alton 4, Anian de Schonaw 1, Rich. Castlecon 2, Ralph Bocking 1, Hugh de Manchester 2, Tho. de Sutton 13, Rich. Clapole or Knapwell 9, Hen. Escheburn 5, Will. de Hotham 7, John Redhead 2, Walter de Winterbourne 4, Maurice 4, Rob. Orford 5, Will. de Macclesfield 13, Tho. Jortz 13, Tho. Sperman 4, Walter de Exeter 1, Nich. Trivet 34, Will. de Southampton 6, Gregory Britain 2, Walt. Jortz 4, Tho. de Langford 4, Tho. de Norwood 2, Rob. de York 5, Simon de Bouralston 6, Tho. Waleis 29, Hugh de Ducton 3, Will. D'Eyncourt 2, Peter 1, Rob. Holcot "the Firm and Unwearied Doctor" 28, Tho. de Lisle 2, Tho. de Ringstead 7, Chr. de Molesey 6, Will. Brunyard 3, Will. de Rothwell 17, Simon de Hinton 13, John Stokes 2, Will. Jordan 9, Tho. Stubbs 14, Hen. Daniell 2, Will. de Bottlesham 2, Tho. Claxton 2, John de Bromyard 12, Rob. Humbleton 2, Simon 4, Robert Josse 5, Walt. Buckden 1, Rog. Dymoke 2, Abraham de Walden 2, Acton (5 ?) 2, Hugh Sweth 2, John Skelton 1, Reind 1, Tho. Palmer 6, Hen. Witfield 1, Rich. Winchelsea 1, Will. Beeth 3, John 5, Phil. Bromyard 2, Griffin 2, Geoffrey the Grammarian 5, Reginald Pipern 2, John de Coloribus 1, John Harley 3, John Hilsley 2, and Will. Perin 3.

Many of these works have passed through the press. The Biblical Concordance was printed the first time we think in 1479 at Bologna. *Tho. Jortz*, "Commentaria super IV. libros sententiarum," those on the first book printed Venetiis 1523; "Com-the devotion of the holy Rosary; and by instructing all in sound doctrine and piety led their hearers into the paths of truth, virtue, and holiness of life. When John Wycliffe

---

mentaria super Psalmos" Venetiis 1611. "In Beati Joannis Apocalypsim Expositio" Florentiæ 1549, but falsely attributed to St. Thomas Aquinas. *Ralph Bocking,* Life of St. Richard of Chichester in the Bollandists' Acta Sanctorum. *Nich. Trivet,* twelve books of his work "In libros Sancti Augustini, de Civitate Dei" with Tho. Waleis's work on the same subject; "Annales sex Regum Angliæ" by Lucas d'Achery in the 8th vol. of his Spicilegium, Parisiis 1668, by Anthony Hall Oxford 1719, and a few years ago by the Royal Historical Society. *Tho. Waleis,* his incompleted work "In decem primos libros e xxii de Civitate Dei St. Augustini expositiones" made up from Trivet on the same subject, Moguntiæ 1473, Tolosæ 1488, Venetiis 1489, Friburgi Brisgoiæ 1494, Lugduni 1520. *Rob. Holcot,* "Super quatuor Libros Sententiarum Questiones," "Quædam Conferenciæ," "De Imputabilitate peccati, Quæstio longa," "Determinationes quarundam aliarum Questionum," all four printed together Lugduni 1497, 1510, 1518; "In Librum Sapientiæ Prælectiones ccxiii" in the infancy of printing without date or place, Spiræ 1483, Venetiis 1483, 1500, 1509, 1515, 1586, Reutlingæ 1489, Basileæ 1489, 1506, 1586, Hagenoæ 1494, Parisiis 1511, 1514, 1518, 1586, and again in abstract under the title of "Phœnix Redivivus ex Relicta facundia Holcotiana palam in lucem progrediens, seu Postilla super Librum Sapientiæ" etc., by F. Raymund Ortz, Coloniæ Agrippinæ 1689; "Explicationes Proverbiorum Salomonis" Parisiis 1510, 1515, Lavingiæ 1591; "In Cantica Canticorum" and "In Ecclesiastici capita septem priora" Venetiis 1509; and the latter work only (which Holcot was prevented by death from finishing) in the infancy of printing without date or place, Venetiis 1509; "Moralizationes Historiarum," Venetiis 1505; Parisiis 1507, 1510, 1513, and with the second 1586 edit. of the work, in Librum Sapientiæ; "De Septem Peccatis Mortalibus," Parisiis 1517; "Philobiblon, seu de Amore Librorum & Institutione Bibliothe-

broached his new and revolutionary opinions he found some of his ablest and most determined opponents in the Dominican body.

The Order of Friar-Preachers had flourished in England for a little more than three centuries, when the nation having left its first charity and made the Church a creature of the state had its candlestick moved out of its place. Henry VIII. found many a ready tool for his breach with the Roman See (which he completed in 1534) among the secular clergy, in universities, and in all the religious Orders. Among the Dominicans there were traitors. A friar of Bristol, who

---

carum," Spiræ 1483; Parisiis 1500; in Tho. James's Ecloga, Oxoniæ 1599; and at the end of the Centuria Epistolarum Philologicarum of Goldastus, Francof., 1610: "Moralitates Verbum Dei Evangelizantibus perutiles," Venetiis 1514. *Tho. Stubs*, "Chronica Pontificum Ecclesiæ Eboraci" in Twysden's Decem Scriptores Historiæ Anglicanæ, Londini 1652: "Officium et Missa de Nomine Jesu" and "Officium et Missa de B. Anna" in the Breviary and Missal. *John de Bromyard*, "Summa Prædicantium," very early but without date or place, Nurimburgæ 1485, 1518, Lugduni 1522, Venetiis 1586, Antverpiæ 1614; "Opus Trivium" on divine, canon, and civil law, very early but without date or place, 1500, Parisiis 1500. *Geoffrey the Grammarian*, "Promptorius Puerorum. Promptorium Parvulorum sive Clericorum. Medulla Grammatice," printed by Rich. Pynson in 1499; by Wykyn de Worde in 1510, 1512, 1516, 1528, and lately by the Camden Society. *John Hilsley*, a Manual of Prayers (or Primer) with the Epistles and Gospels (posthumous) London 1539; De Veri Corporis esu in Sacramento. *Will. Perin*, three godly and most learned Sermons of the most honourable and Blessed Sacrament of the Altar, London 1546, 1548; "Spiritvall Exercyses and Goostly Meditations," London 1557, Caen 1598; a book in defence and for the frequent celebrating of the Mass, which Wood had not seen. Many Dominican works and editions we believe have escaped our notice.

was clever but ambitious, was eager to make himself great at any cost by backing the royal will, and lending his name to every schismatical measure. This was John Hilsley, who was rewarded for his pains in 1535 with the bishopric of Rochester. There were too a Stroddle prior of London, who subscribed the supremacy; a Cosin of Winchester and Dod of Cambridge, who preached error, and a Briggs of Norwich, who yielded to expediency. Hilsley died in his schism in 1538. Stroddle, when he was turned out of the convent of London by Hilsley, inflicted his presence on the unwilling nuns of Dartford under the false plea that he had royal orders to do so; his after career, as that of Cosin and Dod, is unknown. Briggs went among the secular clergy, was made vicar of Bressingham in 1539, of Kenningham in 1547, and of Wymondham in 1559, and after following every change of faith probably died out of the Church. On the other hand, there were numerous friars of the Order, as F. William Hardove, F. Will. Perin, F. Rich. Marshall, and F. Rich. Hargrave, who combated the king's divorce and supremacy with tongue and pen, and suffered in the Church's cause. F. Will. Hardove was imprisoned in 1534, with many more, and the others had to quit the country. In the following year more than a hundred Dominicans chose rather to be driven from their native land than to yield up their faith at the beck of the royal despot. Fontana says, that not one of the young religious forsook the Order; they fled into Scotland and Ireland, and waited there till the master-general settled them in different convents abroad. The destruction of religious communities was begun in 1536 by putting down the small convents, and in 1538 it was finished by the forced surrender or forfeiture of the large monasteries, which were sold to satisfy the avarice of needy courtiers, or squandered on the pleasures of the king. Out of all the houses, only thirteen appear as having surrendered formally.* The remaining friars were turned out of their dwellings into the world without any provision for their support, as they had not even the paltry pensions doled out to the unhoused monks. Some few were secularized, as F. Maurice Griffin, who in Mary's time became bishop of Rochester; most withdrew abroad, but some remained in the service of their Order and of the fallen Church, among whom was F. John Hopton, confessor to the princess, afterwards queen Mary. When under Edward VI. Protestantism was set up on the ruins of the Church, the wreck of the Dominican province was threatened with entire destruction. But that end has never come. A holy hope has ever dwelt in the province whispering the inspired words: "Miseriæ obliviscêris, et quasi aquarum quæ præterierunt recordaberis. Et quasi meridianus fulgor consurget tibi ad vesperam: et cum te consumptum putaveris, orieris ut lucifer." *Job* xi. 16, 17.

* The community of Dartford alone subscribed the supremacy May 14th 1534, if faith can be put in an instrument which has only the seal of the convent, and bears neither names nor signatures.

THE LIFE

OF

PHILIP THOMAS CARDINAL HOWARD.

CHAPTER I.

During the five years of queen Mary's eventful reign, the national religion brought in by Henry VIII. and settled by the protectorate of Edward VI. was abolished. In its ancient faith and ecclesiastical discipline, England was again in communion with the Roman pontiff. In restoring the Church Mary satisfied the many claims it had on her sympathies even in a temporal point of view. In order to give more security to it she laboured to repair the great defences of the citadel of Sion. Several of the religious Orders were revived, and the scanty possessions belonging to ecclesiastical foundations which had escaped the rapacity of courtiers were given back for their hallowed uses. The Dominican Order was then rendering great services in the two Universities, and shared the royal favour. Eighteen years had passed since the convents were destroyed, and most of the Religious who had fled into foreign countries were dead or had become bound to other duties. The Dominican province of England had lost its canonical form of government, and the provincialship was made an honorary title for one of the associates who form the council of the master-general at Rome. Still there was a considerable body of Dominicans in England governed by a vicar appointed by the master-general. Mary called together a remnant of the Order in

1556, and established it in the priory of St. Bartholomew in Smithfield founded about 1102 by Rahere the king's minstrel: and F. William Perin was made prior of the house by the authority of cardinal Pole legate of the pope in England. This father was also vicar-general of the province, and made himself famous as a great champion of the Church during all the stormy period of the schism, and in consequence underwent exile and severe trials all borne with unbroken constancy and courage. He gathered a community of English, Spanish, and Belgian friars in his new convent, where however he soon rested from his labours. He was buried August 22nd 1558 in the convent-church formed out of the choir of the ancient priory which was all then left of the venerable building.

The nuns of Dartford were likewise restored. Out of nineteen choir-sisters pensioned when their house was suppressed seven still survived, and they again formed a community in England. The convent of King's-Langley was given to them in 1556; in 1558 after the death of Lady Anne of Cleves they removed to Dartford, and their own home was once more hallowed with their choral services and witnessed the holiness of life which had made them faithful to their vows for so many years and through such heavy trials. These seven were, Elizabeth Cresner prioress, Catherine Clovyle, Catherine Efflyn, Elizabeth White or Wright, Maria Benson, Elizabeth Exmen, and Magdalen Frere: and their confessor was F. Richard Hargrave an excellent Religious who had never yielded for a moment to the schism.

The death of queen Mary November 17th 1558 was fatal to the Church: her passing-bell was its knell too. Elizabeth was proclaimed queen, and there seemed a well-founded hope at first that no change would be made in religion, as she outwardly professed the ancient faith. But in a very short time Mass was celebrated in her private chapel without the elevation of the Host, and then the Holy Sacrifice was done away with and communion given under both kinds. Protestants from all parts of the continent, and particularly from Geneva the head-quarters of Calvinism flocked into England and spread their doctrines on all sides; and every one could now follow his inward spirit without question. The parliament soon renewed the schism, by decreeing that Elizabeth was supreme governor of the Church of England, and that all who held any benefice or office must swear to maintain her supremacy. The "Act for the Uniformity of Common Prayer" was then passed; and the property of the restored religious establishments was granted to the crown.

After F. William Perin's death F. Richard Hargrave was elected prior of St. Bartholomew's by the unanimous votes of the community; and he was recommended to the master-general by cardinal Pole for the vicarship of the province. The letters-patent of the two offices did not reach England till Easter 1559, when they were sent to F. John de Villagarcia a Spanish Dominican then professor of theology in the university of Oxford; and he forwarded them to the sub-prior of the convent to be put into force. But the sub-prior was a timid man and his moral cowardice made him a traitor. He feared to break the laws enacted against those receiving authority or jurisdiction from any foreign prelate, and carried the letters to the privy council. F. Richard Hargrave went to the convent to take the government, when Lord Rich a nobleman of the privy council had him driven out, and his life was in jeopardy, so he returned to Dartford. The sub-prior kept the convent in his own hands till it was destroyed. Of the friars there, after the decease of F. William Perin some died, others who belonged to the Spanish and Belgian provinces departed into their own countries, and when the convent was suppressed July 12th

(o. s.) 1559* there were only three priests and one young man, "who," to quote the words of F. Richard Hargrave, "chose to remain in England and enjoy the flesh-pots of Egypt to being abject in the house of the Lord."

The oath of supremacy and the "Book of Common Prayer" were enforced from the feast of St. John Baptist (June 24th) 1559. All the bishops except one were deprived, and the political destruction of the Church was completed. Three visitors were chosen out of the privy council and authorized under the great seal of England to suppress the new convents; for all the religious had stood their ground after the act was passed against them, except the Friar-Minors who at once withdrew out of the kingdom and carried away their goods unmolested. King Philip of Spain, through his ambassador the duke of Feria, obtained a safe conduct for the Religious thus driven from their homes and found them means to pass the sea. The visitors soon went

---

* In the archives of the province, an interesting memorial of the convent of St. Bartholomew in Smithfield is still preserved. It is a Collectarium, in small folio, written in black letter, on vellum, and comprising 134 leaves. At the bottom of the first page after the calendar: "Orate p' a'i'a Venerabilis p'ris ff'ris Rob'ti Mylys sacre theologie m'ri ac q^{o}nda' p'uincialis anglie q^{i} hu'c libru' fieri fecit A^{o} x^{i} M ccccc xxiij." Added at the head of the calendar: "Orate pro a'i'a D'ni Thomæ Dowman Sacerdotis eccli'æ lychfyldie's' qui hu'c libru' Conve'tui ordinis predicator' apud Sanctu' Bartholomeu' londini dedit anno 1557 : 12 : Septe'bris." At the bottom of the last page: "Orate pro anima f^{ris} Vincentij Torre S. Theol : Mag^{ri} Pro'ce Angliæ Vicarij Gen^{lis} Ord^{is} ff^{m} Predicatorum, qui huno libr' Dono acceptum ab ad^{m} R^{do} P. Paulo Jordaens Priore Brugensi eiusdem Oord^{is} (*sic*) die 3. Junij 1683, deposuit in Bibliotheca ff^{m} Pred^{m} Bornhemiensiu'. Pro Conventu suo S^{ti} Bartholomæi Londinensi, die 15. Junii 1683."

to Dartford, and calling F. Richard Hargrave and another priest who lived with him tendered the oath and book, and promised great dignities and favours if they would leave the Order and conform to what was required of them. "But that Lord," says F. Richard, "who saved me from schism in the time of Henry VIII. delivered me once more from the lion's mouth, gave me constancy, and kept me from apostatizing either from the faith or from religion." The visitors next summoned the prioress and nuns each alone the better to induce them to yield, but they all refused with unshaken constancy. Then the visitors seeing that they gained nothing had everything in the convent valued, and sold all in the face of the nuns at the lowest rate. They paid the debts of the house, divided the little money over between the prioress and the nuns, took away the common seal and the patents of the revenues, and commanded the Religious to quit within twenty-four hours. Accordingly the nuns departed taking their books and best clothing, and four days after together with the Bridgettins of Sion House* embarked on board a vessel prepared at king Philip's expense and crossed over to Belgium. The band of Dominican exiles was formed of twelve members of the Order consisting of the two priests, the prioress with four choir-nuns and four lay-sisters, and a young girl who had not yet received the habit. These nuns were all aged women the youngest being fifty and three of them eighty years of age: one of them Elizabeth Wright was half-sister to John Fisher bishop of Rochester, whose martyr-spirit she fully shared. They went first to Antwerp and thence to Dendermond, where for two months they lived in a hospital. At length the provincial

* The prioress of the Bridgettin nuns was Catherine Palmer, to whom F. William Perin in 1557 dedicated his beautiful "Spiritual Exercises."

of Belgium who was their only comforter found them a refuge in the convent of Leliendael near Zierikzee, the capital of Schowen one of the islands of Zeeland, the house being in a barren place almost without fresh water, and nearly in ruins. Unfriended strangers they were obliged to ask the master-general's leave for disposing of their few goods to procure the necessaries of life; and they had to petition the duchess of Parma to extend to them her charitable aid. Resources failed, and as the convent of Leliendael could not support so great a burden on its means the English nuns in two months had to return to Antwerp, where they lived on alms. The iconoclastic outbreak in 1566 drove them from that city, and they fled to Bergen-op-zoom. During those times of hardship and suffering Elizabeth Cresner continued to be their prioress, and they observed all the holy offices of their Order. Death gradually reduced their numbers, so that when the master-general made his visitation about the end of December 1573 only the prioress and three nuns were still alive; and he assigned them to the convent of Engelendael outside Bruges, where they soon passed through the gate of death from the *Angels' Valley* to the Mount of God.

Thus was the English province of St. Dominic laid waste. Whilst the nuns were in Zeeland, the vicar-general proposed to return into his native country with three of his religious and try to organize his brethren again. All was fruitless. The oppression of the Church began which in fierceness equalled and in malice exceeded the persecutions of Christianity in the early ages. But the province has never been extinguished. From time to time English Catholics entered the Order in foreign convents, and then came to labour for their countrymen and even to lay down their lives in the glorious but unequal strife with error. They ministered to the spiritual necessities of the faithful, flying from place to place, from town to town, from county to county, as the bloodhounds of heresy harried the land. When Elizabeth's evil reign was over it was hoped that the son of the queen of Scots for the sake at least of his mother's memory would grant toleration to Catholics. The master-general sent additional missionaries into England from the neighbouring provinces and enjoined the provincial of Ireland to lend his aid. But James I. was too weak to be generous, and yielding to the temper of the times he appointed a commission in 1604 for banishing the Catholic missionaries from England. Many of the Dominicans had to withdraw, but several boldly remained at the peril of their lives to console the faithful in secret. For many years the little Dominican body struggled on, recruited from time to time by religious from abroad. In three general chapters of the Order regulations were made for meeting the wants of the English province. In 1615 it was recommended that the college founded by donna Agnes de Gabennas in Andalusia should be assigned to the English; in 1618 probably on the failure of that scheme the convent of Alcala also in Andalusia was deputed for English novices; and in 1628 it was decreed that English novices should be received into the convents of Ronda and Marchena in the south of Spain. The province continued to be governed by vicars-general even down to 1685.

A great many of the Dominicans in England were foreigners attached to the embassies. The most famous of these was F. Diego de la Fuente a Spaniard who resided many years in London as confessor to count Gondomar ambassador of the king of Spain at the court of James I. This good "Padre Maestro" as he was called was a very zealous and learned friar, and was so much esteemed by the secular clergy that when the archpriest Edward Harrison died in 1621 they sought him for their bishop, and it was only his own earnest entreaties that made them cease to press their point. He might have governed the Dominican body in England, but here again he showed his disinterestedness, for at his instance the master-general July 8th 1622* gave the charge to F. Thomas Middleton.

F. Thomas Middleton came on the mission into his native country in 1617, and was usually known by the name of Dade. He was superior of the province for thirty-three years, and under the auspices of queen Henrietta Maria he endeavoured to reinvigorate it by erecting a noviciate in England. He obtained the master-general's patents for this purpose June 24th 1636, but the troubles of the great rebellion probably thwarted his plans. Among others he was commissioned in 1642 by the archbishop of Cambray to enquire diligently into the cause and manner of death of several priests in England who had preferred the faith to their lives. He, too, narrowly escaped taking his own place among the martyrs whose acts he had to record. He was arrested in London on account of his priestly character, cast into Newgate, and brought up for trial along with F. Peter Wright S.J. at the spring sessions of 1651. The lord chief justice Roles sent into the country for Thomas Gage to appear against the prisoners. To ward off this blow the Rev. George Gage an eminent clergyman prevailed on his apostate brother not to sink himself into deeper guilt by steeping his hands in innocent blood. Thomas Gage kept his word as to F. Thomas Dade, for although he bore witness against him that he knew him to be the superior of the Dominicans he qualified his testimony by adding that possibly he was not a priest as St. Francis governed his Order without

* All our dates are New Style, except when it is otherwise expressed. It may be useful to some of our readers to observe, that the New Style in the seventeenth century was ten days and in the eighteenth eleven days in advance of the old. So the date above given was June 28th in England. The Old Style was given up in September 1752.

being one; and as the capital charge was not proved F. Thomas was acquitted by the jury.

In 1634 there were twenty Dominicans in England. By the disastrous civil war which raged for so many years this number was lessened, and during the Commonwealth there were only six Religious who were natives of the country.

F. Thomas Middleton resigned the office of vicar-general in 1655, and closed his life it is said May 18th 1664.

F. Thomas Catchmay whose baptismal name was George was professed in the Order in 1623 and was long a missionary in London. He was appointed vicar-general November 3rd 1655 and was in authority for nearly six years.

F. William Fowler belonged to the family of Fowler of St. Thomas's near Stafford, where he dwelt and died May 24th 1662. He left a picture of St. Dominic and one of St. Thomas in the chapel of the house which was formerly a priory of canons-regular of St. Augustine.

F. Thomas Armstrong was born in Northumberland or in the county of Durham. He entered the English College at Rome in 1631 for the secular priesthood, but was allowed to leave and follow his vocation in the Order of Friar-Preachers. He lived many years at Stonecroft about three miles from Hexham, and laboured chiefly among the nobility and gentry of those parts. He was widely known and much esteemed for his diligence in his religious duties, and through his means John Widdrington lord of Stonecroft left an annuity for maintaining a priest of the Order there. He closed his life May 29th 1662 and was buried at Stonecroft.

F. Robert Armstrong brother of F. Thomas dwelt in a mean cottage either within or close to Hexham. He laboured in his missionary career with plentiful fruit especially among the common people and brought back many families into the church. He was remarkable for holiness of life and for great gifts as an exorcist, so that he became "dæmonibus terribilis." He was usually called by the name of Roberts and died at Hexham May 5th 1663 in the repute of sanctity, for fifty years after "his name still breathed a sweet odour and his memory was in benediction."

F. David Joseph Kemeys will be repeatedly mentioned in the course of our narrative.

Besides these six on the mission there were other English Dominicans in various convents abroad. But the province had now fallen so low that it seemed to be on the brink of utter ruin, when it pleased God in His good providence to call His servant from the highest nobility of the land for bringing about its Restoration.

CHAPTER II.

The Hon. Philip Howard belonged to the most noble family of England. Thomas Howard his grandfather, born in 1585, enjoyed the hereditary titles of his illustrious ancestors, being Sir Thomas Howard, chief of the Howards, Earl of Arundel and Surrey, premier Earl and Earl Marshall of England; Baron Howard, Mowbray, Segrave, Bruce of Gower, Fitz Alan, Clun, Oswaldestre, Maltravers and Greystock. He took for his consort Lady Alethea, third daughter and eventually sole heir of Gilbert Talbot earl of Shrewsbury; and had with others two sons James and Henry Frederick. James, commonly called Lord Mowbray and Maltravers, died without issue. Henry-Frederick on his brother's decease received those titles, and when his father died succeeded to the other dignities of his house.

By his consort Elizabeth daughter of Esme Stuart, duke of Lennox, who was allied in blood to the reigning sovereign of Great Britain and Ireland, lord Henry Frederick Howard had a numerous family, the sons being Thomas, Henry,

Philip, Charles, Talbot, Edward, Francis, Bernard and Esme; and the daughters Anne, Catherine and Elizabeth.

Philip, the third son, is the subject of the present work. He was born September 21st 1629, at Arundel House, the town-residence of his family in the parish of St. Clement Dane without Temple Bar. Up to the age of fourteen years he was under several private tutors* by whom his fine abilities were well developed, whilst his active mind was disciplined in the school of Christ. Some of his tutors were Protestants, but they failed to influence the fair character of their pupil. His education was entirely controlled by his grandfather, who unfortunately for himself had conformed in 1615 to the Church of England, being perhaps led to do so by political motives, for the sincerity of his change may be questioned, as his children and grand-children were brought up in the faith he had forsworn; Clarendon says that "he was rather thought not to be much concerned for Religion, than to incline to this or that party of any," and that "he died in Italy, under the same doubtful character of Religion in which he lived." Thus Philip was educated a Catholic. His mind was deeply imbued with piety, and whilst he was a mere boy he had a gentle but strong influence for good on those around him, so that his grandfather was wont to call him his Bishop; and even then he had ideas that needed only favourable circumstances to bud and ripen into the high vocation of religious life.

Thomas earl of Arundel was greatly esteemed and much employed in the court of Charles I. He was chief justice and justice-in-eyre of the royal forests, parks and chases beyond Trent; lord lieutenant of Norfolk, Sussex and Surrey, Nor-

* When he was eleven years old, Philip with his brothers Thomas and Henry appear to have been entered Fellow Commoners of St. John's College, Cambridge. His and their residence in the University must have been very short.

thumberland, Cumberland and Westmoreland; knight of the most noble Order of the Garter; one of the most honourable Privy Council in England and Ireland; steward of the royal household; and although no soldier, general of all the king's forces in the expedition of 1639 against the Scots; and in 1644 he was created earl of Norfolk. In July 1641 the earl and his countess were appointed by the king to conduct abroad the mother of queen Henrietta Maria, who for two years had been in England. He left his countess with the French queen at Cologne, and spent some time at Utrecht with his grandsons who had been sent there for their education. Again after the marriage of Mary the king's eldest daughter to William second prince of Orange (father of William III.) he was commissioned to escort the royal bride with her mother Henrietta-Maria into Holland. He embarked at Dover, at the end of February 1641-2 and safely led his charge to her destination. The earl never returned into England, for the Civil War broke out and he determined to remain on the continent. From Holland he went to Antwerp, where he was joined by his countess and grandchildren, who were forced to seek abroad the personal safety and religious freedom which the calamities of their native land imperilled.

A Catholic country influenced Philip Howard in a manner easily foreseen in a youth so well disposed. Soon after he arrived at Antwerp he fell in with the Carmelite friars there, and in the first impulse of devotion he wished to join their venerable Order. But his vocation lay elsewhere, so that it is no wonder that his resolution gave way when it encountered the affection of his parents and the extraordinary fondness of his grandfather for him. Still he did not give up his hopes of entering religion, but patiently awaited the time when his course would become clear and practicable.

Leaving the countess at Antwerp (and they never met again) the earl of Arundel began a long tour with some of his grandsons, of whom Philip was one. He visited Spa, passed through part of France, and then went into Italy. At Milan Philip Howard became acquainted with F. John Baptist Hackett, of the Order of Friar-Preachers, who was regent in the convent of St. Eustorgius and taught theology there. The kindness and learning of this celebrated Irish Dominican won the heart and secured the confidence of Philip, who opened his mind to him and declared that he intended if possible to quit the world. Philip very soon felt strongly drawn towards the Order of St. Dominic, and while begging spiritual guidance in the matter he explained how he would be greatly hindered in his design by the affectionate opposition of his family and in particular of his grandfather. In reply F. John Baptist Hackett only repeated the sound and prudent counsel usually given on such occasions. If the vocation was from God there was no reason to dread the contradiction of friends, for He who inspired the holy purpose would by His grace change their dispositions in the end, and make what seemed insurmountable obstacles only serve His holy Will. So the good Father advised Philip to recommend the matter earnestly to God, to increase the fervour of his prayers, to cleanse his conscience thoroughly by a strict confession, and to leave the event in the hands of Providence. Philip was much comforted and encouraged, and remained with his grandfather, but he prudently kept his aspirations secret. He continued the tour through the chief cities of Italy. In his travels he came to the town of Piacenza in the duchy of Parma, where he stayed for some time. He now seized the opportunity to carry out his purpose. With leave from his grandfather to go again to Milan he hastened to his kind guide, to whom he declared that he was determined to join the Order of St. Dominic, and he sought means to do so. F. John Baptist Hackett perceived how difficult and pressing was the case. He had to choose between the danger of a serious and perhaps everlasting injury to the young nobleman and the certainty of stirring up the earl of Arundel's anger and the calumnies of the world against him. He preferred the latter alternative, as it would at least bring the matter to an issue. In his company Philip hastened to the convent of the Order of Cremona, where June 28th 1645 he laid aside his rich attire, put on the simple habit of religion, took the name of Thomas out of devotion to the Angelic Doctor whose extraordinary trials of vocation he was in some measure to share, and entered on the noviciate of a humble Black-friar.

The news of this bold step was immediately sent to the earl of Arundel in letters both from Brother Thomas Howard and F. John Baptist Hackett, and it made a stir in the earl's family which in violence could hardly have been foreseen. In the mind of the earl, the bitterest feelings of pride, anger, and deeply-wounded affection were aroused. His indignation was directed against the Dominicans for daring to receive the novice, and particularly against F. John Baptist Hackett, whom he represented as seducing his grandchild into the monastic state, towards which the youth had never shown any leaning. Unweariedly he took measures for drawing the novice from his retreat and restoring him to his family, and he engaged most powerful friends in his own behalf by stating the case to them with all the prejudices of his own views. The day after the religious clothing the earl sent his account of what had happened to the countess of Arundel at Antwerp, and meanwhile he and his grandson Henry tried to entice the novice from his new career. But their entreaties, promises, and remonstrances were withstood with wonderful firmness and energy, in which the earl could see nothing but obstinacy and disobedience.

By gaining over the supreme ecclesiastical authorities to his side the earl of Arundel thought to frustrate the purpose of the novice beyond the power of any appeal. He called in the aid of John Digby, esq., who afterwards married lady

Catherine Howard, the earl's granddaughter: and this active and interested advocate being then in Rome went immediately to cardinal Francis Barberini protector of England, through whom he got access to cardinal Panfili nephew of the reigning pontiff, and to cardinal Anthony Barberini protector of the Order of Friar-Preachers. All three he enlisted in favour of the earl. Cardinal Panfili laid his representations before Innocent X., and received commands, which, though they fell short of the earl's full wishes, were calculated to discover whether Brother Thomas Howard had been improperly influenced in choosing his new state of life. By the pontiff's order, cardinal Panfili wrote July 17th to the bishop of Cremona and directed him to remove the young religious from his convent, to forbid all intercourse between the Dominicans and their novice, and to keep him in the episcopal palace till his real disposition was found out and the further will of his Holiness made known. Two days after cardinal Francis Barberini expressed to the earl how much he sympathized with him and disapproved of the imprudence of those who had taken such advantage of his grandson's frankness; and he added that he had forwarded the great exertions of Mr. Digby by dispatching Sig. Prospero Meocci, a gentleman in his service, into Lombardy to carry out the pope's instructions.

By the hand of Meocci, cardinal Anthony Barberini sent a letter to the master-general F. Thomas Turco to engage his co-operation, so that the matter which regarded the service of English Catholics might be speedily and silently ended; and the master-general seeing such an appearance of justice at once yielded, and wrote in suitable terms to the prior of Cremona.

Commissioned by these high authorities Meocci hastened to obey his orders. When the prior learned the will of the pope and received the master-general's letter he promptly submitted. Brother Thomas Howard was overwhelmed with sorrow, protested against his removal, and refused to acknowledge his separation from the Order, or even to lay aside the outward tokens of religion. He was taken from the convent July 26th to the palace of Cæsar Monti cardinal-archbishop of Milan. There he had apartments to himself adjoining those of his eminence, and he was surrounded with domestics and strangers, but strictly withdrawn from everyone suspected of influencing him in his cherished purpose. In a few days, Meocci gave an account of his own proceedings to the earl of Arundel, and added that his eminence had several times examined the novice and found him very constant in his resolution.

Meanwhile, this constancy was well searched into by the cardinal-archbishop, who daily spent some hours in conversing familiarly with the novice. To him Brother Thomas Howard laid his mind open, and explained that for three years he had thought of becoming a religious in order that he might help in the conversion of his kindred and countrymen. The cardinal urged against him, that the change from the Carmelites to the Dominicans was a reason for doubting other changes as time went on; the restraints of religious life might be very burdensome at his tender age; he could promote his own salvation in every state; by his example and great zeal he might as a secular do much among the Catholics of England and help to convert heretics, and perhaps he would succeed better with the sword at his side than with the capuce upon his head; the scholars of the Swiss college were not allowed to become Religious, as out of religion they were more useful in their own country; his resolution misrepresented and ill-understood might perhaps be somewhat injurious to the Catholics of England; the delay of a couple of years might strengthen and fix his vocation; and some doubts of his constancy might arise. To all these and other like objections the novice replied in few words, that he could save his soul better in religion than in the world, in England he could do all the more as a religious in the service of souls, and if he waited for another opportunity he was not sure of it. The novice always spoke of the conversion of his friends and countrymen with great earnestness, and with a peculiar bright expression of pleasure lighting up his countenance. The cardinal called in an Oblate who was prefect of the spiritual exercises, and the grand Penitentiary of Milan, who particularly noted all these traits of character; and their knowledge of the spiritual life rendered their decision above all dispute: after repeated examinations they both concluded that the vocation of Brother Thomas Howard was true and came from God.

Cardinal Monti saw all that passed with secret satisfaction, and August 2nd wrote a long account to cardinal Panfili of what he had done in this delicate matter. His letter gave the case in its juster and more favourable aspect, and considerably altered the opinion of the three cardinals. Insomuch that when the earl of Arundel wrote twice to cardinal Francis Barberini thanking him for his ready assistance and urging him to bring the affair to a speedy close, his eminence returned a tardy reply, which though courteous was so reserved as to show how he now looked on the case and that he would not overstep the bounds of strict justice. The master-general too openly took up the cause of Brother Thomas Howard and lent it all his influence.

The earl of Arundel signally failed in attempting to show that the Dominicans had used unwarrantable influence. He now tried again to carry his point by a more particular attack on the affections of his grandson. Henry Howard went to his brother at the cardinal's palace, and he thus describes what passed there in a letter written to the earl on the same day (August 9th). "I had two or three howres talke with him in the Garden alone, & I thinke tould him as much, and as many, and as strong reasons & persuasions as I could possibly thinke of; & could not moue him in anything; onely when I chidd him for his disobedience, and tould him how vnkindly your Ex^{ce} tooke it at his hands, hee seemed to be somewhat mooued to heare how much your Ex^{ce} greeued for his losse, yett not with the least intent euer of quitting his habite, telling me how fully he was resolued to continue his firme purpose during life. I shall not fayle to talke with him, and doe ye best I can to persuade him to reason, to the wch now I finde him very auerse and obstinate." The ecclesiastical authorities became so well satisfied with Brother Thomas's case that he was sent to the Dominican convent of S. Maria delle Grazie in Milan; and Henry Howard foiled in his powerful assaults on his brother's resolution returned to his grandfather.

The subject was again forced on the attention of Innocent X. from another quarter. At Antwerp the countess of Arundel afflicted at the earl's letter, flew to the papal nuncio at Brussels and secured his co-operation. In a letter to the earl she thus expresses her hopes and feelings.

"My Dearest harte, I receaued yesterday your letter of ye 29 of June, with the sadest newes (as with all reason you expresse it to be vnto you, and is no lesse to me,) of Philip, though so much comfort we have, that there cannot be lesse than one whole yeare's time to worke with effect his returne, for wch a letter to the Marques of Velada will, I hope, be sufficient: for he being informed of the case, it cannot but be estemed a thing due in al iustice to have him taken away from those, who have in such manner receaued him. The Marques cannot but in honor and iustice effectually order and vse his authority in it; and if he finde it needefull, that of ye Nuntio's theare; but if nothing else shall serue, I am resolued (if I can geet moneys to free my selfe from this place) to goe my selfe in person (to free you from such an affliction) and to effecte it, and euen follow the Pope's letter for that purpos, rather then it should not be done. For God his sake, my harte, lett us not afflict ourselues: wee shall assuredly haue redresse, as I find to be the iudgment of the most pious and prudent men of all Sortes, who all condemne vtterly such proceedings of theyrs: to w^{ch} [I join] my prayers to our Lord Jesus for all happiness to vs and all ours. I rest

"Y^{r} most faythful louing wife,

"A. Arundel & Surrey.

"Antwerpe, 29 Julij, 1645."

The nuncio accordingly wrote to Innocent X., who wearied with the importunities of the Howard family passed the affair over to the Congregation de Propaganda Fide. Early in September this congregation yielded to the countess's desire so far as to direct Brother Thomas Howard to be removed to Rome that his vocation might undergo a still stricter ordeal.

On learning it was intended to send him from Milan to Rome, Brother Thomas Howard was much alarmed. Hitherto he had only passively resisted the overtures of his family, but now he thought it needful to strike openly and boldly for his religious freedom. He wrote September 18th a formal protest praying and claiming as his right, that if he were again separated from his Order he might be restored to it, as he was fully determined to persevere till death.

The decree of the propaganda revived the earl of Arundel's hopes of soon carrying his point; and before he knew the decision of the congregation he wrote twice to sir Kenelm Digby, through whose influence at the Roman Court still greater importance he thought would be added to his cause. Sir Kenelm's reply was delayed for nearly a fortnight.

"My Lord, Be pleased to receaue by this my dutifull acknowledgement of your $lo^{p's}$, one of the 18, the other of the 25 september. In both of wch y^{r} lo: doth me much more honor then I can deserue. But certainely (my lord) no man liuing desireth more then I to do y^r lo: and y^r noble famely, seruice. I haue, this morning, spoken both wth Cardinall Panfilio and Cardinall Panzirola, to vnderstand when they expect Mr. Phillip here; and they both told me that Cardinal Monti his last letters assured them there should be no time lost in his sending hither, but that he should infallibly come by the first fitting and secure conveniency. And in truth, they expressed themselves exceeding sensible of Mr Phillip's forgetting himselfe to y^r lo: and to his parents, and of the fryars' impudency and other missebeseeming proceedings, and bad me assure y^r lo: that, as soone as he shall be here, they will do their vtmost to serue you in this businesse, as being exceedingly sensible of y^r case. Father Rector will do y^r lo: much seruice herein, both wth his aduice and sollicitation, so doubptlessely will Cardinall Barbarin (in whose house, I conceaue, y^r grandchild is to remaine); and as farre as my small talent reacheth, y^r lo: is sure of my dutiful seruice as long as I stay here. Yet for the credit of the businesse (besides the efficacious helpe), it will be requisite somebody should be here with imediate procure from y^r lo:, wch if you did thinke fitt to haue y^r granchild Mr Henry to be the person, and that no other considerations checke att it, I am very confident the businesse would thriue in his hands; for his great discretion and the much esteeme he hath with all persons here will render him successfull in any thing hee shall undertake, especially when he shall be accompanied wth so much reason and iustice. I will not longer troble your lo:, but beseching God to send you perfect health and happinesse, I rest

"Y^r lo: most humble and most obedient seruant,

"KENELME DIGBY.

"Rome, 7th of 8ber, 1645."

It seems to have been at first arranged to place Brother Thomas Howard in the palace of cardinal Barberini, it was perhaps owing to his own protest that he was sent to the Dominican convent of St. Sixtus. Following sir Kenelm's advice, the earl of Arundel despatched Henry Howard to Rome, who sought to procure a command from the pope shutting Brother Thomas out of the Dominican and every other Order, except with the clear sanction of the Holy See and the leave of his family. The reasons given for so severe a measure were solely that the Howards would be disgraced by one of them turning friar, and that were the matter taken up by the British parliament, the earl might have to suffer imprisonment and the forfeiture of all his property, if he ever returned into England. To such effect Henry Howard wrote a letter in the name of the whole Howard family to cardinal Capponi for the consideration of the sacred college and of the Sovereign Pontiff.

Little ear could be given to such weak reasons for making a vocation void, and Henry Howard saw that he must limit his efforts to the object of stripping his brother of the habit for a time and sending him to a distance, in the hope that change and delay would alter the purpose which all other means had failed to shake. He had however penetration enough to perceive that even do what he might there was still too much ground for fearing that he would be foiled in the long-run by his brother's steadfastness. He thus wrote to the earl of Arundel.

"Deare Grandfather, Since my last letter vnto your Excell^{ce}, I have solicited the business very hard, and find by Cardinall Pamphilio, that we cannot possibly haue any comand from ye Pope to comand my brother absolutely to bee excluded the Order; for Cardinall Pamphilio himselfe sayes, it would bee an extreame scandale to the world, that by mayne force hee should bee hindred from it, if it be a trew vocation from God. Thearefore that wch I cheefly reach at is, that only ye Pope will for the present be pleased to comand his habite to be taken offe, and that he may only be excluded the Order for the present, vntill his holinesse shall againe, by expresse order, give way vnto it, I wishing that, in the meane time, he may be sent vnto Perugia or some other convenient place, wheare for a few yeares he may studey; and if it be a trew vocation from God (as hee sayes it is) then it will continue for euer, although hee bee for ye present seuered from ye Order: and thus much I haue very good hopes to obtaine, yett I feare that I can scarce hinder that, after some yeares' time wch he must employ in studey, if his resolution and obstinacy continue, but that he will then be permitted by ye Pope to enter againe. Yett I thinke that if, for ye present, I can gett off his habite & take him out of ye Dominicans' clawes, I shall doe very well, & I doe really assure your Exce that this businesse is extreamely much more difficult then I could possibly imagine it, ere I was a personall and eye witnesse of it: this is all that I can say of it at this present; wherefore, I shall only most humbly craue your Exce's blessing, & expect your comands, who am and ever shall bee,

"Yr Exe's most dutifull grandchild,

"HENRY HOWARD.

"Rome, 9ber the 7, 1645."

This scheme also failed, and after more than half a year's toil to thwart the divine will, Henry Howard withdrew from Rome and returned to Padua where the earl of Arundel had fixed his abode.* By him Brother Thomas sent the following letter.

---

* John Evelyn was at Padua in 1646, and thus writes in his diary. "It was on Easter Monday that I was invited to breakfast at the earl of Arundel's. I took my leave of him in bed, where I left that great and excellent man in teares on some private discourse of crosses that had befallen his illustrious family, particularly the unhappiness of his grandson Philip turning Dominican friar."

"Deare Grandfather, With this occasion of my deare brother his returning backe to your E., I could not doe lesse then write these few lines vnto your E., to lett you vnderstand how sory I am that your E. taketh it so ille that I haue made my selfe a frier; for God Almighty knoweth that I would neuer haue done any such thing, if hee had not inspired and caled mee theare vnto: thearefore, I humbly desire your E. not to trouble your selfe theareat; for since God hath caled mee vnto such a holy Religion, I make no doubpt but hee will giue me perseuerance thearein: and your E. may bee assured that I doe not faile in praying daly both for you and all my parents: therefore, humbly crauing your pardon both for this and all the rest of my offences, & humbly desiring your blessing, I remaine alwaise, From our Convent of S. Sisto in Rome, this 22 of January, 1646,

"Your Excell$^{e's}$ most dutifull & obedient grandchild,

"FREYER THOMAS HOWARD, of the order of the Preachers."

Due prudence and moderation required that the wishes of the earl of Arundel and of his family should be yielded to as far as Christian justice allowed. At the suggestion of F. Dominic de Marini,* vicar-general of the Order, (the master-general being then on his visitations in Spain) Brother Thomas Howard was withdrawn from the Dominicans of St. Sixtus and placed with the fathers of St. Philip Neri.† Thus the last five months of his noviciate were passed at La Chiesa Nuova under the famous F. Paul Arringhi, who

* He was brother of the master-general F. John Baptist de Marini, and became at last vice-legate and archbishop of Avignon.

† Brother Thomas Howard was received to the clerical habit in the name of the province of England and convent of London; but he now changed his affiliation, and was accepted Feb. 27th for the convent of Cremona.

fathomed the disposition of his novice with fitting trials. At the close of the probation the good Oratorian openly declared that if Brother Thomas's vocation was not from God he did not know what a true vocation was. He gave the same testimony to Innocent X. whose interest was stirred up himself to question the novice. Accordingly Brother Thomas had an audience of the pope, and his prudent and ready answers drove away all doubts from the pontiff's mind. The pope called F. Dominic de Marini into his presence and gave him leave to admit the novice into the Dominican Order. Brother Thomas Howard made the usual protest, Oct. 18th, that of his own free will he entered the Order, and next day he joyfully subscribed his solemn profession at the convent of St. Sixtus, being then in the eighteenth year of his age. His vows were received by the vicar-general of the Order.

CHAPTER III.

From Rome Brother Thomas Howard was sent to the Dominican convent of the Blessed Virgin commonly called La Sanita at Naples, where he studied very diligently for four years, and made rapid progress in piety and learning. A few weeks before he left Rome, he received from Padua the news of the death of his grandfather, who had long been in failing health: and again in 1649 a fresh sorrow overtook him in the decease of the master-general F. Thomas Turco, who had been his firm and valued friend in all the severe trials of the noviciate. A general chapter was summoned to meet at Rome June 5th in the following year for electing another head of the Order. Brother Thomas was sent thither being chosen out of the students to deliver the usual Latin oration before the fathers. When he addressed the august assembly he took as his topic the subject which absorbed his mind and had carried him across the threshold of religion. He pleaded for his desolate country wasted by heresy and persecution and urged that the Order might be made more efficient in restoring it to the communion of the Church. And in a formal petition he humbly declared, that there were only few missionaries of the Order for confirming Catholics in their faith and for converting Protestants, and still fewer existed out of England who might be sent into the mission: and there was no seminary in the Order where others might be received to the habit for that particular purpose. Therefore he most earnestly prayed that the fathers would either set apart some convent for such a seminary, or at least charge provincials and priors to receive English youths who offered themselves for the Order.

The fathers were astonished and moved at the novice's address, and answered his appeal by an Admonition to provincials and to vicars of congregations not to be hard in receiving into the Order, English, Scotch, and Irish youths, when any offered themselves who were fit, but rather to admit them kindly into the noviciates for their own provinces, and after instructing them in regular observance and scholastic studies to send them back to spread the faith in their own countries.

After the general chapter Br. Thomas Howard was sent by advice of F. Dominic of the Rosary (O'Daly) to finish his studies at the convent of Rennes in Bretagne, whither he went with that great Irish Dominican. He was ordained a priest in 1652, with a papal dispensation for two years as he was only in his twenty-third year. The dispensation was applied for (August 22nd) by F. Peter Martin prior of the convent, and procured in Rome by F. Master O'Heyn of the Irish province. The reason for choosing Rennes for his abode was that he might assist his Catholic countrymen who fled from persecution in England. To them he devoted all his energies day and night, consoling them in distress, supporting their faith, and relieving their necessities.

F. Thomas Howard was in the province of Bretagne till near the close of 1654 when he went to Paris. The admonition of the general chapter in 1650 in favour of his country fell far short of his desires for the welfare of England. The want of systematic organization for keeping up and increasing the province was the great bar to the full operation of the Order in England, and this want could be met only by founding a monastery or college exclusively for the province. On such a house F. Thomas Howard had set his mind. The penal laws shut out religious communities from England, so he chose Belgium as being the best country both politically and geographically for his undertaking. He also preferred the discipline of the Order there, as it avoided equally the severity or the laxity of the observance in the French provinces. Into Belgium he bent his steps early in the spring of 1655.

At Brussels F. Thomas Howard took on this subject the advice of F. Ambrose Druwé, as he had great confidence in him who was so renowned for his labours and virtues that his memory has become venerable. F. Ambrose in his zeal for the good of the Order at once approved of the scheme, and bethought himself of the convent of Bornhem which had formerly belonged to his brethren and which he much desired to see once again in their hands. F. Master John Baptist Verjuyse fully agreed with him; and thus F. Thomas Howard's attention was first turned towards Bornhem. But as he had business in England he left the affair in the hands of these two Belgian fathers, and went on towards his native country.

On his way F. Thomas Howard passed through Ghent and seized the opportunity to consult F. Master James van den Heede ex-provincial of Belgium then prior of the convent there. This father entered warmly into the purpose, but did not look on Bornhem as a fit place: he thought a city would be better, as country convents in times of war were much more exposed to the fury of the soldiery and were often crushed in their infancy. He recommended a house in Dendermonde afterwards inhabited by Discalced Carmelite friars. But this would have been very expensive, as the house was in part fallen down and in part destroyed. There was moreover another difficulty in the way. It was feared that the local authorities both ecclesiastical and secular would refuse to admit foreign Religious into the city. It afterwards appeared however that D'Haens rural dean of Dendermonde had a strong leaning to the Dominicans, the more so perhaps as F. Alphonsus Henry of St. Thomas a Dominican illegitimate son of the king of Spain afterwards successively bishop of Osma, Placencia, and Malaga was expected in the country as governor of Belgium. D'Haens had freely given two thousand florins towards rebuilding the convent for Dominicans who knew the language of the country and could serve the city by preaching and hearing confessions, for which duties Englishmen were not very fit. These difficulties stopped F. Thomas from taking any steps as to this house, and he turned in another direction.

A house in Oudenarde called Berlamont was for sale on reasonable terms. It belonged to the count of Egmond, and was near the convent of Sion. It was a very fine building and with some alterations was well suited for a religious community. The garden though small could easily be enlarged, and this was done afterwards by D. Tatton superintendent of the French whilst they had the city. F. Thomas Howard*

* After he entered the Order F. Thomas Howard often used *Arundel* as his surname; but when his family was restored in 1660 and 1661 to the dukedom of Norfolk which had been forfeited in 1572, he called himself *Howard of Norfolk*. To avoid ambiguity hese changes have not been admitted into our narrative.

having already set on foot the treaty for the convent of Bornhem did not think it well to lay it aside. He preferred to negotiate for both and ultimately choose whichever seemed to be the better and more convenient of the two. This matter therefore he left in the hands of the prior of Ghent, who through the assistance of F. Michael Boon bought the house for 12,000 florins, on condition that if F. Thomas did not like it the contract might be made void by paying fifty imperial crowns.

Notwithstanding the great perils which beset the Catholic priesthood in England during the protectorate of Oliver Cromwell F. Thomas Howard remained for a considerable time in his native country, where he consulted the English Dominican fathers as to his undertaking. The vicar-general of the province and all of them fully approved his intentions, and joined in collecting the large sum of money needed for the purpose, in the firm hope of now setting again the bright torch of St. Dominic upon the deserted towers of the English Sion. First of all F. William Fowler gave £200. down, and he resolved to retire into the convent when finished and pass his old age in religious peace, but this plan was frustrated by his death. F. David Joseph Kemeys confessor to the countess of Arundel F. Thomas Howard's mother spoke on the matter to his friend Mr. David Morris a secular priest, and begged him to try and incline for the reviving province any young men of good hope he knew who were well disposed for the clerical state. Not long after Mr. Morris went to Little Malvern in Worcestershire, and there he met with Mr. Martin Russel who belonged to the honourable family of Russel lords of the manor. This gentleman had been educated by the Jesuits of St. Omers, and fought on the side of Charles II. in the fatal battle of Worcester. He was thinking of becoming a priest. By Mr. Morris's advice he went to London, where he was heartily welcomed by F. Thomas Howard, and he resolved to exchange a military life for one of religion in the Order of St. Dominic. In May 1656 he was sent by F. Thomas to the great house of Friar-Preachers at Ghent, and with the especial leave of the English vicar-general he took the habit of the Order June 18th, and passed through his year of probation.

F. Thomas Howard had as part of his patrimony the yearly rent of £97. 10s. 10½d. issuing out of the castle of Folkingham in Lincolnshire held by the earl of Lincoln. As this rent had not been paid for a long time he claimed seven years' arrears, and at his request sir Francis Stydolfe knt. his trustee empowered two gentlemen of the law to recover the amount by legal means. Thus with his own resources and the assistance of his friends he raised about £1600. for his convent. His grandmother died in 1654 before he had formed his plans, or doubtless she would have given much, as she abounded in works of piety and had bestowed £6,000. on the English fathers of the Society of Jesus for founding their college at Ghent. F. Thomas spent much of his time in London in attending to the spiritual welfare of his countrymen. About May 1657 he went back into Flanders without paying a visit to Rome as he thought of doing; but he sent an account of his progress to the master-general, who wrote back June 30th congratulating him on his safe arrival in Belgium and enclosed an epistle for F. Ambrose Druwé to stir him up most actively in the affair of the English convent.

Going first to Ghent F. Thomas Howard was gratified with witnessing the solemn vows taken by B. Martin Russel June 18th, who was professed for the province of England and convent of London because the situation of the house in Belgium was not settled. At Ghent too he deliberated concerning the house at Oudenarde. When he had well weighed the matter he thought Bornhem to be the better, so he broke off the contract for the house and paid the fifty crowns. From Ghent he went on to Brussels and found that F. Ambrose Druwé had carried on the treaty for Bornhem most happily. Still he had much to do to gain the leave of the civil and ecclesiastical authorities for the new convent; but unweariedly he overcame everything that stood in his way, and in the following April he again set up the conventual life which had been withdrawn from the English province for ninety-nine years.

CHAPTER IV.

Bornhem a village of East Flanders lies midway between Antwerp and Aalst, being four leagues south-west of Antwerp, three north-east of Dendermonde, seven east of Ghent, seven north-west of Brussels, and four north-north-west of Malines or Mechlin. It is on the south side of the river Scheldt which has been dammed off it about half a league, whilst the old Scheldt separated from the new by sluices became stagnant as a morass almost close to the village and surrounded all the castle. The parish of Bornhem forms part of a barony; the lord takes his title from this territory and resides at the castle.

In the sixteenth century the ancient castle of Bornhem passed in right of his wife to the marquis Piscarie. The sluices had not then been made, and during floods it could be approached only by boats, so that the marquis became discontent with the place and was wont to say he did not like to live in a swan's nest. So he sold the castle with all the demesnes to a nobleman Peter Coloma supreme receiver of Philip II. of Spain for Belgium and a member of the great Spanish family of the same surname. Peter Coloma now baron of Bornhem began the rescue of the place from the water by means of the sluices, and also to build a convent which was founded in the following manner.

The reform of the Franciscan Order throughout Flanders led several Religious to quit that province. Amongst them one who was a friend of Peter Coloma betook himself to Bornhem and employed his time in teaching youth the rudiments of the Christian faith. The good Franciscan sometimes talked with the baron on this useful and then much-needed work and offered to give himself up still more to it, for which he thought he could easily have leave from his superiors if the baron would build a small religious dwelling with a chapel near the heath. The scheme succeeded far better than he expected, for the baron immediately began a church and convent endowed with rents. This was about 1601. The old inhabitants of the village afterwards told the English fathers how the place was then infested in the night-time with hideous spectres and hobgoblins, so that people scarcely had courage enough to go out in the dark, and when they were driven to do so how they were scared by tremendous visions. In such a swampy country it is very likely that strange things were sometimes seen. The people however were highly pleased with the baron's purpose and lent their carts and horses gladly to carry the building materials, "rectè judicantes," says the annalist of Bornhem, "edificiis tam religiosis spectra dissipanda;" and doubtless the confidence inspired by the consecrated foundation would drive away many a spectre of the fancy.

There was also another reason for building the house. The baron had a large fragment of the Cross whereon the salvation of man was finished, and he wished to place the holy relic where it would be publicly venerated. Anna van Bech abbess of the Benedictine convent of Coninx-dorp bestowed it April 18th 1588 on Don Ferdinando Lopez de Villa Nuova, who two years after gave it to Peter Coloma baron of Bornhem, when Laurence Fabricius titular bishop of Cyrene and grand vicar of the archbishop of Cologne gave leave for it to be carried out of the archdiocese.

The baron of Bornhem did not live to see Religious on the foundation: he died in 1621 before he had leave from the Apostolic See for the Holy Sacrifice to be offered and the divine office to be celebrated there. His son who bore the same Christian name inherited his goodness, and was quite as eager for the house to be filled with persons consecrated to God.

Thus the convent of Bornhem was built for the Franciscans. It was arranged in the usual manner of their establishments. But they never had it, for the question arose whether it ought to fall to the lot of the reformed Franciscans of Flanders or of the old Franciscans of Brabant. And so it happened that the house remained empty for many years: it was put under the charge of an old man named Arthur Roosc, and sometimes when the country was overrun with military, soldiers were quartered in it for the winter.

At length the baron became outwearied with the delay and sought occupants for the house in other Orders. He offered it to some Minims, but the negotiations were broken off. A treaty with some Benedictine nuns was also without effect. The baron who highly esteemed F. Ambrose Druwè at last resolved to place Friar-Preachers there, and the fathers of Brussels readily accepted the generous offer. Urban VIII. gave leave November 9th 1639 for Mass to be celebrated in the conventual chapel, but the bishop of Ghent did not put the brief into execution till November 8th 1641. The baron then turned his attention to the public veneration of the Cross and exhibited the relic to the archbishop of Mechlin, who February 16th 1642 formally attested its authenticity, and afterwards the bishop of Ghent allowed it to be exposed to the faithful.

F. Ambrose Druwè and many of his brethren from

Brussels took possession of the house with some solemnity in 1641, but in consequence of the litigated claim of the Cordeliers they had to leave in 1643. They were allowed by a royal decree June 22nd 1646 to inhabit the cloister that summer, and they gave it up altogether in the beginning of the following year. During that time there were three Dominicans in the house: the baron contributed four pistoles a month towards maintaining them. The house was again void; but in September 1650 royal leave to live there for a time was granted to the Friar-Preachers of Bois-le-Duc, who in 1629 had been driven out of their own convent by the Calvinists. These Religious were at Bornhem till May 1651, when they removed to Mechlin where F. Ambrose had secured them a fixed abode. Meanwhile the Franciscans suffered their claim to fall through, and F. Ambrose was successfully labouring in founding convents at Namur and Mechlin so that he ceased to care any more for Bornhem. The baron thus thwarted in his plans made an agreement with the Gulielmites of Wasia and three Religious from the convent of Bevern took the house. The baron was greatly pleased when he saw his convent thus occupied, though he much regretted the loss of the Dominicans and kept up a friendly intercourse with them. His untimely death happened October 9th 1656: he was succeeded by John Francis Coloma his eldest son.

While F. Thomas Howard was raising means in England for founding his religious house F. Ambrose Druwè and F. John Baptist Verjuyse laboured to secure the convent of Bornhem for him, and they favourably inclined the privy council. F. Ambrose gained over the paramount interest of the governor of Belgium don John of Austria, who was influenced too it is said by the count of Marcin general of the forces in Charles II.'s mimic court at Brussels. F. Ambrose also treated with the baron of Bornhem who respected him so much that they readily agreed.

Great trouble had to be taken for the legal possession of the convent. To have the sanction of the civil power a petition was presented to the Spanish government "by the poor exiled English Religious of the Order of St. Dominic" with the written consent of the Baron attached. The government was fully determined that the colony of foreign Religious should not receive any support from the country in which they were to settle as strangers, and September 10th 1657 they were ordered to show what means of support they possessed. Matthew Bedingfeld an English gentleman who had lived in Brussels since 1646 appeared on their behalf September 28th and certified that they had for the purpose 9000 florins already invested and 11,000 florins in hand, for duly applying which he generously pledged his real and personal property in Belgium.

Mr. Bedingfeld's certificate and the baron's consent were inserted in another petition from F. Thomas Howard, which the privy council placed in the hands of one of them, Van der Becke, and when he had thoroughly gone through the case he referred it Oct. 2nd to the president and provincial council of Flanders. Every effort for success was made. The master-general wrote Sept. 15th to Don Alonzo de Cardinas a privy councillor, who had great authority at the court and considerable power for particular reasons with Sr. la Falla president of Flanders. Cardinas immediately forwarded the undertaking by a letter Oct. 10th to the president. The president himself was much attached to the Dominican Order: this letter and the solicitations of F. James van den Heede led him to bring the matter to a happy issue. The master-general does not seem to have known how deeply F. James was interested in the matter when he wrote Sept. 15th to engage him in it.

Ecclesiastical leave for the foundation was required from the vicars-general of Ghent, the episcopal see being vacant. In this matter F. Thomas Howard found seasonable friends, and he sought the good offices of the papal nuncio at Brussels, to whom the master-general Sept. 15th also recommended him. The nuncio's reply to the master-general Nov. 16th was very favourable, and the leave was granted.

The rank and zeal of F. Thomas Howard gained him all this powerful support, and at last he had everything for settling the English Dominicans at Bornhem. It was necessary to remove the Gulielmites in a formal manner, and this was easily done by the baron, as they were not legally fixed at Bornhem being there on mere sufferance. The king was reminded of this in a petition wherein it was also prayed that they might be removed or made to show the royal leave of admission. The local authorities were directed Oct. 12th to look into the matter, and the Gulielmites had to return to Bevern in the following Lent. They thought themselves harshly treated by the baron, who gave them nothing for their support or expenses. As they had run into much debt in keeping up the house they claimed a right to all the moveables of the convent and carried off even the Relic of the Cross. But the royal apparitor was sent after them, and did not leave Bevern till everything was restored.

The agreement with the baron of Bornhem was concluded in the autumn of 1657. Thereupon the master-general appointed the provincial of Belgium F. John Baptist Verjuyse to be commissary and vicar-general of the convent, as F. Thomas Catchmay in London could not duly adjust the community at so great a distance; and then by letters patent of Dec. 15th he formally accepted the house at Bornhem and made F. Thomas Howard first prior.*

---

* Some dateless ordinations for the province of England clearly refer to this time. In them the master-general accepts the church and house of Holy Cross at Bornhem, *purchased* with the

The royal license was granted March 19th 1658 under conditions much against the privileges of the Mendicant Orders. Still it was thought best to agree, for by opposing them all might have been lost; and the conditions which were binding only as far as the government chose might afterwards be enlarged as often happened in other cases. The fathers were to possess 1000 florins a-year, and the capital was never to be alienated or lessened. They were to have the cloister and church as a refuge only, and not to add to their inheritance in times to come. There were not to be more than thirteen religious, who were never to quest or beg alms in the country under any plea whatever. The Order of St. Dominic was not to claim the cloister so as to place Religious of another nation there if the English withdrew, nor to mingle foreigners with the English. On all Sundays and festivals Mass and the divine offices were to be celebrated with closed doors, so as not to draw off the people from the parish-church: and the fathers were not to exercise parochial

---

patrimony of F. Thomas Howard left him by will by his father Henry earl of Arundel, and by his mother lady Elizabeth. He erects the church into a convent for the English province under the title and invocation of St. Thomas Aquinas, and creates F. Thomas Howard the first prior. The earl and countess of Arundel are declared to be founders and patrons of the convent, and in perpetual memorial of it on the day of their decease (to be marked down on public tablets) the brethren shall celebrate a solemn anniversary for their souls and also for the soul of F. Thomas their son after his death. The earl and countess are received to all the suffrages and merits of the Order both public and private, that God may preserve and protect the Catholics of their family, strengthen them in the faith, and bring those who are wandering back into the bosom of the holy church.

These ordinations were mostly annulled, for they were evidently founded on some misunderstanding.

functions anywhere without the leave of the pastors. But the king might enlarge, restrain, and interpret the conditions as it was found convenient.

The formal donation of the house and church was signed at Brussels April 6th by the baron, and in the name of F. Thomas Howard by F. John Baptist Verjuyse. The noble donor too had his conditions. The fathers were never to diminish the cloister, nor were there to be less than two priests and one laybrother. One priest was to celebrate Mass at the castle whenever a baron or baroness was there, the other was to say a Mass in the convent church at eleven o'clock every day, and on all Fridays this Mass was to be for the baron's intention. After his decease the Religious were to keep his anniversary with the nine-lesson office of the dead.* The holy Relic of the Cross was to be always kept at the convent in the silver and crystal case in which it was given by the abbess of Coninx-dorp, but in times of war it was to be sent for safety to the baron's successors, and to be restored when the danger was over. For their better maintenance, the fathers were to have all the church ornaments and the moveables set down in an inventory at the end of the grant. They were not to alienate the cloister, gardens, and land, without the consent of the baron's successors; and if they did so or left altogether the whole was to revert to the baron or his heirs. And within six months the baron was to be declared founder of the convent with all the prerogatives pertaining to his title as such.

F. Thomas Howard soon found Religious to form his convent; he had already one subject in Brother Martin Russel. Whilst in Brussels he met with F. William Collins, who, born of English parents in Ireland, was then sub-prior

* This anniversary fell on June 24th, and was duly kept as long as the convent remained.

of the Irish college of Holy Cross, at Louvain, but had gone to Brussels intending to change his province. F. Thomas soon engaged him in the great work on hand. John Canning, fourth son of Richard Canning, esq. of Foxcote in Warwickshire, and Gratian Fowler his wife, was sent to join the Order by his uncle F. William Fowler, and took the habit for the convent of Bornhem at Brussels Nov. 11th 1657 from the hands of F. John Baptist Verjuyse. And early in 1658 Lionel Anderson was clothed among the Dominicans of Paris by F. Vincent Baron prior of the convent there, took the name of Albert, and was then sent to the noviciate at Brussels for the English province. He was the son of a Lincolnshire gentleman of good estate, was educated abroad, and on being converted to the faith sacrificed all his worldly pretensions and expectations. Thus there were three English novices at Brussels. F. Ambrose Druwè lent the aid of F. James Lovel and of Brother Peter van den Berghe, who both belonged to the house of Brussels. F. Thomas Howard had also an English attendant named George Daggitt, who served him for about three years, and now entered the cloister with him.

At length after many delays and disappointments all was arranged for beginning the convent. F. John Baptist Verjuyse April 8th 1658 communicated the master-general's patents of priorship to F. Thomas Howard, who then took office, and on the 17th with unspeakable gladness entered the convent of Holy Cross and colonized it for the English province. He had along with him F. William Collins, whom he made sub-prior and syndic or procurator, and Daggitt; and on the 20th he was joined by F. James Lovel, Brother Martin Russel, and Brother Peter van den Berghe. F. James Lovel was the son of an Englishman, and probably went back to his own convent in the course of a year or two as nothing more is said of him. Brother Peter a tailor could readily turn his hand to any work and for two or three years was exceedingly useful to the rising community. These six began the convent of Bornhem.

CHAPTER V.

When the convent of Bornhem passed into the hands of the fathers, the buildings were mean and in wretched repair. The church had an open-timber slated roof, the shattered windows of the house were stopped with straw, and some of the rooms were only roughly partitioned off with boards. In fact the whole displayed the sad effects of so many years of incompletion and neglect. Nor was the furniture of the church and cloister any better. The goods made over to the fathers where only part of what had been assigned to the Gulielmites in 1653, and must have had at least six years' wear. The land attached to the house was less than half an English acre. F. Thomas Howard began first of all to improve and adorn the church and to adapt it to the Dominican rite; afterwards he fitted up cells for the Religious, and formed a library so needful in a studious Order. The work was carried on mainly by Sebastian Reynaets, whom F. Ambrose Druwè sent from Brussels for the purpose. These improvements went on by degrees for several years, and F. Thomas Howard had to lay out great sums of money on them. As he was bound by the vow of poverty, a tender conscience made him fear to apply his own property on his sole responsibility even in restoring his own Order. To remove the difficulty the master-general June 28th 1659 gave him leave to dispose of his patrimony and of gifts as he thought best for the good of his province and convent, and even to use them in other pious works not against the personal poverty his institute required of him.

The convent being now established, F. Thomas Howard

began to gather into it Religious of ability and young men of promise for increasing the Order. He was empowered to call to his aid English Dominicans scattered in various Provinces, and he now sent for F. Thomas Fidden from Bohemia, F. Thomas Molineux from the province of Toulouse, and F. Vincent Torre from Bretagne. The latter was the only one who could immediately obey. The other two reached Bornhem about the summer of the following year.

F. Vincent Torre joined the Order at Dinant in the north of France in 1651, when he was twenty years old. He was professed in 1652, ordained priest in 1654, soon became a lector, and was then made master of novices at Morlaix in Bretagne. He arrived at Bornhem about Aug. 1658, with letters of obedience from F. Peter Martin now commissary and vicar-general of the congregation of Bretagne. He did not continue long at Bornhem; for F. Thomas Howard intended to go to Rome on business, but at last had to send him in his stead. F. Vincent left Oct. 10th for Rome. He had along with him Brother Francis Hayes an Englishman, who shortly before had received the laybrother's habit in the convent. This Hayes was very clever in several languages, and was for some years with the English Franciscans at Douay as their steward or procurator; in times of war he dressed like a hermit and cultivated his beard for more conveniently discharging his office in disguise. From Rome F. Vincent Torre went to be master of novices at Viterbo, where he was also lector of philosophy and theology. Hayes remained for his noviciate in the convent of St. Sixtus: he had not been long there when he changed his mind, put off the habit and returned into France, became a domestic servant to the Spanish ambassador count Fuensaldagna, and died in Paris.

F. Thomas Molineux a native of Kent studied at a good age among the English Jesuits of St. Omer's, and afterwards at the English College in Rome, which he quitted for the

Order of St. Dominic. He was sent by the master-general to St. Maximus in France, where he received the habit, passed his noviciate, and in 1653 made his profession when he was thirty-four years old. He went through philosophy at St. Maximus, and theology at Toulouse being ordained priest in 1656, whence he went to Bornhem.

John Fidden, son of Catholic parents, for three years desired to become a Friar-Preacher and left England for Rome in 1654 to carry out his purpose. The master-general recommended him to the provincial of Bohemia and to the prior and fathers of the convent of Leutmeritz. There he was clothed March 7th 1655, was professed for that convent on the same day in the following year, pursued all his studies, and was fully ordained. Being called to Bornhem he was assigned to it April 26th 1659 by the master-general, and with the commendatory letter of F. Godefrid Marquis provincial of Bohemia and Moravia dated June 6th, soon joined his English brethren.

There were other English Dominicans abroad who did not go to Bornhem: one of them at Ghent led a very holy life. F. Gregory Lovel left his native land for the sake of keeping his faith pure. He dedicated himself to God by the vows in 1637 at Ghent, and through all his life kept up the spirit of regular observance imbibed in his noviciate. He never broke the rule and constitutions and particularly loved solitude and prayer. By words he could not preach to the people as he never mastered the Flemish language, yet he never ceased doing so by his behaviour. Not to break the silence enjoined by the rule he replied by signs and nods if there was a reasonable cause and always with a pleasant countenance; and when speaking was allowed he talked with his spiritual director F. Peter Dierkens a great ascetic but only of God and on divine things, and to stir up each other to regular observance. He was the first and last at the divine office both day and night except when sickness kept him away: all the rest of his time he spent in prayer, so that he had to be sought only in the church and in his cell. Out of tender devotion to the Mother of God he said her rosary every day and with holy care decked her image and altar in the chapter-room. He held so fast to poverty that he only used the worn-out habits others had cast aside. A crucifix, the works of Thomas à Kempis, the spiritual exercises, and a little table and bed were all the furniture of his cell. His humility was so deep that he concealed his good birth and wished to be wholly unknown. As he generously despised human things so he eagerly followed after heavenly; whilst he meditated on them tears of joy coursed down his cheeks, and sighs showed the fervour of his soul. In counselling especially the younger Religious to keep discipline he usually said sweetly to them, "If you only knew dearest brethren how delicate is divine grace, you would carefully guard against the least transgression of the rule even by a single breach of silence." He was given up altogether to mortification and afflicted himself with fasts, hair-shirts, disciplines and other austerities, so as to live for God and not for himself. An Israelite indeed in whom there was no guile, he was always at the beck of his superiors and spiritual director. After an almost angelic life he died November 30th 1673 in the 58th year of his age and the 37th of his religious profession. Such is the account of F. Gregory Lovel given by F. Bernard de Jonghe in his Belgium Dominicanum.*

---

* George Goring, eldest son of George earl of Norwich by a daughter of Edward Nevill lord Abergavenny, was a very distinguished commander in the civil war and appeared early in the cause of Charles I. He was the bravest officer and the most witty and sociable man of his age: Echard styles him also deceitful and profligate, and Clarendon too speaks very indifferently of him. He married Lettice daughter of Richard Boyle earl of Cork, but had no issue. After the fall of the king's cause he went into Flanders

In 1660 F. John Quick an English Dominican of Maestricht was some time at Bornhem, whence he departed to Brussels and then to Maestricht again. At different times he was sub-prior, prior, and for thirty-two years novice-master in his native convent, and died reputed a saint February 24th 1709 in the 89th year of his age, the 71st of his religious profession, and the 63rd of his priesthood.

The noviciate at Bornhem was begun a few months after the house was opened, and F. Thomas Howard was also novice-master. By him Brother John Canning was professed November 11th 1658; as he was the first that entered for the convent of Bornhem he became its eldest son. Brother Albert Anderson went through upwards a year's probation at Brussels, and June 5th following his vows were received at Bornhem in the prior's absence by the sub-prior with the leave of the vicar-general of the house. Brother Lawrence Thwaits was step-son of Mr. William Thompson an English merchant of Brussels and a great friend to the convent: he was clothed at Bornhem August 10th 1658 by F. Thomas Howard, was sent to the noviciate at Brussels, and returning was professed August 25th in the following year by the vicar-general. George Daggitt was clothed as a laybrother July 22nd by F. Thomas Howard; his probation was shortend by dispensation for a year, and he made his profession September 21st 1660 at the hands of the sub-prior. John Jenkin born in Kent was sent on mercantile business into Holland and at

---

and served in the Spanish army. Thence he was called into Spain. There by order of the king of Spain, with great fidelity and resolution he arrested his own general Don Juan de Sylva, who was executed for a treasonable correspondence with France. At last surfeited with the pleasures of the world which he had drained to the dregs, he cast aside his rank and splendid prospects, became a Dominican friar, and after expiating the follies of his youth closed his life about 1660 while his father was still alive.

Antwerp was converted to the faith. For improving his humanities he spent some time at Vilvorde and became intimate with John Canning, whose example led him to join the rank of the English Friar-Preachers. As all his property was in the hands of his friends, he came with F. Thomas Howard into England about May 1659 and sold all he possessed. He was clothed at Bornhem October 6th by F. Thomas, passed his noviciate under him, and was professed by the sub-prior, on the anniversary of his receiving the habit.

These then were the Religious that entered the Order at Bornhem during the first priorship of F. Thomas Howard. Though there was a noviciate at Bornhem, the number of Religious was so greatly limited by the royal grant, that in after-times many were sent to other houses to be tried and to be taught regular discipline.

Founding the convent was not without severe trials, and one of the most vexatious of them was the variance with the baroness of Bornhem. According to the terms of the grant F. Thomas Howard obtained letters-patent dated May 11th 1658 from the master-general, acknowledging the baron to be founder and bestowing on him the graces of the distinction. The patents were handed to him by F. John Baptist Verjuyse; and thereupon the baroness claimed to enter the cloister when and with whom she pleased, as such she asserted was the privilege of founders. F. John Baptist replied that it was indeed a privilege in some institutes, but it was altogether forbidden in the Order of Friar-Preachers, were the foundation 8,000 florins or even enough to support the whole community. But he added the supreme pontiff could make a special concession in the present case. To this the baroness would not listen: in thus wishing to gratify her pride by showing the convent to her friends, she was standing to a right and not begging a favour. She proposed her claim to several Religious, and among others spoke to F. Coomans of the Order of Minims at Brussels. He told her that in his own institute such a privilege was allowed to founders and foundresses, but he did not think it was the same among the Friar-Preachers; at all events it was not a general privilege but was peculiar to those Orders where it had not been recalled by the apostolic see. Other Religious who were consulted on the point replied in the same manner. Nevertheless the baroness continued to be obstinately bent on her whim, and it became a great annoyance to F. Thomas Howard and to his successors at Bornhem for twenty years.

The royal license put the public services of the convent in the power of the pastor of Bornhem. Andrew Denys then pastor was very friendly with the English fathers, and even wished to give them a window for their refectory, but he feared that a popular religious Order would injure his church. So he pressed F. Thomas Howard to give him a written promise for the conditions of the royal grant to be kept to the very letter. F. Thomas refused to do so, as he hoped in time to have the conditions favourably altered. The pastor then referred the matter to the vicars-general of the diocese, by whose order the rural dean De Haens wrote a letter December 23rd 1658 to F. Thomas requiring him to do what was really giving up almost all the privileges of his Order. F. Thomas sent so forcible yet mild a reply on the 25th, in which he only begged time to consult the master-general that nothing more was done. The wishes of the pastor were treated very considerately, and for many years whilst he lived the convent-bell was not sounded except for the 11 o'clock Mass, and even the Angelus was never rung. Baldwin de Backer his successor by degrees allowed many privileges.

After the battle of Worcester in 1650 Charles II. went to live at Paris. When the treaty was on foot between Cromwell and Louis XIV. of France, in March 1656, he withdrew to Cologne for almost two years, and then to Brussels. F. Thomas Howard often visited him, and was always very cordially welcomed on account both of his high family and of his own merits. The prince had the greatest confidence in him and most likely received from him no small share of that favourable impression of the Catholic faith which ended in his being reconciled to the Church on his death-bed.

After Oliver Cromwell died in September 1658, there were great hopes that Charles might gain the throne, especially as a large party in England headed by Sir George Booth were weary of the Commonwealth and desired monarchy. Charles found no one to send into England better fitted than F. Thomas Howard to aid the royal cause. About May 1659 F. Thomas set out for England on this secret service. For making the business surer the prince joined with him one F. Richard Rookwood a convert who had been a priest in the Society of Jesus but was now a Carthusian. This Rookwood was singularly learned and eloquent, but was considered even by his own brethren to be excessively proud, rash, and double-minded; insomuch that the Carthusian prior of Nieuport warned Charles not to trust him in any of his affairs. But Charles would not even suspect treachery, and charmed with the bland address of the man let him into his confidence, and united him with the prior of Bornhem in the commission to the royalists of England. But F. Thomas Howard well knew the real disposition of Rookwood, and on that or some other account would not go along with him. Rookwood went to Nieuport to take the packet-boat for England, while F. Thomas Howard with Mr. John Jenkin went round secretly by Zeeland, where he had to wait about a month owing to contrary winds. Meanwhile Rookwood reached England, bent on making himself great by the basest treachery. He went direct to Richard Cromwell who had succeeded his father as protector, and disclosed to him, that F. Thomas Howard bearing a most extensive commission from prince Charles to the royalists was expected every day in England. He believed he would take the same route as he himself had done, as he had received a letter at Nieuport from the sub-prior F. William Collins saying that the F. Thomas Howard would be there in a few days; and he advised that scouts should be set to watch and arrest him on landing. But F. Thomas Howard came into England by another and unexpected way, yet his arrival was not so secret but that it was bruited about London, and a warrant was issued for apprehending him. Fortunately F. Thomas Howard was warned of the danger by friends: he found he could not possibly carry out his instructions and must look to his personal safety without loss of time. It so happened that the Polish ambassador was then leaving the country. F. Thomas Howard went immediately to him and frankly told him who he was, whose commission he bore, and his present peril. The ambassador kindly took him under his protection, and F. Thomas putting off his English dress for a Polish, undetected by the scouts went on board among the Poles, and with a favourable breeze reached Belgium; full of thanks to God, says the annalist, who thus rescued him from the jaws of death.

The annals of Bornhem here explain an important point in English history, which writers on the subject have hitherto failed clearly to explain: it is now shown how the royalists' insurrection in Cheshire was so suddenly discovered by the government and so rapidly put down. Though F. Thomas Howard escaped the snares of the traitor, such was not the good fortune of those who were organizing the revolution in favour of Charles. Through Rookwood's information the rising of Sir George Booth was quashed. General Lambert with about 20,000 soldiers was sent with all speed to Chester, the infantry being hurried forward on horseback; Sir George's forces being surprised were taken or scattered, and he was imprisoned in the tower of London. Charles was reported to be in England, but he had only come as far as Rochelle; he had to return to Brussels and wait for another chance of attempting the kingdom. Rookwood received a very large reward which he did not long enjoy, for he soon had what he most richly deserved. Charles after being recalled in the following May into England commanded him to be arrested, and as he did not like to punish him directed that he should be sent for correction to his convent. But Rookwood slipped off into Holland, whence he passed into Germany, and at Heidelburg for some time he acted the part of a Protestant minister and taught Calvinism. Then forsaking Minerva, quaintly says the annalist, he took to Venus and Mars, and married the widow of a German colonel, who procured him from the palatine her late husband's embassy. He rose into such favour and influence that the elector sent him as his ambassador into England. Charles was as angry as he could be, would not hear even his name, and peremptorily ordered him to get out of the country. At length in 1673 while defending a place of the palatine, Rookwood was slain by the French, and ended at once his life and his crimes.

Soon after he was safely back at Bornhem,* and

* At this time F. Thomas Howard placed in the library of Bornhem convent the precious book of devotions, splendidly illuminated and written about 1475, which has been noticed in the Gentleman's Magazine of 1789 and 1790, and made the subject of a very able article by the Rev. Joseph Hunter, F. S. A., in the 45th No. of the Archæological Journal. A memorandum in the book runs thus: "Conventus Anglo-Bornhemiensis, dono-datus ab Em^{mo} Dno Cardinali de Norfolcia fundatore ejusdem Conventus, 1659.-V. T." This note is in the hand-writing of F. Vincent Torre, and must have been put in either in or after 1675, most probably between 1679 and 1683. The work could hardly have belonged to F. Thomas Howard earlier than 1659, or he would have placed it in the library when first formed the year before; at which time too we find his brother Charles Howard making a donation of books.

F. Thomas Molineux and F. Thomas Fidden had joined the community, F. Thomas Howard began a college at the convent for educating English Catholic youth in all branches of scholastic and polite learning, from which they were rigorously shut by the penal laws in their native land. A college was a ready means too for recruiting the province with subjects. In this and the next year six students went to Bornhem, among whom was Esme Howard, F. Thomas's youngest brother: and they had suitable masters placed over them. So important did F. Thomas Howard think this college to be, that as the convent was much too small he tried to buy a neighbouring house called the Delft to be turned into a school, and offered 20,000 florins for it, more than double the real value. But the owner Honorius Coene asked 2,000 florins more, and F. Thomas Howard refused so extravagant a sum.

About this time Francis seventh son of Henry Frederic earl of Arundel joined the Order. He was born in 1639, and when he was fourteen years old went July 8th 1654 with his brothers Edward and Bernard to the English college at Douay. There he had a very severe illness in 1656, and when the physicians despaired of his recovery and he seemed to be at the gate of death he was wonderfully recalled to life by the relics of John Southworth a secular priest martyred in England two years before. In 1658 he went with Francis Hayes from Douay to Bornhem and stayed some time with his brother F. Thomas Howard, who gave him the habit March 21st 1660 and with it the additional name of Dominic. He made his solemn profession March 22nd 1661 to the vicar-general of the house, studied

---

The work was probably given to him by his mother or some of the family; and a new interest is added to its history if he carried it with him when he fled out of England.

philosophy at Douay, and after he had been ordained deacon returned to Bornhem to prepare for the priesthood. He was scrupulously pious and had quite a morbid dread of the priestly office. This unfortunate state of mind together with maladies which seized him in Lent 1662 and again in 1668 stopped his ordination. He spent his time in Paris, Louvain, Brussels, Bornhem and other places, and died at Geele February 27th 1683 in the forty-fifth year of his age.

In 1660 F. Thomas Howard again thought of consulting on the affairs of the province with the master-general, and had letters of obedience from him dated March 20th for going to Rome. But many important affairs turned up and the chief of them was the restoration of Charles II., so that he contented himself with sending F. Martin Russel in his stead. This Religious entered the priesthood in the Ember-days of September 1658, and very early in the next year was sent from Bornhem to Brussels for his philosophy. His present journey into Italy served a two-fold purpose, for after he had acquitted himself of his commission he passed through his theological courses at St. Eustorgius in Milan, and then being made lector taught philosophy in the convent of Rimini. F. Thomas Howard was exceedingly anxious to have the convent of Bornhem thoroughly well organized and the studies carried on as the Order required. He found it best to have a proper novice-master and begged the master-general to send back F. Vincent Torre from Italy. F. Vincent returned about the end of August while F. Thomas Howard was away; the vicar-general of the house immediately put him into the office, and also September 24th made him and the sub-prior F. William Collins the lectors of philosophy; and they directly began the first course of regular instructions.

Meanwhile F. Thomas Howard was again in England on a more pleasing mission than the last. Charles II. gained his throne, and made his public entry into London May

29th (*o. s.*) 1660. Whilst at Brussels the prince had often declared that if he ever came in for his kingdom he would marry a Catholic princess. On this account F. Thomas Howard followed his royal master into England, in hopes of forwarding a match so promising for English Catholics, and for nearly two years he actively promoted the marriage treaties with Spain and Portugal. Spain offered a princess of Parma with a royal dowry: the alliance pleased the king and the articles were settled on both sides, when the French mindful of some injuries on the part of the Spaniards upset all through chancellor Hyde and proposed Catherine of Braganza infanta of Portugal, whom Charles accepted with a large dowry including the city of Tangier in Africa.

CHAPTER VI.

Regular observance would not have been fully restored in the English province without Religious of the Second Order. A convent of sisters entered into the broad schemes of F. Thomas Howard. In England he found some ladies of gentle birth who desired to dedicate themselves to God under the rule of St. Dominic, and others in Belgium had also the same holy aspirations. Among them was his cousin Antonia Howard; and her elder sister Elizabeth too seemed much inclined for a life of perfection. Being sure of subjects F. Thomas Howard March 6th 1660 asked the master-general for leave to erect a convent in Belgium, and April 3rd it was readily granted.

Though F. John Baptist Verjuyse advised it to be delayed till the convent of Bornhem was more firmly settled, F. Thomas Howard immediately set about founding the house. He received due authorization for it from the sovereign pontiff Alexander VII. and enlisted the kind services of the

Dominican nuns of Tempsche not very far from Bornhem but on the opposite side of the Scheldt. To that convent he sent Antonia Howard about June 1660, "she being the first English," say the English nuns' chronicles, "that had to our knowledge taken the habit of our Holy Father St. Dominic since the unhappy fall of religion in England;" and after a twelvemonth June 11th 1661 he clothed her in the habit there. He then hired and afterwards bought for 5,000 florins a house near the vicarage of the Friar-Preachers at Vilvorde, a small town of South Brabant on the river Senne two leagues north of Brussels and between that city and Mechlin. This house he formed into a convent, and with the license of the bishop of Ghent to whom they were subject, three nuns of Tempsche gave their services, Sr. Louisa de Hertoghe or Paddeschoot and Sr. Clare van Elst being choir-religious and the other a lay-sister. The three with Antonia Howard (now Sr. Catherine) removed to Vilvorde, and there joined by another novice Elizabeth Boyle began strict observance. To the eldest of the Dutch Religious Sr. Louisa de Hertoghe F. Thomas Howard gave the office of prioress.

Sister Catherine Howard was the youngest daughter of colonel Thomas Howard of Tursdale in the county of Durham (of the family of the Howards of Carlisle) and Margaret Evers his wife. She received the habit at her own most earnest entreaties though she had a very delicate constitution and was only sixteen years old. A little more than three months of her noviciate passed when it pleased God to send her a tedious and fatal sickness borne with singular patience and perfect resignation to the divine will. Six days (October 2nd) before her death when no hope of recovery was left she took the solemn vows of religion that she might enter heaven with the higher prerogatives of the consecrated brides of Christ.

"Her death, to the best of my memory," says an eye-witness,* "passed in this manner. The day before, she said several times that she should depart out of the world that night, and demanded often if the confessor were returned, who was that day gone to Brussels: we not perceiving her to be worse than she had been ten days before, [or] when she made her profession and received the rites of the Church. She appeared to be glad when she heard the confessor was come home, saying she had much to do that night, every hour of which she observed the clock, and a little before twelve desired that the confessor might be called to hear her confession and to bring her the Most Blessed Sacrament, for it would be soon time for her to communicate. This was performed, and she confessed and communicated with great devotion, and an entire confidence in the infinite mercies of our dear Redeemer. She then desired the holy candle, and a little while after fell into a trance, in which for about a quarter of an hour she appeared quite dead. Then smiling she opened her eyes, with great signs of joy, and presently after fell into another trance which lasted not so long as the former, but the signs of joy and satisfaction which she then expressed far exceeded what she had shown before. This moved the father to ask her the cause of her joy, to which she made no reply, but looked on him and us that were by her very cheerfully and made some signs with her hands which we could not understand. Then her confessor much surprised to see this strange satisfaction so very unusual at such a time said thus to her, 'Child, I command you in virtue of holy obedience to declare the cause of your joy at this dreadful time when you are going to give a strict account of every thought, word, and deed, which God exacts with such severity that the greatest saints have trembled to think of it.' She without any change of

* We have not doubt that the unnamed writer of this narrative was Sister Barbara (Elizabeth) Boyle.

countenance answered, 'I see it.' 'Child,' said the father, 'what do you see? Tell what you see.' She said, 'I see our Blessed Lady, with a crown in one hand and a rosary in the other: a fine crown!' 'Child,' said the father, 'have a care what you say: Do you see our Blessed Lady?' She very cheerfully replied, 'Yes, I *do* see our Blessed Lady with a fine crown and rosary. O fine crown! O fine rosary! I desire to see no more of this world.' Then the confessor who was the Very Rev. Father William Collins a very learned and exemplary religious man said to her, 'Child, would you have the absolution of the Rosary?' She answered, 'I made signs for it many times when I could not speak: pray give it me.' Then devoutly preparing herself to receive it, he gave it to her, and presently after with a pleasant smiling countenance she left this wretched life (as we have great reason to hope) to pass into eternal felicity. I though most unworthy of it then felt a joy and satisfaction so great that I did not then resent any sorrow for her death, though I loved her with such tenderness that I could never before think of her death without being extremely afflicted. All that were present felt an extraordinary joy. Her face retained the same beauty she had when alive."

Thus died this holy girl October 8th 1661 "cum opinione sanctitatis," as F. Bernard de Jonghe says. As the nuns at Vilvorde were in a hired house and could not inter there, the body was removed in a wooden coffin to Bornhem by order of F. William Collins and buried in the cloister. As to Elizabeth sister of Antonia Howard, she never joined the community but after spending a few years at Brussels in the convent of Berlamont returned into England and was soon married.

Elizabeth Boyle, of the family of the earls of Cork and Burlington, was daughter of Thomas Boyle esq. and Alice Modant his wife relict of Mr. Piney. She was born in

Ireland in 1624, came into England whilst young, and then settled in Belgium. She was educated a Protestant but by God's grace became a Catholic. She met with F. Thomas Howard and resolved to join the Order of St. Dominic; so she went to the house at Vilvorde when she was thirty-six years old and took the habit with the name of Barbara.

Very great and wearisome difficulties were met with in overcoming the unwillingness of the archbishop of Mechin and the opposition of the temporal authorities for an English community to be established at Vilvorde. Full three years passed before F. Thomas Howard gained their consent, though he was very pressing in the matter; and whilst they held back the monastery made no real progress, for the vows of religion could not be legally administered.

CHAPTER VII.

The first priorship of F. Thomas Howard was drawing to a close when the master-general by patents of November 20th 1660 placed him in the office again for another three years, and the fathers of Bornhem immediately accepted the appointment. He was in England when the patents reached him. He continued F. William Collins sub-prior, who April 17th 1661 professed Brother Sebastian Raynaets. Raynaets was the Belgian sent in 1658 by F. Ambrose Druwè to overlook the repairs and improvements of the convent; and afterwards he became a lay-brother in the house. He was clothed at Brussels May 15th 1659 by F. John Baptist Verjuyse, and was sent to Bornhem where he passed his noviciate.

About the beginning of May 1661 F. Thomas Howard returned from England to Bornhem. He found F. Thomas Fidden in weak health, so he sent him into his native country and stationed him in London. F. Thomas Fidden left June 28th, and was the first in the long list of missionaries apostolic supplied by the convent of Bornhem to England. Soon after, F. Thomas Catchmay gave up his office as vicar-general of the English province, in favour of F. Thomas Howard, whom the master-general appointed to it during pleasure with full jurisdiction both in England and Belgium and power to remain prior of Bornhem till his term in that office expired in the usual course: and now F. John Baptist Verjuyse ceased to be vicar-general of the convent. The patents dated July 24th came to hand just before he again left Belgium for England towards the end of September. Important affairs at the English court were constantly calling him away, and whilst he was absent the government of the convent fell to the sub-prior: F. Thomas Howard got power from the master-general July 21st to delegate and sub-delegate as he thought proper all his powers both ordinary and delegated. He had already gone from the convent when Brother George Daggitt was carried off September 3rd by the pleuritic fever, of which for some time he had lain ill. This lay-brother was of a very obliging disposition and exceedingly laborious even beyond his strength. He was the first that died at Bornhem, and he was buried in the cloister near the church-door. At his funeral F. William Collins blessed the cloister and declared the convent to be canonically enclosed; but it was afterwards doubted whether this act was really valid. Sister Catherine Howard early in the next month was buried in a grave at his feet, "ad introitum portæ, quæ ducit ad sacristiam."*

Belgium was now gladdened with the peace declared

* When the foundations of the church were being repaired about 1823, the graves of some Religious were unavoidably opened. Two skeletons were found in the place thus marked out, but they were not identified.

between France and Spain, and the people were restoring their ruined houses and building new. During his stay in the convent F. Thomas Howard shared in the general joy; and as he thought that the happiest fortunes were in store for the Church in England, he again turned his attention on improving the accommodations of the secular college. The Delft would have formed an excellent school-house both as to size and situation, for the building afterwards put up on the west of the convent would have been on the east and a direct fenced road made from it to the college. But Honorius Coene refused to abate anything off the 22,000 florins; he was afterwards well punished for his exorbitancy, for when he was overwhelmed with his difficulties the house was sold by royal decree for 10,500 florins less than F. Thomas Howard had offered. The Religious of Bornhem were engaged, some in teaching others in studying philosophy, and some in directing the secular college. As the Delft could not be had, F. Thomas Howard fixed on enlarging the buildings of the convent, and had Herman de Wauters a very skilful Dominican lay-brother of Ghent to draw out the plans; when he departed for England he left the work in the charge of the sub-prior to begin them early in the following year. A third set of buildings were added in 1662.

Brother James Goodlad, of the Holy Cross, and F. Joseph Vere both made their solemn professions November 8th 1661. Goodlad, an Englishman, had lived for a long time at Antwerp, and was perfectly familiar with the Flemish language. He was clothed at Bornhem October 6th 1660 by the sub-prior, and was the first student of the college that entered the cloister. Henry Vere was a secular priest of Douay College, who had spent some years as a missionary in England. He received the habit at Bornhem November 8th 1660 from the sub-prior. About this time many strove to become lay-brothers, and among them were Peter Hasselman of Tempsche, Lawrence van Hove of Bornhem,

Lambert den Ubael cook of the convent, James from Antwerp baker, Peter of Dixmude cook, and Ivo Williensen or Willerms; but the last was the only one who went so far as to put on the habit.

In 1662 F. Thomas Howard visited Bornhem at the beginning of the year, taking with him Edward Bing to join the Order. This gentleman born in 1625 had been an officer under Oliver Cromwell during the civil war, and after the Restoration was a lieutenant in the body-guard of Charles II. He was converted by Mr. Whright a priest, who seems to have served the army, being commonly known as captain Wright. His wife was now dead, and his only daughter was in the care of her Protestant aunt. As he made up his mind to leave the world he was recommended by the same priest to F. Thomas Howard. At Brussels F. Thomas agreed with the Baron (now Count) of Bornhem for half a bounier of land on the east side of the convent, and it was afterwards turned into a garden, while the ditch was filled up to form the broad way leading from the highroad to the bridge. This land, subject to the yearly rent of a viertale of rye to the poor of Bornhem, was taken on a lease of twenty years with power of purchase within that time for 450 florins, and it was thus bought in 1667. At the convent F. Thomas Howard gave the habit February 22nd to Edward Bing, George Mildmay, and Ivo Williensen. George Mildmay, son of Francis Mildmay, esq., of Amersden in Oxfordshire, and Mary Brook his wife, was born in 1638. He learned his humanities at St. Omers, and entered the Order, being so counselled by his cousin Mr. Matthew Bedingfeld. Williensen was a Brabantine, and had for some years served the Carthusians of Lire; he left Bornhem early in Lent, 1663, married at Antwerp, and died near Louvain where he dwelt. F. Thomas Howard about this time deeply interested himself in the welfare of the English nuns of the Third Order of St. Francis, and lent them his powerful aid to remove in 1662 from their unhealthy dwelling at Nieuport into the noble and ancient palace called Princenhoff at Bruges.*

The number of Religious in the convent was now so much increased that all the cells were occupied, and such was the regular observance and so great the charity towards one another, that in the opinion of the annalist, the primitive ages of the Order seemed to have come back. The Religious rose at 5 o'clock and said Matins. Then followed meditation during the first Mass. At 7 o'clock the schools of humanities, and at 9 those of philosophy were opened. At 10 o'clock, Mass was often sung. After dinner at half-past twelve, there was free conversation for an hour, the priests and novices apart. At 4 o'clock p.m. the schools were closed, and for the most part Vespers were then said. Complin was sung every day with the Salve in the nave of the Church, according to the custom of the Order. At 6 o'clock all went again to the refectory; at 8 the bell was rung for profound silence, and the suffrages were said; and at a quarter to 9 the signal was given for the lights in the cells to be all put out. Moreover at a signal given by the master, those in the noviciate, on the evening before holy communion took the discipline from their own hands; and all outside the noviciate had become so used to the exercise that none scarcely ever laid it aside. The noviciate was closed to all without: and so strict was the profound silence that the convent seemed to be deserted. The observance greatly edified the students, so that some and among them Esme and John Howard spoke openly of their wish to join the community, and they would have done so if the college had remained on the same footing.

F. Thomas Howard was created a master of theology March 7th 1662 by the master-general. About the same time he

---

* This community now flourishes at Taunton-lodge in Somersetshire.

returned into England; for the marriage of Charles II. with the Infanta of Portugal, which he had done much to forward, had been settled and was to be speedily celebrated. Catherine of Braganza arrived at Portsmouth May 13th (*o. s.*) and was joined on the 20th (*o. s.*) by the king. The marriage took place on the following day. Catherine was earnestly solicited to dispense altogether with the Catholic rite, but she was firm and expressed her will rather to return into Portugal than to accept the Protestant ministry. The royal pair were accordingly married by lord Aubigny in the strict privacy of Catherine's bed-chamber, and the public ceremony was afterwards formally gone through by the bishop of London. The queen had her own ecclesiastical establishment so that she might freely practise her faith. Lord Aubigny was her chief almoner, and through his interest F. Thomas Howard his nephew was made her first chaplain. This appointment required F. Thomas to reside continually at the English court.

In the beginning of 1663 F. Thomas Howard attempted to found a second English convent of the Order, as Bornhem was quite full. This house was to be in France and one about an hour's distance from Dieppe was pitched on. F. Vincent Torre with Brother Lawrence Thwaits went to arrange for it, but when they got to Dieppe they found that Carmelite Fathers were already living there. While on his way back to Bornhem Brother Lawrence was laid up for a month at Douay by illness. John Atwood and Henry Errington received the clerical habit February 22nd from the sub-prior. The former was a native of Warwickshire, was educated at St. Omer's, and in religion took Peter as his religious name and his mother's surname as Pitts; the latter in two months returned to the world and to England his native country.

F. Thomas Howard paid his yearly visit to his convent about the end of Lent in the same year, and again took with him Brother Herman from Ghent to make good the cellars which were deluged with water. The annalist gives a curious account of his method with the most difficult of them, how he wisely set the floor with drains and three layers of rubble, mortar, and cement an inch thick, and then stopped up the last hole with a stone wrapped in linen steeped in a melted compound of candle-ends and of toads and sulphur pounded together in a mortar; after which the cellar remained dry, "gratias Deo, fratrique Hermanno!" Immediately after F. Thomas Howard arrived theses in universal philosophy were defended at the convent, in the morning by F. John Canning, F. William Collins presiding; and in the afternoon by Brother Lawrence Thwaits, F. Vincent Torre presiding. There were present F. Master Moitings and F. Master Nightingale from Antwerp, and F. Master Henry Collins from Brussels, all three very learned and eminent Dominicans, with many others. The theses were dedicated to the count of Bornhem and to his brother the baron of Marianser, each of whom made a donation of fifty patiçons, and F. Thomas Howard gave them an entertainment in the greater dining-room at a cost of nearly 200 florins. F. Thomas April 15th received the vows of Brothers Edward Bing and George Mildmay, who had put off their solemn profession for nearly eight weeks so that they might have the pleasure of making it at his hands.

About the end of April F. Thomas Howard set out again for England. On July 2nd following F. John Jenkin died of icteric disease in the 27th year of his age. He had been ordained priest and chosen procurator of the convent within a twelve month before. He was little in stature, but was very useful to the community as he was perfect in the French and Flemish languages, wrote a fine hand, and was an excellent accountant. Both before and after him the sub-priors had to be procurators. His loss was severely felt by the community as he was reckoned its greatest hope, but he was well succeeded by Brother Hyacinth Coomans a lay-brother who made his profession within three weeks after.

Giles Coomans was born in 1635 at Brussels. He seems to have come of a very respectable family and certainly had a good education: his father-in-law Matthew de Haese was a merchant at Brussels, and rendered many important services to the Fathers of Bornhem especially as to their landed property. Entering the convent of Bornhem he took the lay-brother's habit and the name of Hyacinth November 15th 1661 from the sub-prior, who also received his solemn profession on the feast of St. Mary Magdalen 1663. He was a diligent writer, and compiled in Flemish the History of the Convent of Bornhem down to 1675 (now lost) from which F. Thomas Worthington in 1710 abridged the Annals that form a very valuable source of information in the present compilation.

CHAPTER VIII.

F. Thomas Howard discharged the duties of first chaplain in the royal household of Catherine of Braganza with such care and zeal as to call forth the praises of the queen in a letter which she addressed in November 1663 to the master-general; and the master-general wrote to him December 22nd following, expressing his satisfaction at it and his pleasure on hearing of the great friendship between him and F. Christopher of the Rosary, a Portuguese Dominican of the highest repute and confessor to the queen.

Although so far from Bornhem F. Thomas Howard still continued his jurisdiction over the convent even for many years after his second priorship had come to an end, for such was the respect of his brethren that they would not elect another in his place. At the end of summer 1663 he appointed F. Vincent Torre sub-prior, whose patents of office were read and accepted on the Nativity of the Blessed Virgin. F. William Collins was made confessor to the nuns at Vilvorde, who till then had been only casually supplied with a director.

Brought up in the strict observance of France F. Vincent Torre seems to have imbibed all the spirit of what it is clear the annalist thought its supererogatory austerity with its *penchant* for that outward edification which sits so gracefully on our French brethren, but grates so harshly in the reserved and less demonstrative Englishman. He took up their practices, but missed that delicate tact in governing without which it is impossible to lead souls along the highest and most rugged paths of perfection. Yet he was a man of very great and singular piety, and won the full confidence of F. Thomas Howard, though he was certainly somewhat too credulous, and perhaps was one of those ascetics who wrapped in self-contemplation measure all spirits by their own. There was indeed much in the discipline of the convent to alter before it would come up to the full constitutions of the Order, for observance was sacrificed in many points; but as far as he could he followed out his views with a headstrongness that brought great troubles and well-nigh ruined the foundation. F. Thomas Howard allowed him in a great degree to carry on his plans, as they were most praise-worthy in themselves though now injudiciously enforced.

There is no doubt that the secular college must have somewhat interfered with strict discipline. It was at once put down. The scholars were few in number, but there was every likelihood of more: they were sent to the vicarage of the Brabantine Friar-Preachers at Vilvorde to study under the confessor of the nuns, who lived in that house and would thus usefully fill up his leisure-hours. The convent of Bornhem found all their expenses and had nothing in return: and

John and Esme* Howard and Charles Atkins, three very promising youths who had seemed bent on joining the Order, changed their minds with the change of place. "Condonet ipsis Deus, quicunque authores fuêre consilii Provinciæ adeo perniciosi," exclaims the annalist, "damni minus attulissent, si conventum in cineres reduxissent; damnum enim illud reparabile, hoc numquam reparari potest."

After the defensions of philosophy it was debated whether theology should not also be taught at Bornhem. F. William Collins before going to Vilvorde, and F. Master Carney a very learned Irish Dominican who died at Liege in 1667, tendered their services, which were not accepted. F. Vincent Torre began his school of philosophy again, and all had to be present even those who had already gone through that branch of study. But such an ill arrangement could not be continued long, and the religious students were soon scattered.

About the end of November F. Antoninus Wichart and F. Albert de Groet being sent for went to Bornhem. Both were sons of the convent of Bruges, but had lived some years in the strict observance of France, which made them very welcome to the sub-prior. A well-grounded report soon spread through the convent that the French observance was speedily to be brought in, and some of the Religious signified to the sub-prior that in such a case they would pass over to the Carthusian Order. He replied only that he should soon know the will of the Vicar-General in the matter. The mind of F. Thomas Howard may be gathered from the fact that no change took place.

It is clear however that an attempt was made to alter the community. The greater part of the Religious were

* Esme Howard returned into England and married. He died June 3rd (*o. s.*) 1728 in the 83rd year of his age. His only daughter Elizabeth died unmarried in 1737 aged 61, and was buried with her father and mother at St. Pancras, Middlesex.

placed in various houses of the Order, partly it is true for the sake of theological courses. Brother John Canning was sent to Louvain, Brother Lawrence Thwaits to Brussels, Brother Francis Howard with Brother Henry Packe to Paris, Brother James Goodlad to Burg St. Winox (Bergues) near Dunkirk,* Brother Edward Bing to St. Omers afterwards to Burg St. Winox, Brother Hyacinth Coomans to Ghent, and F. Thomas Molineux into England. Thus of the professed Religious there remained in the convent besides the sub-prior and the two fathers of Bruges only F. Joseph Vere who left after six months, F. George Mildmay, and the lay-brother Sebastian Reynaets, so that the sub-prior had all in his own hands. In hopes to make up the numbers with new subjects Brother Edward Bing was sent to Douay and F. Thomas Molineux to St. Omers, to see some Englishmen who they thought might have a vocation to religion. But the two returned without success to their former places.

Henry Packe an Englishman was clothed at Bornhem as a lay-brother August 6th 1662 by F. William Collins, and was professed at the age of 35 years November 28th 1663 by F. Vincent Torre. Brother Peter Atwood was professed Feb. 22nd following by the same sub-prior.

On Whitsunday (May 29th) 1664 F. Thomas Howard reached at the convent from England, and stayed till August. He did not make any changes in the community. He was chiefly taken up with the affairs of the nuns, and at last his unflagging zeal removed every hindrance on the part of the

---

* F. James Goodlad, being ordained priest, left Burg St. Winox June 26th 1666 for the English mission. He returned to Bornhem in Feb. 1668 with F. Thomas Molineux, and in March 1669 was made sacristan. In November 1676 he became companion to the nuns' confessor at Brussels, was appointed procurator at Bornhem in 1683, and died in that office April 2nd 1684 in the 44th year of his age.

temporal and ecclesiastical authorities to their settling at Vilvorde. He received the royal leave of Philip IV. for the convent to be founded, which the king granted gratuitously, with the simple obligation of some prayers for the good estate of the royal family of Spain.* Sister Barbara Boyle was now allowed to take the vows, which she did July 13th at the hands of F. Thomas Howard, who at the same time gave the habit to Sister Magdalen Sheldon and to Sister Catherine Mildmay. Bridget Sheldon was daughter of Edward Sheldon, of Little Ditchford Worcestershire, third son of Edward Sheldon, esq., of Beoley in the same county, by Margaret his wife daughter of Lionel Wake, esq., of London, of the family of Wake, formerly of Kent, and sister of the famous Carmelite Nun of Antwerp Sister Mary Margaret of the Angels, who died in 1678 reputed a saint. She entered the house at Vilvorde early in June 1663, took the name of Magdalen, and at the age of twenty-five years subscribed the solemn vows July 14th 1665 along with Sister Catherine Mildmay, who had gone to Vilvorde at the end of August 1663, and was fourth sister of F. George Mildmay. Owing to F. Thomas Howard living in London, it was thought best for the convent of Vilvorde to be under a well-qualified member of the Order, who was always at hand and could readily help it in all the doubts and difficulties which beset every newly-organised religious body. The master-general gave the important charge to F. John Baptist Verjuyse then prior of Antwerp.

Before leaving Belgium F. Thomas Howard assigned F. William Collins to the English mission, who probably accompanied him back to London, and F. Joseph Vere went

---

* In return for this grant the nuns as long as they remained in Belgium offered up the daily Salve and a general Communion on the first day of the year.

from Bornhem to be the confessor of the nuns. F. Martin Russel was called back from Rimini and reached Bornhem in November. He had been only a few days in the convent when he was sent by the sub-prior to Burg St. Winox. After some weeks F. Thomas Howard summoned him into England. There was a small Dominican convent in Tangier, and when that city as part of the dowry of queen Catherine of Braganza passed into the hands of the English, the Portuguese Religious there became useless. The master-general September 10th 1664 made over the house to the English province, and enjoined F. Thomas Howard to station at least two Religious there for the sake of the Catholic soldiers who were chiefly Irish. F. Martin Russel was the only one that could then be sent. He was decked with the title of prior, reached Tangier April 15th 1665, and took possession of the convent, where he dwelt without any companion all the time, and supported himself on the pay of a common officer.

CHAPTER IX.

Louis Stuart lord Aubigny, son of Esme duke of Lennox, died in 1665, and F. Thomas Howard succeeded him as Grand Almoner to queen Catherine of Braganza. By his new office he had now fully to superintend her royal oratory at Whitehall, while too he had a state apartment for his use.* For his services he received the yearly salary of

---

* Pepys went January 23rd 1666-7 (*o. s.*) to St. James's, to see the organ. "I took my lord Brouncker with me," he writes, "he being acquainted with my present lord almoner, Mr. Howard, brother of the duke of Norfolk..... The almoner seems a goodnatured gentleman. He discoursed much of the goodness of the musique

£500, with an additional £500 for his table, and £100 for the necessaries of the oratory. He was now always addressed by the title of "my Lord Almoner."

Amid the occupations that engrossed his attention at the English Court, F. Thomas Howard never forgot that he was a Religious and a Dominican, and always kept at heart the welfare of the province in his charge. He tried to obtain from the master-general the convent of St. Clement in Rome as a house of studies for the English Dominicans. This could not be granted, on account it was alleged (April 4th 1664) of the connection of that house with St. Sixtus.* The master-general recommended the place of education to be either in Belgium or in Bretagne where the controversy called for on the English mission was more in vogue than at Rome. Again, F. Thomas Howard July 13th 1668 asked for powers like those just given (September 16th 1667) to the Irish province, for founding houses subject to it alone anywhere on the continent, where Irish, English, and Scotch Religious might be freely educated, to be also granted to England. The master-general August 18th declined doing

---

in Rome; and of the great buildings which the Pope (whom, in mirth to us, he calls Anti-christ) hath done in his time." After visiting the Capuchins' establishment the visitors "went away with the almoner in his coach talking merrily of the differences of our religions, to Whitehall, where we left him." Of the lord almoner's apartment the chatty diarist says, "I doe observe the counterfeit windows there was, in the forme of doors, with looking-glasses instead of windows, which makes the room seem both bigger and lighter I think." And again, "here I observed the deske which he hath, made to remove, and is fastened to one of the arms of his chayre."

* St. Clement with St. Sixtus was given in 1677 to the Irish province.

so, as such unusual faculties had been given only under very extraordinary circumstances; but he freely allowed two other favours begged at the same time, that an English father might be placed at Paris for managing business, and that one might be received as a student in the convent of the Minerva at Rome.

Meanwhile the convent of Bornhem was making only slow progress. From time to time F. Thomas Howard sent over large sums of money to help it in his financial straits. In 1665 F. William Collins returned to it from England, taking with him Brother Francis Dominic Howard from Paris and Brother Hyacinth Coomans from Ghent. None of them remained there long, for F. William Collins came back into England, and Brother Francis Howard with Brother Hyacinth, who became his companion for four years, went to Vilvorde and were there all the winter. In this year F. Vincent Torre professed two Religious, Brother Antoninus van Antryve April 19th, and Brother Dominic Gwillim November 1st. The former whose baptismal name was Anthony was a Belgian, born near Ghent, and had received the lay-brother's habit May 10th 1663 from F. William Collins.* The latter, Edward Gwillim or Williams, was born in Monmouthshire; he was one of the earliest students in the college of Bornhem where he finished his education, but had to return home for the sake of his health. After he had recovered from his sickness he betook himself to the cloister, and was clothed at Bornhem, October 28th 1664 by the sub-prior, under whom he passed his noviciate. With the habit he changed his name to Dominic, and when he uttered the vows (being then twenty years old) he added to it "of the Most Holy Rosary." F. Vincent Torre had been sub-prior

* This lay-brother died April 17th 1693 in the 55th year of his age.

for the usual two years, and now willingly laid down his charge. F. Joseph Vere declined the office, so F. Thomas Howard sent F. Thomas Fidden from England, who was installed Nov. 16th; and early in the following year F. Vincent departed for the mission in London.

In 1666 several changes were made amongst the Religious. In the beginning of the year F. William Collins was claimed by his native province, being chosen prior of the Irish Dominicans of Louvain; he took the office very unwillingly only after he had a formal precept to do so from the master-general. F. Lawrence Thwaits, having been the year before ordained priest, went from Brussels to Antwerp for finishing his theology; Brother Francis Dominic Howard with Brother Hyacinth Coomans from Vilvorde to the Irish Dominicans of Louvain; F. James Goodlad June 26th from Burg St. Winox to the English mission; F. Edward Bing from Douay to Brussels; Brother George Mildmay from Bornhem to Antwerp, where he had a burse in the convent and began his theology; and Brother Peter Atwood to Louvain to study with F. John Canning. On September 8th the sub-prior gave the habit to F. Thomas Cowper a secular priest of the English college of Douay, who now took the name of Vincent Hyacinth, and September 14th to Alexander Thursby, who had just gone through his grammar, being sixteen years old, and became Lewis in religion; and he professed September 29th Brother Ambrose Graham or Grymes and William Michael Bertram, both of whom had been clothed September 27th the year before by F. Vincent Torre.

Brother Ambrose Grymes was of a high family. He was born about 1647, his baptismal name was Richard, and he was the heir to a baronetcy; but entering the Dominican Order he waived his right, preferring an everlasting crown and inheritance to a temporary title and wealth.

The plague ravaged the parish of Bornhem in 1666, but

by God's mercy the convent escaped the infection. The inhabitants of the castle dreading to face the contagion by going to the parochial church begged a priest from the convent to celebrate Mass in the castle chapel on all Sundays and festivals, and the fathers freely granted the request. F. Thomas Fidden restored the time of the evening collation to 6 o'clock, which F. Vincent Torre had fixed an hour later. He also tried to bring in the custom of publicly exposing the Relic of the Cross and singing some canticles in honour of it, but F. Thomas Howard put this down as an innovation on the constitutions of the Order.

Early in 1667 F. William Collins a second time left Louvain, and returned to the English mission. On his way he visited Bornhem, taking with him Brother Francis Dominic Howard and Brother Hyacinth Coomans, who staid at the convent for a short time and in June went to Brussels for the whole summer. FF. John Canning and Lawrence Thwaits having gone through all their studies also returned to Bornhem. In the early part of the summer FF. Antoninus Wichart and Albert de Groet departed, the former to Louvain the latter to his native convent at Bruges.

Meanwhile, F. Thomas Howard was in Holland with the English ambassadors-extraordinary to assist at the congress for re-establishing peace between England and the United Provinces. With the embassy he left England April 29th (*o. s.*), made a splendid public entry into Breda May 21st (*o. s.*) and went to the conference, which began in the castle June 8th (*o. s.*), the pacification was concluded June 29 (*o. s.*), signed July 23rd (*o. s.*) and proclaimed in London August 24th (*o. s.*) with great solemnity. Before the conference he visited Bornhem, and afterwards went to Vilvorde, and he meant to have spent the whole summer in his convent had not the siege of Dendermonde by the French forced him to change his plan.

At Vilvorde he found the little flock of sisters had increased, four Religious having joined since he was last there. Jane Bergmans a lay-sister was professed September 14th 1665. Frances Peck, third daughter of Mr. Thomas Peck and Jane Farwood his wife, took the holy habit November 16th 1664 when she was forty-three years old, and the vows exactly a twelvemonth after. Columba Pound a lay-sister was professed March 4th 1666, and Ann Busby, daughter of Mr. Joseph Busby of Yorkshire and Mary Dancer his wife, subscribed the vows April 26th following at the age of twenty years. A small and fervent community was formed, numerous enough indeed to govern themselves without the aid of the Dutch nuns who now went back to Tempsche, and Mother Barbara Boyle was made prioress of the convent. F. Thomas Howard probably gave the habit to his cousin Catherine, third daughter of Colonel Thomas Howard and sister of Antonia Howard: she was professed May 15th 1668 at the age of thirty-two years. F. John Baptist Verjuyse who had charge of the house died September 21st 1667, and it then fell under the ordinary jurisdiction of the vicar-general of the English province.

The close neighbourhood of the war at Dendermonde greatly alarmed the Religious of Bornhem, and not without good cause. One day a troop of French soldiers entered the village of Bornhem, slew the son of one of the inhabitants, and drove off many horses and cows. Four soldiers went to pillage the convent, and as they could not find any beasts on the premises broke open the sacristy-door, overran the whole house, and betook themselves to drinking and to seeking for money. F. Thomas Fidden spoke to one of them who was an Irishman, and then went up into his cell for a bag of money to bribe off the unwelcome intruders with a part of its contents, so that still greater evils might be avoided. The Irishman spied the bag under the sub-prior's scapular, seized on it, and then ordered off his companions, very probably keeping to himself the whole booty of about sixty florins. On this occasion the four novices, Grymes, Bartham, Cowper, and Thursby, particularly Cowper, were so terrified that next day the sub-prior took them all to Antwerp, where they remained for a short time.

The danger which thus threatened the convent made F. Thomas Howard wish for a city-refuge for his Religious, and he immediately set about finding a fit house in Antwerp which would serve also for a secular college or school. He consulted the bishop of Antwerp, the abbot of St. Michael, and F. Godefrid Marquis prior of the Dominican convent there, who all encouraged his purpose: as to the purchase of the house he spoke with Mr. Hartopp, Mr. Shaw, and other English merchants. There were many different opinions as to where the house should be, as some preferred one in the neighbourhood of St. George's, some, one near the river, and others, one adjoining the Dominican convent-garden which the English might use and at the same time attend the convent choir. F. Thomas Howard chose the last plan as the best. But the petition for the English Religious to enter the city was rejected, and probably by some of those who seemed at first most favourable. Although he thus failed in trying to benefit his brethren F. Thomas Howard had twice seen how much could be done by steadily pushing on, and he made up his mind to try again at a better time. He returned into England in September, bringing with him F. Hyacinth Revel from Antwerp. F. Hyacinth son of an English officer was born at Brussels, joined the Order young at Louvain, and then taught philosophy at Antwerp. He was always very much attached to his father's countrymen, which led him to become a missionary in England; but he fell into ill health, returned the next year into Belgium, and died at Antwerp.

F. Vincent Hyacinth Cowper and Brother Lewis Thursby were solemnly professed September 14th 1667 by the sub-prior, and not long after F. George Mildmay ended his studies and went back to his own convent. In the same month Brother Dominic Gwillim was placed at Antwerp for his theology, and shortly after BB. Ambrose Thomas Grymes and William Michael Bartram at Brussels for their philosophy.

The convent of Tangier in Africa was attached to the English province for a little over two years. F. Martin Russel laboured there with unwearied zeal and suffered many heavy trials and privations. It happened in 1667 that two Protestants were condemned to death for some capital crime, F. Martin charitably visited the men in their prison and converted both of them, so that while they were being led to execution and at their death they boldly and openly professed their new faith. The English governor was so angry and carried on such bitter bickering, and threatened so much that F. Martin was driven altogether out of Tangier.* He withdrew to Malaga in Spain, whence he sailed to Calais in a ship employed in carrying Italian soldiers into Belgium, and from Calais he crossed over in an English vessel to Dover, and so went to London for the sake of seeing F. Thomas Howard. From the Italian soldiers he caught a fever which harassed and enfeebled him for a long time. F. Thomas Fidden's term as sub-prior was now drawn to a close, so F. Thomas Howard gave the office to F. Martin, who accordingly went to Bornhem, and November 27th the day after he reached it undertook his new duties. F. Thomas Fidden after some weeks was called to London and made procurator of the province.

In February 1668 Brothers Ambrose Thomas Grymes and William Michael Bertram were called from Brussels to

* The convent of Tangier was given in March 1668 to the Irish Dominicans, and was held by them till 1681 when the city was destroyed and abandoned by the English.

go through all their studies at Rennes, whither they went a little before Easter.* At the same time FF. Thomas Molineux and James Goodlad went back to Bornhem, but the former was soon again on the English mission. Not long after Brother Lewis Thursby was sent May 27th to Louvain for his courses.

F. Thomas Catchmay was now old and was so broken by his unwearied labours on the mission that his memory failed him much, though in other respects his mind was quite unimpaired. He was a very learned man, and his conversation had a particular charm about it. He resolved to spend the short time that still remained for him in religious retirement, and was taken over to Bornhem by F. Thomas Fidden who left him there and immediately came back to England. But the veteran missionary did not long enjoy the peace of conventual life, for he died July 22nd 1669 in the 72nd year of his age, the 47th of his profession, and about the 44th of his priesthood: he was buried in the cloister at the feet of F. John Jenkin.

In the summer of 1668 F. Joseph Vere† went for two or three months to Bornhem, and F. George Mildmay taking his place at Vilvorde served the nuns. The plague was then ravaging that town and neighbourhood, and almost all the Brabantine Dominicans of the vicarage fell by the scourge ready victims of their charity and religious duties. F. Bauens

---

* F. Will. Mich. Bertram returned in 1675 to Bornhem, and early in the next year was made sub-prior. From 1681 to 1686 he was at Stonecroft near Hexham. He died in his convent April 19th 1691 aged 48 years.

† F. Joseph Vere returned to Brussels about the end of October 1668, left in 1674 for England, two years after was again the nuns' director, and died at last May 13th 1683 in England.

was sent from Brussels to help the people and took up his quarters in the public hospital so as to be always at hand for the sick. One day he sent for F. George Mildmay to hear his confession, who accordingly went to the hospital early in the day before he had broken his fast. Immediately after he went and celebrated Mass for the nuns. When it was over he complained of feeling somewhat unwell and begged to have a little wormwood tea. He went back to the vicarage, fell ill of the plague, died on the third day (October 26th) and was buried there being then in the 31st year of his age. The next day the news of his death was carried to Bornhem where his loss was much lamented, for great expectations were centred in him as he was deeply read in general literature and was thoroughly acquainted with the Flemish language. Yet the sorrow of his brethren must have been softened with the consolation that he had sacrificed himself in conscientiously and fearlessly fulfilling his duties.

F. Thomas Howard was again employed in 1669 as a public functionary. The September before, the marquis Castel Roderigo by command of the king of Spain gave up at Mechlin the government of the Low Countries to Don Pedro de Velasco grand constable of Castile. Early in the year F. Thomas was sent to Brussels by Queen Catherine to carry her royal congratulations to the new governor on his taking the vice-regal power, who however was still at Mechlin, as the plague was in Brussels. He took advantage to see after his two foundations in Belgium. The situation of the nuns made him very uneasy, as they were exposed to great perils in time of war; so he determined to remove them from Vilvorde to Brussels, and set about finding a suitable house for them. Some advised a place in Rosbank near the little stream, others, one in the Walsplat where a convent would be more readily allowed by the magistracy, as it was much desired to improve so desolate a spot by building good houses there so as to draw inhabitants in that direction. But F. Thomas Howard chose a large castle-like edifice called Het Spellekins-huys, the pin-house, because it was at first a pin manufactory, a name commonly shortened into Spellekens or corrupted into Pelikans. It had passed into the hands of the fathers of the Oratory, who built a small chapel and fitted up the house with cells, chambers, and all that a convent required. It stood in a healthy place in the Rue du Chêne, and had a very spacious garden shaped like an amphitheatre which commanded a very fine prospect especially towards the west. The Oratorians wished to dispose of it as they had just built themselves another house nearer the great church of St. Gudule, and they agreed to sell it to F. Thomas Howard for 20,000 florins. The sharp opposition of the magistracy against the nuns being in the city was overruled by the governor (March 14th) who said that as other religious communities were allowed to have property in Brussels he did not see why the English nuns should not occupy the Spellekens. Amé Coriache vicar-general of the archbishop readily gave his consent (March 28th) so that every hindrance was thus removed. F. Thomas Howard in Lent led the nuns himself from Vilvorde to their new asylum. The Religious who removed to Brussels were Mother Barbara Boyle prioress, Sisters Magdalen Sheldon, Catherine Mildmay, Frances Peck, Ann Busby, and Catherine Howard; and the lay-sisters Jane Bergmans and Columba Pound. The building underwent great improvements at considerable expense: the house at Vilvorde was sold and the money used for a guest-house. King Charles II. of Spain Dec. 15th 1693 granted amortization of the house gratuitously, in return for which the nuns, of their own good-will, gave the Mass on every Easter-Sunday and a daily Exaudiat.

In the mean time F. Thomas Howard met with the provincial of Belgium F. master Matthias Marquis, who found him a new subject for the English province. Mr. Jonston a Scotchman was a secular priest, and then entered the Benedictine Order abroad in which he continued for eleven years. He now sought to become a Dominican and was sent from Rome to join the Belgian province. But the provincial thought it better for a Scotchman to be with the English than with the Belgians. F. Thomas Howard sent Mr. Jonston to Bornhem, and following soon after gave him the habit March 13th with the name of Dominic of St. Thomas and placed him in the noviciate at Ghent. As vicar-general and prior F. Thomas Howard had much to do for Bornhem. Whilst he was at Brussels he presented F. Lawrence Thwaits to the bishop for faculties. F. Lawrence was the first of the convent who thus had power to hear confessions at large in the diocese of Ghent, for before him F. William Collins had leave only for the three festivals of Holy Cross, of St. Dominic, and of the Most Holy Rosary. F. Thomas Howard took back F. Edward Bing from Brussels to his convent. F. Martin Russel had not recovered his health since his voyage from Tangier, and his elder brother at Little Malvern being lately dead his sister-in-law pressed him to come into England; F. Edward Bing too was very anxious to see after the welfare of his daughter whom he had left in his native country. So F. Thomas Howard released F. Martin from his office of sub-prior, and sent him March 13th with F. Edward Bing by way of Ghent into England. The same day too he departed to Brussels after he had made, F. John Canning vicar of the convent till he could arrange for another sub-prior, F. Lawrence Thwaits procurator, and F. James Goodlad sacristan. At Brussels he was joined by F. Antoninus Wichart whom he brought with him into England. This father knew nothing at all of the English language, but he had continued to be on very friendly terms with F. Vincent Torre, who always corresponded with him and led him thus to betake himself to the English mission. It was attempted now to affiliate him and F. Albert de Groet to the English province, and F. Thomas Howard got the leave of the master-general and the full consent of all the fathers of Bruges for this purpose; but something or other was wanting on the part of Bornhem which made the proceedings void and afterwards in the opinion of the annalist came very seasonably into use.

In May shortly after reaching England F. Thomas Howard sent the patents of the sub-priorship to F. John Canning who was the first son of the convent that had the government of it: he rendered great services and first invested the capital of the house in real property. At this time F. Peter Atwood returned having done all his studies at Louvain. Some time after B. Francis Dominic Howard who was much worse than ever in health went to live with the dean of Geele hoping he might recover through the intercession of St. Dympna: he gained only in part what he thus sought. The sub-prior April 7th 1670 received the profession of F. Dominic Thomas Jonston.*

For five years F. Thomas Howard was so much taken up with his office of grand almoner at the English court that he could not visit Belgium; and during this time there are only a few scattered facts about the convent of Bornhem, as Brother Hyacinth Coomans with his recording pen was away. In 1670 F. Lawrence Thwaits fell into ill health and was sent May 1st into England, as it was thought that the climate of his native country would do him good; he died in London June 22nd in the 29th year of his age. He was a mild and learned Religious and was thoroughly well acquainted with the Flemish and French languages.

In 1671 the roof of the church was raised five feet and arched over with masonry; the count of Bornhem had his

* This Religious died at Bornhem April 11th 1685.

armorial bearings put into the windows. The area in front of the church was enlarged, for it was so narrow that a carriage could not be turned in it. The commissary of Rupelmonde required the fathers as English strangers to pay all secular imposts. Against this exaction the fathers petitioned the council of Flanders, whilst the commissary on the other hand contended that the matter ought to be taken before the royal ministers of Ghent who supported his claim. The council April 14th provisionally granted immunity and sent the cause to Ghent; but nothing more was then done and the fathers were left in their former liberty.

In May 1672 a secular college was again formed at Bornhem and four or five boys of respectable families were sent to it, but it was given up about the end of the following year. F. Edward Bing was made chaplain in an English regiment under the duke of Monmouth, and during the invasion of Holland he paid a visit to his convent. In 1673 Roger Powell a fine and modest Welsh youth was clothed August 4th as a cleric by the sub-prior; but while he was in the noviciate of Ghent he became half silly through over-done and ill-regulated devotion, so that in about six months not without some difficulty he was sent back into his own country. F. Dominic Gwillim was instituted sub-prior September 1st, as F. Joseph Vere was called into England by F. Thomas Howard, and F. John Canning became confessor to the nuns at Brussels where he died July 19th 1676 in the 36th year of his age.

George Gibson clothed December 20th 1672 by the then sub-prior was professed December 26th in the following year by F. Dominic Gwillim and became in religion George of St. Thomas.* He belonged to the honourable family of

* F. George Thomas Gibson in 1682 was made sub-prior of Bornhem, and was vicar till 1685. He came into England and was chaplain to Ralph Clavering esq. and also had Stonecroft

Gibson of Corbridge in Northumberland, settled in 1693 at Stonecroft near Hexham which they then bought of John lord Widdrington. The Gibsons have been distinguished for their unwavering attachment to the faith and for the number of ecclesiastics they have given to the Church.

Brother Sebastian Reynaets died April 22nd 1674 when he was in the forty-fourth year of his age: he was a very hard-working laybrother and aided very much the rising convent. About the end of summer the same year F. William Collins went to Bornhem, on what account is not recorded; but he was soon called back into England. Shortly after an unfortunate affair happened with F. Vincent Torre, who wrought a great miracle as he thought it, the fame of which was buzzed about far and wide, whilst its spuriousness made it a scandal to religion and a derision to Protestants. He was obliged to hide himself for some time in London, and then F. Thomas Howard sent him out of the way to the Spëllekens. It is probable that F. Antoninus Wichart returned into Belgium with him, for he was at Bornhem in 1675; but how long he stayed there and what became of him do not appear.

---

in place of F. Will. Mich. Bertram. He died at Stonecroft December 19th (*o. s.*) 1696 and was buried at the little church there.

CHAPTER X.

At the English court F. Thomas Howard was in the highest esteem: his abounding charities led him to be called "the common father of the poor." The king always addressed him as "My lord." He alone was allowed to appear in public habited as an ecclesiastic, and by dispensation he wore the dress of a French abbé. He was often the guest and companion of Cosmo de Medici in and around London, when that prince of Tuscany visited England in 1669, who thus speaks of him in his published travels. "It has been wished at Rome to consecrate as titular bishop in England some ecclesiastic of integrity and talent a native of the kingdom who may watch over the missions, as is done in Holland. For this purpose they cast their eye upon Philip Howard grand almoner to the queen, having ascertained that the king was no way averse from such a step; but the affairs of the kingdom being in a condition not very favourable to the Catholics owing to the inveteracy of the Parliament, it was thought unseasonable, and was judged more prudent, the same having been hinted by the king, to put off the execution of such a proceeding to some other more favourable opportunity. In the mean time the bishops of Ireland perform the episcopal functions for the benefit of the Catholics and come over occasionally to exercise their charge in the best manner in their power."

Fearful times indeed were coming on for the persecuted Church in England. There were mutterings and threats against it throughout all the land and in high places, which grew louder and foretokened the greatest evils as time went on and showed that a Catholic sovereign would mount the throne. When the convent of Bornhem was in danger from the arms of France F. Thomas Howard interested the French ambassador in London in behalf of it, and also wrote December 29th 1673 to the marshal de Bellefond, pleading that the house he had founded might be saved for his retreat when his country would no longer receive him. This letter shows how clearly he foresaw the issue of the deadly hatred which was more and more rapidly gathering against the Church and in a great measure against himself. His zeal and his influence at the court made him very much disliked by Protestants, especially as he had a great hand in the royal Declaration of Toleration for liberty of conscience published March 15th (*o. s.*) 1671-2, and almost daily complaints were brought against him of reconciling persons to the Church. At length he drew upon himself the anger of the dean and chapter of Windsor by converting John Davis one of their minor-canons and chaplain of Magdalen College Oxford, and also John Greene a young protege of theirs of much talent whom they had sent to the same college to be brought up for the Establishment. Such liberty of conscience could not be suffered for a moment: and when the chapter had taken deep offence it was easy to gather other charges against F. Thomas Howard which would make their cause seem still more important. They accused him of being the promoter of the Declaration of Toleration, and of having printed in some English books of piety the pontifical bulls of indulgences granted to the Most Holy Rosary. This last charge was the most serious of all, as the penal laws made it high treason to publish papal bulls and decrees. In vain he tried to justify or excuse himself by alleging that he had only followed the example of the Capuchin chaplains of queen Henrietta Maria: the chapter was not to be appeased, raised a mighty uproar and threatened to carry the matter into parliament. For a time F. Thomas Howard withstood the storm, but it thickened around him and raged so violently that it was rash to outbrave it. He sought the king's leave to withdraw abroad lest he should entangle the faithful and even the royal household of the queen in all the troubles of a national religious strife. Charles granted his request, and F. Thomas Howard giving much of his personal property into the care of the provincial procurator F. Thomas Fidden, but carrying with him his valuable ecclesiastical ornaments together with some sums of money which the king and queen bestowed on him to relieve his exiled Catholic countrymen, sought an asylum at Bornhem where he arrived about the middle of September 1674.

Mr. Davis and Mr. Greene who had been the innocent cause of so great a stir followed F. Thomas Howard to Bornhem and reached the convent October 3rd shortly after him. John Greene was born in 1655; his mother's maiden name seems to have been Westby, by which he was afterwards known on the mission, as persecution made it needful for a priest to screen his family and himself under another name. He spent a great part of his youth in the royal household at London and Windsor, where when he was seven years old he was much noticed by Cosmo de Medici afterwards grand duke of Tuscany. He received the habit of St. Dominic and the religious name of Raymund December 9th from the sub-prior F. Dominic Gwillim, by whom he was professed December 15th in the following year after he had passed through his noviciate in the convent of Ghent. John Ovington his elder in age by a year and in the Order who entered Bornhem November 10th, was clothed, passed his noviciate and made his profession along with him.* Mr. Davis never tried even to take the habit: he left Bornhem April 29th after he had stayed there nearly seven

* F. John Ovington was sent to Brussels June 1st 1678, and to Nantes in Bretagne June 4th 1682 for his studies. He was made procurator of Bornhem September 21st 1686, vicar-in-capite of the

months, and his after-history has escaped our researches. With him went a Mr. Butler, who had gone there November 4th, had been clothed with Ovington and Greene, and March 9th following quitted the noviciate at Ghent.

---

convent in 1688, prior in 1691, and died at Bornhem March 25th 1696 in his forty-third year.

F. Raymund Greene was professed along with the last December 15th 1675 by the sub-prior and vicar F. Dominic Gwillim. He studied his philosophy at Bornhem and his theology at Naples. He then taught both these sciences at Rome and Bornhem, and so skilful was he in them that being companion to the provincial for the general chapter held at Rome in 1686 he made such an excellent defension embracing the whole sweep of theology before the assembled fathers, that the newly-elected master-general F. Antoninus Cloche raised him to the grade of a *præsentatus ;* and in the general chapter of 1706 he was laureated master of theology. In 1707 he went to the college at Louvain and taught there for five years. He became confessor to the nuns at the Spellekens in 1693, 1712, 1719, 1722, and 1732; was elected prior of Bornhem in 1694 and 1697; and was appointed provincial in 1716. In 1700 he twice attempted to cross the sea into England, but was taken both times by enemies (for much warfare was then raging) and forcibly landed in the Netherlands. In 1720 he was on the mission for two years, and in 1726 became chaplain in the Catholic family of Knight in Lincolnshire till 1730 when he removed to London. In June 1736 he was made rector of the college of St. Thomas at Louvain where he died July 28th 1741 in the eighty-sixth year of his age. For the last seven years of his life he suffered much from hemiplegia. He was the last of the province who was personally acquainted with cardinal Howard, whose memory he cherished with the greatest veneration.

In the library of the Duke of Norfolk at Arundel castle is a beautifully executed Processionale of the Order, "Written out for the use of the most truly Vertuous and very Religious Sister Sr. Dominica Howard of Norfolke, By her unworthy Brother and Ser-

At Bornhem F. Thomas Howard took up his duties as prior. One of his first acts was to agree with the fathers of the conventual council September 20th in declining a perpetual foundation for the soul of Frances Coloma, widow of Christopher de Medina Montoya chevalier of the Order of St. James in Spain. By her will December 7th 1659 she desired her body to be buried in the convent church of Bornhem, and directed six hundred Masses to be said for her, half by the English fathers and half by the Friar-Minors of Mechlin, at privileged altars. She also bequeathed 110 florins a-year to Bornhem for celebrating daily for her soul in perpetuity. The fathers complied with the other conditions; but the foundation offered them by the count of Bornhem and his brother Peter Coloma baron of Mariensart was much below the honorarium fixed by the bishops of the Netherlands.' What was afterwards done does not appear in existing records. The baron of Mariensart was a great benefactor of the convent, and perhaps he came to some arrangement, for a daily Mass for Madame Medina was regularly celebrated till about 1804, when the loss of the rent through the French Revolution destroyed the foundation. F. Thomas Howard April 28th 1675 received the profession of Brother Pius Westcote alias Lyttelton, whose baptismal name was Gervase. He belonged to the honourable family whence descend the Lytteltons barons of Frankley in Worcestershire, went to Bornhem February 26th 1674, was clothed March 28th by the sub-prior F. Dominic Gwillim, and two days after began his noviciate.* F. Thomas Howard intended to travel some

---

vant, the most unworthy of all the Children of St. Dominique, Br. Raymund Greene, Professed at Bornhem in Flanders among the English Dominican Fryars Preachers, the 15 day of December, In the yeare of Grace 1675." The MS. was finished in 1694.

* F. Pius Westcote was procurator of the convent of Bornhem

time in France, and then settle down in his convent for the rest of his days and dedicate all his energies to the welfare of the English province.

The year of jubilee arrived in 1675, and F. Thomas Howard sought the master-general's leave to visit Rome, so that he might partake there of the fulness of the Church's spiritual gifts. But before he could receive an answer an event happened which changed every scheme for the future. On Trinity Sunday (June 9th) a traveller drew nigh to Bornhem and enquired for the English Dominican convent. When he saw how poor and small it was he paused for some time fancying he had wandered out of the right road and had mistaken the house. As he found he was not wrong he entered the convent, and announced that he had been officially sent direct from Rome ten days before with the message, that among the six dignitaries whom Clement X. May 27th had added to the Sacred College, F. Thomas Howard had been created a Cardinal-Priest. The news was received with great joy by all except by F. Thomas Howard himself, who was thunder-struck as he was wholly unprepared for it. He remained dumb with amazement for some time and then burst into tears. He heeded little the congratulations of his brethren and hardly would admit into his presence the messenger with the letters of promotion. He was at a loss to conceive to whom he owed this great honour, little suspecting then that the great friend of his early years F. John Baptist Hackett had some hand in it; though his former tutor now the pope's confessor mainly brought it about, as a token of

---

from 1681 to 1683 and then came into England. He led a wandering life ministering to the faithful from place to place till 1696, when he settled at Stonecroft. Failing health forced him within ten years to give up that mission, and he became chaplain to Marmaduke baron Langdale at the Holme in Yorkshire, where he died June 10th 1723 in his seventy-fifth year.

respect for his rank, a reward for his religious zeal, and a recompense for the exile into which persecution had driven him.

The first wish of F. Thomas Howard was to learn the will of God in such a weighty affair, and he withdrew into his cell where he remained alone for three or four hours in meditation and prayer. The next morning he celebrated Mass and exposed the venerable Relic of the Cross, in order to draw down divine aid and light; and then he resolved to consult the bishop of Antwerp F. Marius Ambrose Capello a Dominican in whose wisdom, piety and prudence he reposed the greatest confidence. In the company of Brother Hyacinth Coomans he went to Antwerp and first visited the Dominican convent, receiving there on bended knee the blessing of the prior F. master Godefrid Marquis, to whom the whole affair was unknown. The prior asked him to dine there as it was about two o'clock in the afternoon, but he excused himself and took his way to the bishop's palace. He found the aged bishop was just taking his siesta, so not wishing to disturb him he turned aside to the professed house of the Jesuits to wait his leisure. Meanwhile the news began to fly about all the convent and to make no small stir there. During vespers Brother Hyacinth Coomans went into the choir to ask the prior's leave for going out, and unable to keep his overcharged tongue still whispered what had happened and added that he thought F. Thomas Howard would not accept the dignity. The prior did not believe a word and took no notice. Brother Hyacinth had told all before to the less doubting porter of the convent Brother Philip van Hoof, who in his turn went to F. lector de Brew and pointed out the messenger. F. de Brew had been in Rome and knew the man again, and when he learned of him the truth he too ran off to the prior who was still in the choir. The prior putting on his cappa, immediately hurried off with the lector to the bishop's palace to meet F. Thomas Howard and to offer him his hearty congratulations. When the two arrived F. Thomas had not returned from the house of the Jesuits, so that they had time to tell the bishop of the honour done to the prior of Bornhem. The bishop called together all his household to give a fitting reception to the new cardinal. F. Thomas Howard soon came in; he knelt for the blessing of the bishop who in his turn knelt for that of his eminence. He laid open all his difficulties and anxieties regarding his promotion, and declared he would refuse the cardinalship if his lordship so advised him. The bishop led him into the private chapel; after praying there for a few minutes he stood up and entoned the *Te Deum* with a loud and joyful voice, and F. Thomas Howard arose from his knees a Prince of the Church of God. The bishop then led the cardinal into some private apartments in the palace. In the evening the cardinal returned in his lordship's carriage to the convent where he remained two nights. The first night he spent there he had a characteristic conversation with Brother Hyacinth Coomans. He remarked, "I am afraid my promotion will prove more hurtful than advantageous to the convent of Bornhem, as I have not means to keep up a cardinal's dignity properly." "I hope," replied Brother Hyacinth, "that his Catholic Majesty will provide a valuable bishopric for your eminence." "No, no!" he exclaimed, "I will not bind myself to anybody; for if a man once attaches himself to a prince by receiving a favour he is always and in everything at the prince's beck, even though it may go against his conscience." The cardinal soon acted on this high principle, for the messenger from Rome brought him the present of one hundred gold crowns from Cosmo de Medici grand duke of Tuscany, and the same sum from cardinal Altieri. He declined the gift from the grand duke, but thought it best to take the one from the cardinal who was the patron and protector of the Dominican Order. And throughout all the rest of his life he religiously kept to his resolution, for when Spain, France, and Germany offered him many benefits he firmly refused them.

From the convent his eminence returned to the bishop's palace where he was most kindly entertained for some time. Meanwhile Monsignor Con arrived from Rome bringing the cardinal's biretta, which the bishop publicly placed upon the head of the elect with the usual ceremonial in the cathedral of Antwerp, when numerous spectators were present.

Amidst all this excitement the cardinal never lost sight of the English province and of his own cherished foundations in Belgium. Whilst he was now at Antwerp it seemed a very good time for him to try again to have a house and college in the city joined with the convent of Bornhem. He spoke about it with the bishop and abbot, who counselled him against proposing anything in the matter to Mr. Hartop or Mr. Newport. Brother Hyacinth Coomans was sent in secular clothes to look at some houses, and he found two adjoining in the Iserway called de Gulde Panne and St. Jacques, which seemed most suitable and were tenanted by relatives of M. de Witt a Norbertine and pastor of Duerne. M. de Witt himself advised the cardinal to buy them, and it was agreed to give 11,500 florins for them, twenty-five patiçons being added in favour of some Devout Daughters who dwelt there. The cardinal sent 12,000 florins to Brother Hyacinth, who took possession of the houses in the name of his step-father, and in the middle of August the purchase was completed. The houses were amortized by the king May 30th 1682, and sometimes served as a refuge in perilous times, but beyond this no good came out of the scheme and the houses were at length sold in 1697. The cardinal also endeavoured to have the endowment of the convent enlarged and the number of Religious increased from thirteen to twenty; and for that purpose he petitioned the privy council for leave to buy lands and to have them amortized, and even went privately to speak with the supreme president on the subject. But an unfavourable answer was returned and the matter was altogether laid aside. The financial state of the convent was the cardinal's greatest trouble, for out of the foundation-capital 5,000 florins had been borrowed to buy the nuns' house at Vilvorde, and 12,000 florins were now used for the two houses at Antwerp which never brought in anything, as the rents (when there were any) were swallowed up in repairs and other expenses. So the convent was almost without the legal endowment; yet as it never drew at all upon the country the government let the matter alone, and the convent had to struggle on for many years in deep poverty before its revenues were fully recruited.

Before quitting the country the cardinal paid a last visit to Brussels and Bornhem, and the countess of Bornhem seized the occasion to press again her long-fostered claim to enter the cloister at pleasure as foundress of the convent. Moreover she demanded that the *aspersorium* should be offered her, so that she might take the holy water with her own hand. This latter privilege had been yielded to her vanity by D. Legaw of Hosdunk, but was denied by D. de Backer pastor of Bornhem, which so piqued her that she would not go any more to the parish church. The cardinal replied that offering the *aspersorium* was directly against the pontifical rubrics and was allowed only to a bishop in his own diocese; and that while he was grand-almoner to the queen of England it was never done, but it was the custom to sprinkle first the deacon and sub-deacon and then the queen; and he could not allow the Religious to take up another practice. As to the countess entering the cloister it was quite out of his power to grant it; but when he got to Rome he would speak to the sovereign pontiff on the matter. The countess was not contented and went off in a pet, declaring afterwards that she would never again enter the convent-church, and she desired that a Religious would say mass every day at the castle. In a day or two the cardinal returned to Anwerp accompanied by the count of Bornhem and the baron of Mariensart, both of whom pressed him to give in to the countess's whims; but he excused himself from granting what in fact he could not.

On the following morning which was a Sunday the countess sent her steward to the convent to announce her will that a Religious should celebrate at the castle. The sub-prior sent back word that he could not obey her order, for the Mass must be said in a place where those hearing it would fulfil the obligation of the day. On receiving this message the countess lost her temper, and the steward hurried back to the convent and begged Brother Hyacinth Coomans to go and speak to her with all speed. He found her in the castle-garden overwhelmed with tears, and he boldly but respectfully begged her if she would not give scandal to her children and to the baroness of Mariensart who were present to repair at once to the convent, as it was not fit for upwards of a hundred persons to be bereft of Mass, as it was now eleven o'clock and they were staying for the last celebration. The countess at length gave way and getting into her carriage attended the church. A day or two after when the count and baron had returned from Antwerp Brother Hyacinth waited on them, and the question of celebrating Mass in the castle-chapel was gone into with some sharpness. The count believed that his chapel was consecrated and that the obligation of hearing Mass could be fulfilled there as had been often done without contradiction. Brother Hyacinth said that the chapel was not consecrated, and that an abuse could not avail in the argument; and on examining the altar they found inscribed on it the year and day of its consecration but nothing about the chapel. The count was amazed, and wondered how Brother Hyacinth knew so much about it. The good lay-brother had been made so bold in what he said by his having noted that there were no dedicatory crosses on the walls. He even went farther and asked if papal leave had been given for Mass there at all, and the count had to own that he had not, got it. Thereupon brother Hyacinth* offered if it was agreeable that he would obtain it at Rome. The count would not agree at the time, as he perhaps wished to have the opinion of others. The bishop of Antwerp was consulted, who said that formerly bishops had power to give such a leave, but it had long been reserved to the Apostolic See; still it would be easy to have it from Rome: and with this opinion the count was contented.

The cardinal left at the Spellekens all the personal property he had carried out of England; and he told the nuns (October 5th) that if he did not hereafter dispose of it under his hand and seal it would belong to them. The goods forwarded by F. Thomas Fidden after lying some time at the bishop's palace in Antwerp were placed with the rest at Brussels. To the convent of Bornhem he gave a fine silver sanctuary-lamp and a silver thurible and incense-boat which had probably belonged to the royal chapel at Whitehall; they are still kept as memorials of the great man to whom the province owed its restoration. He also ordered wooden confessionals and sedilia to be made for the convent-church. F. Vincent Torre was to go with the cardinal to Rome as his confessor. But at that time F. David Joseph Kemeys chaplain to the countess of Arundel and a good and prudent Religious had gone over into Belgium to carry the congratu-

* Brother Hyacinth Coomans was for many years procurator at Bornhem, then at the college of St. Thomas at Louvain. He died at Bornhem July 12th 1701 in his sixty-seventh year. Besides his Annals, he wrote: 1. "A Booke of Avthentike Copys Concerneing the Concession, Donation, Fundation, Rents, and Revenues of ye English Cloyster of the Dominicans at Bornhem," began in 1672 and continued. 2. "A Formall Discription of the Lands and Woods that ye English Dominicans at Bornhem have to their Vse," etc. etc. 1694. 3. A genealogical history in Flemish of the family of Howard of Norfolk, 1696 (title page gone).

lations of the countess to her son on his promotion, and he seized an opportunity to speak with his eminence on this matter, as the fame of the false miracle was spread as much about Rome as about London; and choosing F. Vincent as confessor might seem to be approving and patronizing "such folly." The cardinal yielded; and not long after F. Vincent with tears expressed his sorrow to Brother Hyacinth Coomans that he was not going to Rome, but would shortly be sent back into England as vicar-general of the province. This last appointment F. William Collins and other missionary fathers tried to prevent; but the cardinal overruled their objections, and as the master-general took up his recommendation F. Vincent Torre was soon again in London.

The cardinal now got ready to leave Belgium for Rome. Among the distinguished company that attended him in his journey were, his uncle William viscount Stafford who lost his life on the scaffold in 1680, Mr. John Howard the viscount's son, lord Thomas Howard his eminence's nephew and son of Henry earl of Norwich afterwards duke of Norfolk, monsignor Con, and Mr. John Leyburn president of the English college of Douay who became his secretary and auditor. The cardinal went through Flanders to Douay and took up his quarters in the college, where he was received with very great state and entertained with every mark of respect by Mr. Leyburn. Next day he visited St. Gregory's college of the English Benedictines in the same city, and being met by the whole community was led into the church in solemn procession, when the *Te Deum* was sung and the ritual for such receptions fully carried out. From the church he passed into the cloister and was regaled with a splendid banquet. A panegyric was then addressed to him by Richard (Brother Wilfrid) Reeves a religious student of the college, which shortly afterwards was printed in twenty pages folio. "All which," says Anthony à Wood, "was so well performed that Visc. *Stafford* was pleased to say, that it was the only fit reception his Eminence had met with in all his journey." From Douay the cardinal went to Paris where he remained a short time in retirement. "At length," continues our author, "with other Nobility and Persons of Quality added to the former company, he journeyed to *Rome*, and made his entry: for the defraying of which and his journey, he had the assistance of the Pope, and not of King *Charles* 2. and Queen *Catherine*, as the common report then went."

There is no doubt that this last statement of Anthony à Wood is correct, but the cardinal owed no little to the kindness of his brother Henry earl of Norwich, who for once dared (such were the dangers of Catholics in those unhappy times) to write to him. The earl's letter is dated, "London, $\frac{1}{2}\frac{4}{4}$ June, 1675," and from it we make some interesting extracts.*

"Although I had much difficulty at first, and when I spake with Coll. Balati about your Em. affaires, how I could correspond with you, for feare of offending our masters here, yet I found it so necessary, not alone in order to your Em. service, but to the preservation of mine and families interest and credit abroad, that I write to yourselfe, and also to L[d] Padrone† and Barbarino, that I have swallowed all apprehensions of difficulties at present, and henceforward never more to correspond more then to order Mr. Hay to write to Mr. Thomas Grane,‡ who will informe your Em. of all my con-

* This letter with the foot-notes is taken from Tierney's "History of the Castle and Town of Arundel," (Vol. II.) p. 530.

† Cardinal Altieri, to whose influence, in conjunction with that of cardinal Barberino, Howard appears to have been principally indebted for his advancement to the purple.

‡ The name which the cardinal henceforth assumed in most of his correspondence with England.

cornes.........I was out of towne at the arryvall here of the express you sent, and came, the day ere yesterday, to towne. All yesterday and this day, I spent in preparing what you desire, and, this very night, am going to supp with his ma^{ty} and the duke, at the prince of Newburgh's, where, since I cannot now meet them at Westminster, nor conveniently go to Whitehall,* I will make your compliments, and ask if they desire you should write or not. Next day I will go to the Portugall embassador, and, by his advice, address to her ma^{ty}, and, by lord Peterborow, to the dutchess. I send the two letters for Rome, with a blank for the filling up of the day of the moneth, though els I had put the $\frac{14}{24}$, and have wrote them both all with my owne hand. I would have said much more of the *causa di Dio, &c.*, but I durst not: and pray let their Em^{ces} know, I would, had I durst, have expressed the joy, gratitude, and concerne of my family herein much better: but time will show that I am sensibilissimo del honore......I desire your Em. to reckon upon it, that I ever will be a true friend, as well as a kind brother, to one who has ever bin so kind and sincere to me in all my concernes. And I reckon upon it also, that one in your Em. condition now and ever will be as just and kind to me, and the concerns of our family, as all other persons in their posture. And, for the first earnest of my part, I am providing, and, next post, (certainly depend upon it) I will send your Em. a bill of a thousand pounds sterling, payable at sight in Antwerp, of which if you will receive all or part in Italy, it depends on your pleasure: and I hope one day, at your owne best leasure, your condition will be so good, as that, before, or at,

* In January, a proclamation had been issued, declaring that any papist or reputed papist who should presume to enter the palace of Whitehall or of St. James's, should, according to his rank, be committed either to the tower, or to one of the common gaols. Kennet III. 301.

your death, you may with ease repay it to me, or those I leave behind me to receive it: and, if not, I freely remitt it from the hower forward as I send it. I am going, in August next, into Cumberland, and hope, at my returne, I may furnish your Em. with a thousand more, on the same terms, of which though I am not certaine as to the time precise, yet you may as well reckon upon it as soon as I can get it, and, I believe it, suddainly. I am glad to see in Mr. Hay's letter of the generous offer or presents of the cardinal padrone, and the great duke, in which particular I cannot, at this distance, take upon me to advise what to do, but answear only for myselfe, that, at every turne, I will be a sure carde not to faile you in time of the greatest need. And if you can but rubb out for the present, I hope some veschovate,* or other church livings, will so capacitate you as to need little more hence. As to your going into Italy, it's best, I think, if your chiefe padrone† continue in any reasonable health, that you deferr it till the heats be over, or els that you rest at Padoua, in your brother's house, where, let your traine be what it will, 20, or 30, I will see all defrayed as long as ever you please to be there: and, in sede vacante, in 24 howres you may be thence in Rome. I have also thought, as soon, or in what time you please, to add to your traine your nephew Tom, wherere you'l goe, and to allow him, at my cost, to keep a camariero,‡ a coach and two horses, and two foot footmen, and all in your livery, and to pass as if it were at your cost, though I pay underhand for it. And also agree, and like extreamly the name of 'Card. of Norfolke,' as Vendosme§ and others did. If

* 'Vescovádo,' a bishoprick.

† The pope.

‡ 'Cameriére,' a valet.

§ Louis, Duke of Vendome, grandson of Henry IV. of France, who, after the death of his wife, Laura Mancini, in 1657, took

my letters to the two cardinals get any replies, pray open, keep by, and read them, and send only to Mr. Hay the breviat of what they purport......I hope her ma[ty] will still continue your office under her, which, I think, will be no solecisme for either, for I am really in pain to know how, for the future, you will be annually supplied. You know my condition, and how I am tyed up with entails &c., whilst the Duke of Norfolk lives, who is likelyer to do so long then I; els I had more elbow-roome. Besides, I feare our miseries and disorders here are much more likely to increase then decrease, of which God alone can foresee the event. ......I should be glad finally that Mr. Grane would write to Mr. Hay, how he believes your Em. proposes to live for the future, and out of what fonde or yearly revenue, that my opinion and help may be best applyed. I believe Dr. Yerbury* has, by this, good store of silver plate, and some very good moveables, in Padoua. I freely offer all that to your present service, to go to Rome for a yeare, two or three, till your owne condition may be better: and do consent, if you please, to put out the armes, if any were now graven upon such plate, and put yours in the place, the which, at your return of it hereafter, may againe be altered, and no hurt neither if it remaine."...........

The arrival of the new cardinal in Rome was hailed with great joy, and numerous congratulatory verses were as usual composed in his honour. F. Vincent Fontana was then just completing his great "Monumenta Dominicana," and he

---

orders, and obtained the purple. He was known as the cardinal of Vendome.

* Dr. Henry Yerbury, fellow of Magdalen college Oxford, and doctor of physick in the university of Padua. He seems to have been professionally employed in the care of Thomas, Duke of Norfolk. See an account of him in Wood, Ath. Ox. II. 860, and Fasti, 124.

added two leaves in order to commemorate the great event and insert the heroic verses of James Alban Ghibbes,* poet-laureate of the emperor of Germany.

Ad Eminentiss. atqve Reverendiss. Principem
Fr. Philippum Thomam
Hovvardum
Ducis Norfolciae
Perpetvi Angliae Marescalli,
Germanvm fratrem;
E Sacro Praedicatorum Ordine
S. R. E.
Cardinalem Creatvm
Anno Iubil. 1675, *Mens. Maij* 27.
Gratvlatio.

Maius à celsâ titulos haud iustiùs vnquàm
Maiestate tulit, neq; tanto veris honore
Se iactauit ouans, regalia germina quàm cùm
Stirpis *Arundeliæ* Romano murice tinxit,
Atq; sacrum Patribus lectis adscripsit *Hovardum.*
Nempè bono par mensis erat nec degener anno,
Saturni regnum referens, & Virginis astrum
Sub specie *Alteriæ* Stellæ. Nam respuit imas
Pacto alio a Superis Astræa reuisere terras,
Clementis Patris obsequio & moderamine læta.
Rem miram vnius monstrant hæc tempora secli
Angligenis, laxare parat quo maximus orbis
Arbiter, atquè idem præses sublimis Olympi,

* James Alban Ghibbes or Gibbes was, says Wood "a most celebrated poet" born of English parents at Rouen. His father a convert was physician to queen Henrietta Maria. He followed the same profession, and in 1644 went to Rome. He was made professor of rhetoric at the Sapienza in 1657 by pope Alexander VII., and poet-laureate in 1667 by Leopold emperor of Germany, and in 1673 as a mark of honour was created M. D. of the university of Oxford. He died at Rome in June 1677.

Scrinia Divorum, ac cœlestia munera pandit
Thesauros latè spargens mortalibus ægris;
Te quoq; neglectam venisse, *Britannia*, dudùm,
Currit ab insigni quàm longum tempus Alano,
Præcipuam in partem, rubro dignata galero,
Speraris cùm tale nihil, vel credere posses.
Albion, ipsa facis polluto nomine mirum,
Quam seiuncta loco, Latijs tam dissita sacris.

Attamen vnus homo, prauæ telluris alumnus,
Propositi ille tenax & spectatissimus æqui,
Heroüm soboles, ac longo sanguine Princeps,
Grandior ac patrio censu virtutis auitæ,
Nec fidei desertor iners, nec transfuga campi
Cognitus, excubias ad propugnacula seruans
Maiorum exemplo pro Relligione satelles:
Pro qua mille neces, quæcunque pericula vitæ,
Omnes fortunæ vultus, vncosquè, rotasquè,
Pauperiem, & vilem cultum, durosquè labores
Constanti nunquam dubitauit fronte subire;
Hic tibi restituit famam, sanctæquè vocamen
Insulæ Oceano in vasto; veniamquè rogauit
Cœlicolas, rursùm vt fieres *Dos Virginis* almæ.
Scitur, Aranidæ quantum miseratus ab alto
Detulerit soli Deus ob pietatis amorem.
Totas sæpe vrbes texit iustissimus vnus
Nec rarò populis renouauit fœderis arcum.

O benè! diuinæ sed quis penetralia mentis
Explicet, æternos aut possit voluere sensus?
O decus arcanæ sortis, memorandaquè fastis
Gloria, virtutem profugi velut vmbra secuta,
Post tergum quæ sedit eques! Nouus aduena terram
Dùm premit ignotam, non miti lege Senatus
Pulsus in exilium nupèr, *Norfolcius* heros,
(Causa tulit; CHRISTVM Romanè fassus abito,
Contià qui steterit, capital fecisse putator:)
Eccè Quirinali, vel sic, occurritur ostro
Menapios intra fines ad litora Scaldis,

Ingratæ patriæ iussus præponere Romam
Principis imperio, frænat qui Tibridis arces.
Nostri odio natale solum te quandò repellit,
Noster eris: Fratres inter numerabere nostros,
Te maior primo, procerum cùm maximis ires.
Exilium felix, Capitolj habuisse triumphum:
Illius invidia reparat sic Roma minutos.
Ocyùs hùc eià, Ausonium & nunc indue coccum.
Scripserat hæc Genitor: tabulas fert nuncius albas
Præcipiti cursu, Bruxellæ in sede moranti.
I, *Fama,* altisonæ notissima filia Clius,
Exere pennarum remos librata per auras,
Atquè his immensum comple clangoribus orbem
Ante, suus tantos quàm sentiat author honores.
Vltimus esto ipse; ignaro gratentur vt omnes;
Ac plausus pompis veniant Laurentibus apti.
Talibus haud facilem dictis accommodat aurem
Ille quidèm, & fastus odit, quos fugerat olim
Penè puer, regum altorum, prognatus ab ipsis:
Præ cunctis opibus, tectisquè illustribus optans
Veste sub obscura, contractæ in limite cellæ
Magni sancta sequi *Calarogæ* iura Magistri.
Sed quid agat? Superùm frustrà pugnatur amori
Addictos si laude volunt cumulare clientes.
Mentem aperit cœli Interpres: parere necesse est.
Exemplum graue cedendi paulò antè *Gravina*
Præbuit assultu simili, dum ferre latebras
Mallet adoratas pariter, *Guemannia* pubes:
Multa diù luctatus, objt præcepta parentis.
Ergo agite, egregij Fratres virtute, vel ortu,
Nobile stemma Ducum; cleris incumbite cœptis,
Atquè augete genus præstantis lumine vitæ.
Oebalio niteant Ledæi sidere Diui;
Oebalio nexi cinctu splendete sodales.
Vos ego, cantando si quicquam nostra Camæna
Proficiet, veniensuè olim demisit in æuum,

Alite Mæonio secli miracula tollam ;
Nullaquè post ætas meritos obducet honores.
Pars mihi laudis erit, *Claustrum* vertisse *Theatro.*

Eminentiæ Tuae
Humillimus seruus

Romæ, ex Musæo meo, Cal. Jun. 1675.

Jacobus Albanus Ghibbesius, Poët. Laur. Cæs.

CHAPTER XI.

The cardinal's hat was placed on the head of F. Thomas Howard by the pope, and the new cardinal took the title of *S. Cecilia trans Tyberim,* which after the death of the great cardinal of Retz in 1679, he changed for *S. Maria supra Minervam.* Clement X. declared him March 23rd 1676 assistant of the four congregations, of Bishops and Regulars, of the council of Trent, of the Propaganda, and of Sacred Rites. Innocent XI. afterwards placed him on the congregation of Relics. He was generally called the "Cardinal of Norfolk," or the "Cardinal of England."

In England F. Thomas Howard had been in close friendship with sir Henry Tichborne, who dedicated a work of his to him. On being made cardinal he pressed the baronet to join his company to Rome. Sir Henry could not then do so, but early in the following year he visited his eminence in Rome, as he thus mentions in his quaint Diurnal of Pilgrimage. In his reasons for the pilgrimage the baronet says, "Besides, to lead as well as to drive me to this resolution, the Cardinal Norfolk, then Philip Howard, Lord Almoner to the Queen, who had honoured me with a particular friendship and acquaintance, and banished not only from that office and honour, but from the nation also, whom they were not worthy of, was pleased to give me a kind invitation to accompany him to Rome, then going thither to receive the honour of the purple, which sacred dignity was conferred on him, not only in recompense for these losses, but in respect of his great merit and virtue, and nobleness of Ducal Family, whereof he is descended. But so it was, that my affairs would not permit me to go as soon as his pressed him forward; but hoping to overtake him by the way, if not, to meet him at Rome."...... Sir Henry Tichborne reached Rome December 26th 1675, and first of all visited the tomb of the apostles. He then goes on, "the principal and first business of my long journey done, I went to perform the other part of it, which was to wait upon our English Cardinal Howard, to whom having delivered letters of recommendation, I was kindly and familiarly received by him: he brought me to Cardinal Altery, ye patron, and several other Cardinals; to whom having made the reverence due to the sacred purple, he carried me to St. John Latteran's, the most ancient Christian church in Rome." Sir Henry went to Naples, returned to Rome, and then resolved to visit Loretto. He says, "having obtained my last audience of his Holiness, where being particularly alone with him by myself, he was pleased to entertain me a long time, a good deal longer than ordinary, giving me several graces which I begged of him:.........kissing his foot, I took my leave of him April 14th 1676; so visiting Cardinal Barberini, the Cardinal of Norfolk, who gave me several relics of great value of St. Maximus and St. Longinus with others. Then I visited Princhipe Vicivaro, Sigr. Manuco, and many others my friends &c. and left Rome on the 16th of April."

Although raised to so high a dignity in the Church and far away from the scenes of his former undertakings, cardinal Howard never ceased to have at heart the welfare of the province to which he had devoted his life. He had long wished for his brethren to have an establishment in Rome, and immediately after he settled there or early in 1676 Clement X. at his request gave the church of SS. John and Paul with the house joining it on Mont Ceilo for a convent of English Friar-Preachers.

This church is one of the most ancient and interesting in Rome. It was first built in the fourth century by St. Pammachius on the site of the dwelling of the two brothers John and Paul, who were martyred under Julian the apostate, and whose relics still repose beneath the high altar. Several sovereign pontiffs greatly favoured it particularly St. Gregory the Great, and it was made the *station* for the first Friday in Lent. It was restored several times by the cardinal-priests who took their title from it; and it is now remarkable as a pure specimen of the Romanesque style of the north of Europe. Nicholas V. about 1452 gave this church to the Gesuati or Jesuats of St. Jerome founded by St. John Columbino and approved in 1367. When the Jesuats were put down in 1668 by Clement IX. the church and house, both of which were going to ruin, returned into the hands of the sovereign pontiffs and the house remained void for eight years. The Irish Dominicans wished to have this foundation, and their procurator-general F. master John O'Connor would have gained his point respecting it had not the cardinal unwittingly tripped him up. The disappointment of the Irish Dominicans was fully made up in the following year when they secured the church of St. Clement with St. Sixtus. Cardinal Howard immediately set about repairing the buildings. He laid out more than 15,000 Roman scudi (about £3000) in restoring the fine but much decayed campanile which stands to the south-west quite alone upon the ruins of the Curia Hostilia, and in ornamenting the church and cloisters. Over this new foundation he watched with ceaseless care, forwarding its interests with his powerful influence and aiding it with his purse in its struggles against poverty.

All the records of the English Dominicans of this house are unfortunately lost and we glean only scanty particulars concerning it from scattered sources. The convent had a noviciate and was the college of studies for the English province.

It is probable that this convent was colonized with the assistance of the Irish province. F. Felix MacDowell taught theology there before 1680, and F. Lawrence O'Farrell followed him in the professor's chair. The community seems to have been governed at first by F. Thomas White, an English Dominican who spent all his life in Italy where he changed his name into the language of the country and was usually called Bianchi. He was a very learned man and had the degree of master of theology in the Order. There is scarcely any doubt that it was he who September 30th (*o. s.*) 1673 celebrated the marriage of James duke of York (afterwards James II.) with Maria Beatrice Eleanora d'Este sister of the reigning duke of Modena. The earl of Peterborough who was the duke's proxy on the occasion says in his Genealogy of his Family, that when the bishop of Modena refused, this "poor English Jacobite," having nothing to lose and on whom the terror of excommunication did not much prevail, undertook the ceremony. In truth the court of Rome was against the match unless the princess could have her private chapel and the free exercise of her faith: but no excommunication was uttered on any priest marrying the parties, though some fears on that head might have got abroad. F. Thomas White was brother of F. Jerome White also a Dominican who afterwards served the duchess of York as her chaplain and confessor. Cardinal Howard who became archpriest of St. Mary Major, got him made a penitentiary apostolic in that basilica. He held this office till the master-general in 1688 chose him provincial and commissary-general of the English province, when he gave it up for a time to F. Ambrose Mc Dermott (an Irish

Dominican afterwards bishop of Elphin) purposing to take it again when his provincialship was over, but death hindered him from doing so. He lived in Rome where he was at the general chapter of 1694; and where still provincial he closed his life November 19th in the same year. He bore for his arms as his provincial's seal shows, *in a border of eight bezants, a chevron between three popinjays:* this points out the good English family of South Warnborough, Hants, to which he belonged.

Of the other Religious who joined the Order in this convent under the eye of cardinal Howard the notices are very few.* F. Dominic Pegge took the vows about 1677, three years later was ordained priest, became a lector of theology, was chosen prior of this house, and died in office December 21st 1691 in the thirty-fifth year of his age. F. Patrick Ogliby was professed 1679 and died in 1685 in his forty-second year. F. Thomas Cottam went to be director to the sisters at the Spellekens, and closed his life October 3rd 1693 at Brussels in their service. F. Joseph Broughton took the vows in 1683, and died at Bornhem April 26th

---

* In a letter to the prioress at the Spellekens September 20th 1687 cardinal Howard thus writes from Rome: "The noble pious Earle of Salisbury with his Camerado Mr. Charles Hales went hence yesterday towards England and ye Priour of S. Jo: Paul's theyr confesseur with them, and perhaps they may goe to Brus^ls^ to see you, wch if they doe pray make them very welcome. Fat^r^ master Tho: White will be Priour of S. Jo: Paul's in his place, as soon as his place of Penitentiary in Santa Maria Maggiore in Rome will be provided for. Fat^r^ Bachelior Raimond Greene having ended his Courses of Philosophy and Divinity, both wch hee taught at S. Jo: Paul with greate applause, will next weeke beginne his voiage towards Bor^m^, wheare he will stay for some time."

James Cicil earl of Salisbury, his countess and two brothers, were converts.

1696 in his forty-second year. F. John Been became a missionary apostolic in Ireland where he died in 1690. Brother Robert Procter died August 30th 1690 while he was still a subdeacon.

Among the English Catholics who frequented the palace of cardinal Howard in Rome few secured more of his esteem and friendship than did the three sons of the poet-laureate John Dryden. Counselled by the cardinal the youngest of them entered the Dominican Order in the convent of SS. John and Paul. The history of F. Thomas Dryden gives a curious example how the penal laws worked against the Church in England.

The honourable family of Dryden seated at Canons-Ashby in Northamptonshire had a baronetcy given it November 16th (*o. s.*) 1619 by James I. John Dryden grandson of the first baronet by a younger son was the poet-laureate of Charles II. and James II., and added everlasting glory to his earthly laurels by his conversion in 1686 to the Catholic faith. He was followed by his three sons. Charles was usher of the palace to Clement XI., and while visiting England was unfortunately drowned August 18th (*o. s.*) 1704 in the Thames at Datchet-ferry, and two days after was buried at Windsor. John died of a pleurisy in his father's life-time at Rome. Erasmus Henry was born May 2nd (*o. s.*) 1669, and after he joined the Church made up his mind to be a secular priest. He spent some time at Douay college, but in 1690 went to the English college at Rome. Being called to a stricter life he quitted the college for the English convent, where he changed his name into Thomas in religion and in 1692 took the vows. Two years after he entered the priesthood and studying with much success became a lector.

In 1697 F. Thomas Dryden went to Bornhem. He was made sub-prior, and in 1700 between two priorships he was vicar-in-capite of the house. He then came on the mission in London.

Sir John Dryden fourth baronet of the family died in May 1710, and the title fell to F. Thomas. On hearing of his cousin's death F. Thomas Dryden went to Canons-Ashby where he was saluted by his kinsmen as Sir Erasmus Henry Dryden. They could not strip him of the title, but he gained nothing more than that empty honour by becoming the head of his family. Sir Robert Dryden third baronet foreseeing that a popish priest and friar would succeed the next heir John Dryden (whose only son was killed by a fall from his horse), by his will dated July 5th (*o. s.*) 1708 about a month before his decease, had passed over F. Thomas Dryden and settled the patrimonial estates of Canons-Ashby worth about £2,000 a-year in next succession on Edward son of F. Thomas's uncle Erasmus, relying it seems on the great likelihood that this Edward would succeed F. Thomas in the title. But by the speedy death of the latter the title went to the uncle Erasmus, who moreover outlived his son, and thus by the studied shutting out of the Catholic heir the title and the family estates were separated for eight years till the son of Edward inherited both by his grandfather's and father's deaths. F. Thomas might perhaps have had the inheritance had he chosen to apostatize; but he would not make the false and costly sacrifice of his faith. As it was he could do nothing, for a penal statute of 1699 disabled any papist from inheriting landed property and his estates were to be enjoyed by his nearest Protestant kinsman. F. Thomas Dryden had a pittance allowed him at the good pleasure of his uncle. Malone says, "From the time his kinsman Edward Dryden became possessed of the family estates in 1708, Erasmus Henry was probably an inmate at Ashby, where he appears to have resided after he succeeded to the title; and from various entries in the account books of his uncle Erasmus respecting the rents of his patrimonial estate in Northamptonshire (at

Blakesley) which were regularly received by him for the use of his nephew, though he himself was on the spot, I imagine he was in a state of mental imbecility derived perhaps from his mother, who became insane after the poet's death." F. Thomas Dryden's *imagined madness* is easily explained. He was suffering from a lingering phthisis and had not been long at Canons-Ashby when he sank under it. While his life was fast ebbing he sent word of his state to the provincial F. Thomas Worthington in London. The provincial hurried to Canons-Ashby where he was received with outward courtesy by the family and saw the dying friar-baronet. F. Thomas welcomed his superior with great joy, told him that he had received the last sacraments from a neighbouring priest, and now gladly shared in the blessings and gifts the Order bestows at the gate of death. He then pressed the provincial to quit the house with all speed, as he dreaded treachery on the part of his protestant relatives. The provincial bade a last farewell to his fellow-religious and sorrowfully hastened back to London. Very soon after F. Thomas Dryden went to receive it must be hoped the hundredfold for what he lost, in the everlasting inheritance which neither cruel penal laws can reach nor grasping relatives debar. He died December 3rd (*o. s.*) 1710 in the forty-second year of his age, and was buried next day in the church of Canons-Ashby which stands not far from the mansion: consecrated ground being once part of an Augustinian priory, whence the place takes its distinctive name.

Two others joined the convent of SS. John and Paul in the time of cardinal Howard. F. Albert Lovell was professed about 1692. He went to Bornhem, and in 1704 was made lector of controversy there. Then he was chaplain to one of the foreign ambassadors in London. Falling into the clutches of the penal laws he narrowly escaped prison by flying into the country, as the ambassador could not shield him, though he was loath to part with him and promised to receive him again when the storm had blown over. He suffered much while wandering up and down as an outlaw, sent for help to the count of Bornhem, and got over into Belgium. Afterwards he was tutor in the family of lord Clifford of Ugbrooke in Devonshire, and in 1738 was elected provincial. He was chaplain to the Dominican nuns of Brussels during his time of office, came over to London in 1742 for the provincial chapter, fell sick, and died there June 1st (*o. s.*) F. Alan Pennington of the family of Pennington in Lancashire left the English college at Rome in 1692 to become a Dominican. In five or six years he went to Bornhem, where at several times he held many offices, being made procurator in 1703, sub-prior in 1707, prior in 1708, and sub-prior again in 1718. He taught all the time in the secular college there and was prefect for more than twenty years. He was again made prior in 1726, and died in office March 31st 1728 in the fifty-ninth year of his age.

Though he was thus founding and supporting the convent of SS. John and Paul, cardinal Howard was as deeply as ever concerned in his Belgian houses and did not let slip any occasion of forwarding their welfare. At his prayer Charles II. king of Spain by royal letters dated May 20th 1682 amortizated the convent of Bornhem with the gardens and 566 virges of land: to this grant was attached July 26th in the following year by the government of the Netherlands the yearly obligation of two solemn masses, one (March 19th) in honour of St. Joseph for the health long life and prosperity of the kings of Spain; the other (September 23rd) for the souls of their illustrious predecessors. The cardinal wrote to his brother Henry duke of Norfolk August 30th 1681 earnestly recommending him to educate some of his daughters at the Spellekens: and when one of those daughters lady Catherine Howard shortly after her father died desired to enter religion he advised her April 30th 1684 to try her vocation there, and if it proved true to join the community; but he yielded to her choice of another Order in Flanders. Through his kindly advice and aid a daughter of his uncle William lord viscount Stafford, and the two elder daughters of his brother colonel Bernard Howard became Dominican nuns at Brussels. Mary Delphina Stafford-Howard was professed March 2nd 1677 and died January 12th 1714 aged 56 years. Elizabeth (Dominica) Howard and Mary (Rose) Howard both took the vows February 10th 1695. The former was twice sub-prioress, and also mistress of novices and died December 17th 1761 at a very great age, having been professed sixty-six years: she was an exceedingly skilful miniaturist. The latter was chosen prioress in 1721, and closed her life April 18th 1747 in the seventy-first year of her age. The third and youngest daughter of colonel Bernard Howard, Catherine (Mary Joseph) also entered the Spellekens, taking the vows August 17th 1701 and dying February 2nd 1753 aged seventy years. Indeed the noble house of Norfolk was linked with the English Dominican province for more than a hundred years and helped it with a bountiful hand. Elizabeth duchess of Gordon second daughter of Henry duke of Norfolk and niece of cardinal Howard gave the English fathers large means to found a mission in Scotland with the aim of restoring the Scotch province; but while the the fund was in the bank of Paris it was lost in 1719 when commerce was wrecked by the failure of the great Missisippi scheme. In our days this friendship with the house of Howard comes again and calls up olden times into memory. The church at Littlehampton built in domestic affection for a loved and honoured one, and placed under the invocation of St. Catherine on whose feast he slept in Christ, is now under the pastoral care of the fathers of that province which one of his family restored.

CHAPTER XII.

After F. Thomas Howard had been forced to fly from England in 1674, the puritanical spirit of the age had deepened the hatred of Protestants against the Catholic Church into a frenzy which was perfectly fiendish, and which now could hardly have been imagined had not an echo of its cry resounded in our own days when the Catholic hierarchy was restored in England and the "Papal Aggression" scared the nation for a time out of its good sense. In Charles's time this hatred was joined with fear, as James duke of York had openly declared himself a Catholic, had married a Catholic princess, and was the presumptive heir to the throne. When the whole realm was ready for anything that pandered to its religious passion the astounding news came that a great popish plot was on foot. Titus Oates a clergyman of the Establishment suspended for his disorderly life and heterodox opinions, had feigned himself a Catholic and spent some time among the Jesuits in their colleges at Valladolid and St. Omer's out of which he was turned for his immoralities. "In those seminaries," says Macaulay, "he had heard much wild talk about the best means of bringing England back to the true Church. From hints thus furnished he constructed a hideous romance, resembling rather the dream of a sick man than any transaction which ever took place in the real world. The Pope, he said, had entrusted the government of England to the Jesuits. The Jesuits had, by commissions under the seal of their society, appointed Catholic clergymen, noblemen, and gentlemen, to all the highest offices in Church and State. The Papists had burned down London once. They had tried to burn it down again. They were at that moment planning a scheme for setting fire to all the shipping in the Thames. They were to rise at a signal and massacre all their Protestant neighbours. A French army was at the same time to land in Ireland. All the leading statesmen and divines of England were to be murdered. Three or four schemes had been formed for assassinating the King. He was to be stabbed. He was to be poisoned in his medicine. He was to be shot with silver bullets. The public mind was so sore and excitable that these lies readily found credit with the vulgar." And when sir Edmondsbury Godfrey the justice of the peace who had taken the depositions of Oates was found murdered either by his own hand or by a private enemy, the whole nation went frantic. "Everywhere justices were busied in searching houses and seizing papers. All the gaols were filled with Papists. London had the aspect of a city in a state of siege. The trainbands were under arms all night. Preparations were made for barricading the great thoroughfares. Patroles marched up and down the streets. Cannon were planted round Whitehall. No citizen thought himself safe unless he carried under his coat a small flail loaded with lead to brain the Popish assassins." Oates was called the "saviour of his country" and was pensioned with £1200 a year. His success stirred up rivalry, "and soon, from all the brothels, gambling houses, and spunging houses of London, false witnesses poured forth to swear away the lives of Roman Catholics. One came with a story about an army of thirty thousand men who were to muster in the disguise of pilgrims at Corunna, and to sail thence to Wales. Another had been promised canonization and five hundred pounds to murder the King. A third had stepped into an eating-house in Covent Garden and had there heard a great Roman Catholic banker vow, in the hearing of all the guests and drawers, to kill the heretical tyrant. Oates, that he might not be eclipsed by his imitators, soon added a large supplement to his original narrative.

He had the portentous impudence to affirm, among other things, that he had once stood behind a door that was ajar, and had there overheard the Queen declare that she had resolved to give her consent to the assassination of her husband. The vulgar believed, and the highest magistrates pretended to believe, even such fictions as these. The chief judges of the realm were corrupt, cruel, and timid." "The juries partook of the feelings then common throughout the nation, and were encouraged by the bench to indulge those feelings without restraint. The multitude applauded Oates and his confederates, hooted and pelted the witnesses who appeared on behalf of the accused, and shouted with joy when the verdict of Guilty was pronounced. It was in vain that the sufferers appealed to the respectability of their past lives: for the public mind was possessed with a belief that the more conscientious a Papist was, the more likely he would be to plot against a Protestant government. It was in vain that, just before the cart passed from under their feet, they resolutely affirmed their innocence: for the general opinion was that a good Papist considered all lies which were serviceable to his Church as not only excusable but meritorious."

More than two thousand Catholics were arrested under the monstrous charges of Oates. Twenty-six, the greater part being priests and Religious, suffered the penalty of death, nearly twenty were condemned but reprieved, and some died in prison. Oates threw the plot on the Jesuits, because their power was most dreaded by the people, and he knew by name more of them than of any others, as he had lived in their colleges abroad. It is honourable to the English Dominicans that they held a high rank in numbers among the Regulars he dragged into the arena of his bloody tragedy; in fact they were made the arch conspirators with the Jesuits, and representatives of the other Orders. When he was examined on oath at the bar of the House of Lords October

31st (*o. s.*) 1678 Oates named more than eighty priests, secular and regular, who were engaged in the plot. Of the "conspirators" in the latter class, 43 were Jesuits, 9 Dominicans (besides cardinal Howard), 3 Carmelites, and 2 Franciscans. He gave in the following list of the Dominican "conspirators," and where they were at the time; to which we add the correct names.

"Joseph David Keymash, in Engl'd.	F. David Joseph Kemeys.
Mr. Dominick, in England.	F. Dominic Maguire.
Mr. Collins, in England.	F. William Collins.
Mr. Vincent, in England.	F. Vincent Torre.
Mr. Fidding, in Engl'd.	F. Thomas Fidden.
Mr. Mansell, in England.	F. Albert Anderson *alias* Munson.
Mr. Cooper, at Rome.	F. Vincent Hyacinth Cowper.
Mr. Lunsdall, in England.	F. Alexander Lumsden.
Captain Bingly, in England."	F. Edward Bing.

Oates swore that in a congregation of the Propaganda held about December 1677 Innocent XI. had declared all the dominions of the king of England to be part of St. Peter's patrimony and to be forfeited through the heresy of the prince and people, so as to be at the free disposal of the Holy See; and that cardinal Howard was appointed legate to take possession of England in the name of his holiness. The throne was to be given to a Catholic, and the five principal offices of state were to be entrusted to the Catholic lords, William Herbert earl Powis, Henry lord Arundel of Wardour, William Howard viscount Stafford, William lord Petre, and John lord Bellasyse. Moreover the Protestant ecclesiastical dignitaries were to be deprived and Catholics put into their places. Oates declared that Innocent had issued a bull dated either the November or December before, a copy of which had been shown him, whereby the pope was pleased to dispose of the bishoprics of England. Of those twenty sees, five were to go to the Dominicans, five to Jesuits, two to Franciscans, one to a Benedictine, and the rest to the secular clergy. The archbishopric of Canterbury was given to cardinal Howard, with an augmentation of forty thousand crowns a-year to maintain his legatine authority: Ely to Vincent provincial of the Dominicans; Peterborough to Gifford a Dominican; Bristol to Minison [Munson] a Dominican; and Bangor to Joseph David Keimash a Dominican. The tales of Oates stirred up the Commons to madness against the Catholics; and April 3rd (*o. s.*) following they impeached for high treason all the parties concerned in the "Popish Plot." This impeachment was sent on the 7th to the house of Lords: besides the Catholic noblemen named above, it included cardinal Howard, Vincent commonly called provincial of the Dominicans in England, and all the rest of the conspirators in order. Of the Dominican "traitors" five were arrested, two were beyond the jurisdiction of the Houses, one fled out of the country, one escaped being taken, and one died amidst the troubles.

Cardinal Howard was fortunately at Rome, far away from the dangers that threatened his life in his unhappy country. If he had been in England he would have found, not only a lord high chancellor to trample his hat underfoot, but a headsman to strike him with the fate which overtook his uncle William viscount Stafford.

F. David Joseph Kemeys was charged by Oates with being one of the popish conspirators who planned the burning of London in 1666, and with enticing him to join the Church in order to escape the mighty blow which was soon to overthrow the throne and the Protestantism of the country. Being arrested and cast into Newgate, he was arraigned January 17th (*o. s.*) 1679-80 at the Old Bailey before the lord chief justice Scroggs, not on account of the conspiracy, but for the high treason of being a priest and remaining in the country contrary to the law. He pleaded "Not guilty;" but being aged and weakened in health by his imprisonment he was scarcely able to stand, and could not speak in his own defence, particularly as no time had been given him to prepare for it. Scroggs was obliged to put off the trial and order the gaoler to take the prisoner back and get him a bed. F. David Joseph lived only a few days longer, dying January 27th (*o. s.*) in Newgate.

F. Dominic Maguire an Irish Dominican joined the Order in Spain. He became honorary chaplain to the Spanish ambassador in London, and as we shall soon see was brought up before the House of Lords as a suspected person. Innocent XI. made him archbishop of Armagh, in place of Dr. Oliver Plunket who was executed at Tyburn July 1st (*o. s.*) 1681 the last victim of the 'Popish Plot.' He governed his church till 1691, when he was exiled with many others at the Hanoverian invasion, and died in 1708 at Paris.

F. William Collins was also sheltered in the household of the Spanish ambassador. He was charged with high treason before the House of Lords by a low villain who was willing enough to share anyhow in the profits of the Plot. William Greene on oath at the bar of the house deposed November 14th (*o. s.*) 1678 that about August he took a letter to one Collins a popish priest, sent out of Flanders, wherein there was this passage: That there would be a war between England and France. Whereupon Collins replied, We should have war enough at home. This Collins, he said, lived in the Spanish ambassador's house. The Lords immediately prayed the king for Collins and Dominic Maguire to be delivered up, and for Greene to go along with the messenger as he knew Collins when he saw him. The next day the king's answer came, that the ambassador had promised to send the two persons when and where his majesty pleased; "expressing himself sensible of the occasion upon which they were demanded, that if he knew his own Son was engaged in it, he would deliver him up." F. William Collins was brought to the bar on the 16th and asked, whether he knew one William Greene. He answered: No; but when Greene was called in and he saw him he confessed that he did know him. Greene repeated what he had said two days before at the bar; which F. William denied. Then Greene deposed that Collins had confessed to him, That he was a Romish priest. The House commanded F. William Collins to be committed to the Gate House prison till farther order. F. Dominic Maguire being brought to the bar said that he was born in Spain and not naturalized. As there was no charge against him and as he was a Spaniard it was ordered that he should be returned to the Spanish ambassador.

It does not appear that F. William Collins was brought to trial. He was probably set free by the king after the parliament was dissolved. Charles II. was the only one who had a grain of common sense in the matter of the Plot. He always declared his disbelief of it and did what he could to unmask the perjurors. He often used his royal power to rescue some of the victims, but he was wholly powerless to stem the torrent of the national fury. F. William Collins returned to Bornhem, became prior of the convent in August 1685, was affiliated to the English province in 1691, and died at Bruges November 17th 1699 in the 78th year of his age. "He writ," says our MS., "somewhat against y[e] sectaries of y[e] times," but we have not lighted on any of his works.

F. Vincent Torre fled when he was impeached for high treason, and found a safe shelter at Bornhem. In 1682 he took the government of the convent. He left August 20th in the following year for Rome, and spent almost all the rest of his life in the convent of SS. John and Paul. He was still vicar-general when the master-general's associate

F. Leonard Hansen, who had borne the titular dignity of Provincial of England for about twenty years, closed his life March 28th 1685. At the instance of cardinal Howard, the master-general made F. Vincent Torre provincial of England, who thus became the first one since the fall of the faith under Henry VIII. In this character he assisted in the chapter at Rome in June 1686, when the great F. Antoninus Cloche was elected head of the Order. He held the office till his decease. In 1687 he quitted Rome,* and August 3rd arrived at Bornhem, where he died on the 24th of the same month, in the 57th year of his age.

F. Thomas Fidden died in London September 4th (*o. s.*) 1679 in the heat of the Plot, when he was in his 55th year.

F. Albert Anderson *alias* Munson after he had gone through all his studies and was ordained returned into England as a missionary, and abode for the most part in London. He was much esteemed by many of the nobility and persons at the Court, and even Charles II. sometimes enjoyed his pleasant conversation. He took little part in the affairs of the time beyond publishing one or two pamphlets against the temporal power of the popes, and in favour of the oath of allegiance then proposed for Catholics, which he in

---

* Three months before F. Vincent Torre left Rome cardinal Howard gave him some relics of the martyrs of Christ taken out of the catacomb of St. Castulus, and consisting of the whole arm of St. Vincent and relics of St. Bonus. The letter of authentication dated April 14th 1687 is now in the Bodleian library. With it in the same collection of "Miscellaneous papers, being chiefly original letters from K. Henry 8, Theodore Beza, Archbp. Whitgift, Bp. Morton, Cardinal Howard, [etc.]" is a long article on the jurisdiction, rights, and privileges of a cardinal. No name is given, but it is in the handwriting of F. Raymund Greene.

common with many others including several of the greatest doctors of the Sorbonne thought could be lawfully taken. For these writings he was blamed by his own brethren, and severely censured by the numerous and more powerful party rightly opposed to the views he took. In the frenzy of the Plot he was imprisoned in the King's bench and thence removed to Newgate. Along with F. David Joseph Kemeys, F. Alexander Lumsden, and several secular, Benedictine, and Franciscan priests, he was tried at the Old Bailey January 17th (*o. s.*) 1679-80 before the infamous lord-chief justice Scroggs. Dangerfield, Oates, Bedloe, and Prance gave evidence against him and swore most positively to his saying Mass and giving the Sacraments. The vileness of the witnesses' characters, their reckless oaths and clear falsehoods raised his temper, and though he was in poor health he defended himself with great warmth and freedom which even the brow-beating of his unjust judge could not put down. The verdict of Guilty was brought in, and he was condemned to death by the halter and to the butchery of quartering. He heard his sentence with great firmness. Many of his and of the other prisoners' expressions were left out or mis-given in the report of the trials printed by authority; but they were afterwards published by the parties themselves in a pamphlet entitled, "Some of the most material Errors and Omission in the late printed Tryals of the Roman priests at the Old Bailey, Jan. 17, 1679."

When he had been in Newgate under condemnation about a year he humbly petitioned Charles II. that the sentence of death might be carried out. The king changed his punishment into one of banishment for life. It is certain that once if not twice he made a pilgrimage to Jerusalem, and perhaps it was at this time he visited the Holy Land. Spite of his judicial condemnation he returned to London. James II. April 6th (*o. s.*) 1686 granted him a free pardon. At the Hanoverian invasion he fled with king James and remained for some time abroad, but again he took up his charge in the metropolis. In 1710 he was seized with a fever which in about a week ended his life. Strengthened in the last struggle by the sacraments, and surrounded by many of his brethren, he died October 21st (*o. s.*) in the 91st year of his age. Next day he was buried at St. Giles'.

F. Vincent Hyacinth Cowper after his profession came into England, but about 1676 he was sent to the newly-formed convent of SS. John and Paul in Rome. Then he was again in England, where he died April 21st (*o. s.?*) 1690 in his 61st year.

F. Alexander Lumsden was arrested at Whitehall, and tried at the Old Bailey along with F. Albert Anderson. He was then fifty-eight years old. Oates, Dugdale, and Prance appeared against him, and Oates and Prance swore to having seen him say Mass at Wildhouse the residence of the Spanish ambassador. But as he was a Scotchman born in Aberdeen, and was prosecuted under a statute of queen Elizabeth passed when Scotland was an independent kingdom, the jury brought in a special verdict, and he was not sentenced to death. He was still on the mission in 1687.

F. Edward Bing, though he lived most of his time in London, seems to have escaped the fangs of the law during the Plot. After the decease of F. Thomas White, the master-general March 8th 1695 made him provincial of England for four years. Shortly after he was arrested, tried, and condemned, on account of his priesthood. His life was spared, but he was driven out of his country. He withdrew to Bornhem and died in the convent September 25th 1701 in his 77th year.

F. Maurice Gifford was fifth son of Thomas Gifford esq. of London, by Ann daughter and co-heiress of Gregory Brookesby esq. of Frisby in Leicestershire; his elder brother Henry of Burstall in the same county was made a baronet November 21st (*o. s.*) 1660, but the title soon became extinct.

He was professed among the Friar-Preachers of Antwerp, and was on the English mission before 1672. At the time of the Plot he baffled his foes. By letters-patent of the master-general dated February 9th 1692 he was affiliated to the English province. He died in London March 25th 1699. Jonghe ranks him among the illustrious fathers of the convent of Antwerp.

The 'conspirators' were not the only fathers of the Dominican province that suffered in Oates' persecutions. All the rest on the English missions being looked on as traitors to the state were in jeopardy, and being hunted up and down the country had to fly or to conceal themselves from the pursuit of their enemies.

F. Thomas Molineux seems to have been at some distance from London as he was unnoticed by Oates, and we do not find that he fell into any troubles. When old age hindered him from his pastoral duties he withdrew to Bornhem. After a few years of repose from his toils he was seized with a catarrh, and after receiving the sacraments peacefully died at the convent December 10th 1708 in the 90th year of his age.

F. Martin Russel laboured among the Catholics about Malvern and the Western counties of England. He was very zealous and laborious in all his duties. During the Plot he withdrew to Bornhem, but left the convent August 23rd 1680 and came again into England. On Christmas-eve 1690 he was taken for being a priest, and imprisoned about three months in Hereford gaol along with another of the Order who afterwards died in the convent of SS. John and Paul at Rome. He underwent many hardships in prison and was brought up to be examined by the Protestant bishop of Hereford. Now this bishop was an apostate Catholic. His father was sir Robert Croft of Croft-castle in Herefordshire, who was converted to the faith, and had a little cell within the ambits of the English Benedictine college at Douay, where he spent the rest of his life in religious exercises and died in 1622. His younger son who bore both his names was brought up in the Catholic faith, but soon turned a rigid Calvinist, was rector of Uley in Gloucestershire, then dean of Hereford, and from 1661 to his death in 1691 occupied the see. F. Martin Russel parried the bishop's questions very skilfully. Dr. Croft asked him how he was bred.

F. Martin. When a little one, I heard people say I was reared like other children with milk and pap. When I grew bigger I remember a butterum and a piece of cheese served.

Dr. Croft. This is not to your purpose. I ask your education.

F. Martin. When I was grown up I served my king, and fought for him in Worcester battle where you durst not show your face.

Dr. Croft. You were educated beyond seas, were you not?

F. Martin. I hope, my lord, that is no crime. Your lordship was so too.

Dr. Croft. What did you study there?

F. Martin. How to get back again. I served the king at Tangier and suffered there much for his sake.

Dr. Croft. Come, come, tell the truth.

F. Martin. That I will and the naked truth.

Thereupon one present took F. Martin up and presented a bill of indictment against him. He was sent back to Hereford gaol and thence to the assizes, and stood fair for his trial and condemnation, had not the gentry of the country (warned probably by the prosecutions under Oates) turned his friends by becoming jurymen in his cause and hindering the witnesses from coming in against him.

Another time F. Martin Russel was met by the king's officers, who questioned him whence he came. "From Cracovia," he replied. "And whither," they asked, "are you going?" He said jestingly, "To Cracovia:" nor would he give them any serious answer. That time they departed not knowing him. Afterwards many searches were made for him, but he gave them the slip and escaped their hands. To the last he continued his fugitive life, serving the scattered faithful from place to place as duty called him. He had been about forty-two years on the mission when he peacefully closed his life September 8th (*o. s.*) 1711 in the house of a Catholic family named Pickering at Stanton-Lacey near Ludlow in Shropshire, being then in his eightieth year. He was buried at the village church where he died. A plain stone marked the grave of this first subject and early friend of cardinal Howard: on it was inscribed simply,

D. Martinus Russel O. P.
R. I. P.

F. Peter Atwood was placed on the English mission in 1672 by F. Thomas Howard, and generally lived in London. In Oates' Plot in 1679 he was imprisoned, tried, and condemned to death for his priesthood. Just as he was stepping on the hurdle which was at the prison-gate waiting to carry him to the butchery of hanging and quartering at Tyburn, a reprieve came which some Catholics had obtained of the king who well knew his innocence. When he was told that he was delivered from death he burst into tears and exclaimed, "Alas! alas! my friends, to-day they have bereaved me of the kingdom of heaven: the crown of martyrdom has fallen from my head." All the rest of his life he went about in deep sorrow for his loss. But though he missed the martyr's crown, he won at least the martyr's spirit. More than once he suffered chains and loss of freedom for Christ's sake, all which he bore most patiently. He was vicar-provincial of England from 1696 to 1708 while the provincials were in Flanders. At last he died in London

August 12th (*o. s.*) 1712, in the seventieth year of his age. He was buried two days after at St. Giles'.

F. Cornelius O'Heyn an Irish Dominican studied at the Minerva in Rome, and for many years taught philosophy and theology at Prague where he was made a master of theology. He came into England and was *socius* and *commensalis* to F. Christopher of the Rosary confessor to queen Catherine of Braganza. At the time of the 'Plot' he was forced to seek safety abroad, but as soon as the country had calmed down he came back to London. Burke in his Hibernia Dominicana styles him "celebris," and says, "fuit valde candidus, doctus, ac proficuus Catholicis Anglis." The Bornhem records mention him among the English Religious, so that he must have been incorporated into the province; and they add that his death took place in 1686, while Burke dates it a year earlier.

CHAPTER XIII.

From the first year of Elizabeth's reign the Church in England underwent an oppression scarcely surpassed in the history of persecution. From time to time penal laws were framed against it more harassing and cruel than open warfare would have been. Catholics were forbidden the freedom of worship even in their own private houses and in the solitude of their chambers. They were denied a fitting education either at home or abroad. Stripped of their rights as citizens and subjects they were shut out from their elective franchises, from every public office however mean it might be, from practising the liberal professions as a means of support, and even from being executors or guardians, or mere witnesses to a contract. They were kept prisoners to the neighbourhood of their dwellings; and they ran the risk of their lives if they dared to look unbidden on the face of their sovereign. The oaths of allegiance and supremacy closed against them the houses of Lords and Commons and all the local corporate bodies, and embarrassed them even as common soldiers and sailors in the army and navy; while added to the oaths those thirty-nine articles which declare fundamental doctrines of the Church to be vain, corrupt, and blasphemous, drove them from the gates of the universities. At the malicious pleasure of a private enemy or the covetousness of the vilest informer and foresworn witness the Catholic was doomed to death, was put out of the protection of the laws, or was condemned to banishment, to imprisonment, to the loss of real and personal property, to ruinous penalties, and to every civil disability: for disbelieving in the royal supremacy; for believing in the spiritual supremacy of the sovereign pontiff of Rome; for bringing in or publishing any papal bull or decree even on devotional matters; for being a priest; for harbouring, concealing, or aiding a priest; for saying or hearing Mass; for believing in transubstantiation, the invocation of saints, and the sacrament of the Mass; for reconciling another or being reconciled to the Church of Rome; for having any controversial work in favour of popery; for buying, selling, or having any popish book written in English; for having an Agnus Dei, a relic, cross, crucifix, popish picture, or beads;* for not attending the

---

* There was some show of reason for forbidding Rosaries. Thirty years after Elizabeth had set up Protestantism they were still used openly in Wales. The common people said that they could read upon their beads as others did on their books, and made such "clappings" with them in the church that it was complained the minister could hardly be heard for the noise.

Confraternities of the Most Holy Rosary flourished secretly

parish church at least once a month; for not receiving the sacrament of the Church of England; for being married or having a child baptized otherwise than openly in the Church of England; for having a fellow-Catholic buried elsewhere than in the church or churchyard; for keeping a school; for having a popish schoolmaster in private; for sending anyone or being sent abroad into any popish college, seminary, or family to be educated; for practising law, physic, or any liberal art or science to gain a livelihood; for keeping arms; for going to the royal court without the command of the king or the warrant of the privy council; for going within ten miles of London; or for being five miles beyond his dwelling without the leave of four justices of the peace.

Such was the condition of the Catholic body in England when James II. came to the throne in 1685. The penal laws had been put into force during the reigns of Elizabeth and James I. so fiercely that the faith must have been driven altogether out of the land if avarice had not overruled all godly considerations, and allowed the Catholic nobility and gentry by compounding for their recusancy to buy at great prices the secret practice of their religion and to shield from persecution the humble dependants of their houses and estates. When a Catholic queen shared the honours of the court of Charles I. the penal laws were not so much carried out, and Catholics enjoyed fitful seasons of calm broken from time to time when at the instance of some needy informer a priest was offered in bloody sacrifice to glut the bigotry of the country. In the great rebellion the deep devotion of Catholics to their monarch's cause earned for them the lasting esteem of the royal family. Charles II. spite of the loud complaints of the whole nation would fain

---

through all the times of persecution and aided powerfully to foster the heroic spirit of the faithful in setting at nought the rack, the gibbet, and the knife.

have granted toleration to them and to all dissenters. By his Declaration of Indulgence (for promoting which F. Thomas Howard suffered so much) he set aside the penal laws against Catholics and against Protestant nonconformists, granting to the former the *private*, and to the latter the *public*, exercise of their religion. But in the fierce intolerant spirit of the time the Commons denied to the king that prescriptive right to use the royal prerogative of mercy which had not been questioned before, and obliged him forthwith to cancel the declaration and promise solemnly that it should never be made a precedent. Nor was this enough. The Commons immediately passed the Test Act directed avowedly against Catholics, by which every person holding any office civil or military had to receive the sacrament of the Church of England publicly and to sign a declaration against transubstantiation. A few years after they added to the test a further declaration against "the Invocation or Adoration of the Virgin Mary, or any other Saint, and the Sacrament of the Mass, as they are now used in the Church of Rome."

James II. did not stretch his royal prerogatives farther than the kings who went before him had used their acknowledged powers; but he carried them beyond the bounds of moderation and prudence when the temper of the whole nation was so obstinately set against the Church. He relied too much on his supremacy and on the loud professions of passive obedience which were rife among the English Protestant clergy. Moreover he was driven on to the measures he took by traitors in his court, who at the same time were planning his downfall and courting the favour of his Protestant successor. The king had Mass and the rites of the Church celebrated in all their grandeur at the palace and attended them with royal pomp. He sent an ambassador to Rome and publicly received a papal nuncio. He called four Catholics, one of whom was a Jesuit, into the privy council made up of forty members. He admitted Catholics into the army spite of the Test Act. He authorized a few Catholics to hold some preferments in the Protestant establishment, and appointed seven commissioners for governing it. He forced Catholics on the universities of Oxford* and Cambridge, gave the deanery of Christchurch Oxford to a Catholic, and sanctioned the time-serving renegade master in bringing over University college: he turned out the fellows and scholars of Magdalen college, and when

---

* The original of the following is in the archives of the English Dominican province.

"To the Right Reverend Father in God, Samuell, Lord Bishop of Oxon, President of St. Mary Magdalen Colledge, in Our Vniversity of Oxon, or in his absence to the Vice President of Our said Colledge.

"JAMES R.

"Right reverend Father in God, We greet you well. Whereas there are severall Fellowships now voyd in that Our Colledge of St Mary Magdalen; We haue thought fit hereby to signify Our will and pleasure to you, that you forthwith admit Our trusty and welbeloved Richard Short to be a Fellow of Our said Colledge, with all the Rights, Priviledges, Profits, Perquisits and Advantages to the same belonging or appertaining, without administring unto him any Oath or Oaths but that of a Fellow, any Law, Statute, Custom or Constitution to the contrary in any wise notwithstanding, with which We are graciously pleased to dispense in this behalfe. And for so doing, this shall be your Warrant. And so We bid you heartily Farewell. Given at Our Court at Whitehall, the 14th day of March 168$\frac{7}{8}$, in the fourth yeare of Our Reigne.

"By his Majty's command.

"SUNDERLAND, P.

"Mr Richard Short to be a Fellow of Magdalen Colledge."

Rich. Short became an eminent physician. An account of him is given in Dodd's Church History.

the bishop of Oxford died, appointed a Catholic bishop to be president, so as to make it entirely a Catholic institution. He put forth April 4th (*o. s.*) 1687 a Declaration of Indulgence removing the penal laws and freely allowing public worship to all classes of nonconformists, so that Catholics built chapels and convents in some parts of the kingdom. He repeated this declaration April 27th (*o. s.*) 1688 and enjoined it to be read in all churches, and when his order was disobeyed he sent seven of the English bishops to the tower of London. And he remodelled the self-elective corporate bodies of cities and boroughs formed under the penal and test codes, and opened them and every civil office to members of all sects. The nation was aroused, and the English clergy soon unlearned their doctrine of non-resistance, James now saw his danger. He strove to undo his great errors by withdrawing his acts against the Protestant Establishment, abolishing the court of High Commission he had revived, and giving up Magdalen college: and he restored the corporate bodies to their former state. But all was too late. The Revolution was fully organized. Insurrections occurred throughout the country. William prince of Orange landed and gathered a military force around him. The army was disaffected. James had to fly and the Calvinist stadtholder seized the government and for ever shut out the Catholic House of Stuart from the British throne. The penal laws were brought again into force and increased in severity, and the state of the Church in England became worse than ever.

Cardinal Howard took deeply to heart the ecclesiastical affairs of England and forwarded them with every means in his power. At his instance Innocent XI. extended the feast of St. Edward the Confessor, which had been kept in England only, to the universal Church: a decree of the congregation of rites May 29th 1679 ordered it to be on October 9th, but another decree of April 6th 1680 changed it to the 13th of the month, being the anniversary of the Translation of the Saint's relics in 1161. Francesco Barberini cardinal-protector of England died in 1679. Charles II. prayed Innocent XI. to give the charge to cardinal Howard, who accordingly undertook the welfare of the Catholics of England. The English secular clergy congratulated him on his appointment in a letter dated, Paris March 15th 1680. In his answer April 10th he commended them for their zeal in defence of the faith, for which many of their predecessors and even some in the persecution then on foot had lost their lives, whom he proposed to their imitation. At the same time he warned them that it was not lawful to take the oaths of allegiance and supremacy, though some of their brethren had abetted them so as to cause reflections on the whole body of clergy and some uneasiness at the court of Rome and in the mind of the sovereign pontiff. As cardinal-protector of England and Scotland he also addressed an admirable epistle dated Rome April 7th 1684 to the clergy of the two countries. Among other things he recommended to them the "Institutum clericorum in communi viventium," founded about 1644 by a German priest Bartholomew Holtzhauser. The institute was eagerly taken up in England and flourished for some years, but was broken up at last through a misunderstanding between the members and the rest of the secular clergy: still it gave rise to some important and valuable funds for relieving over-aged or disabled priests, which have continued to the present day. Under the protection and the watchful eye of the cardinal were carried on the fine new buildings of the English college and of his own adjoining palace in Rome. The famous Legenda and Carlo Fontana were the architects of the buildings, which were finished in 1685. Here were only his state rooms. Though he had a pension of 10,000 scudi from the pope and apartments in the Vatican he chose the cloistral life in the Dominican convent of St. Sabina, where to the time of his death he shared the humble fare of the friars in the common refectory. The palace of cardinal Howard has always been interesting to English Catholics in Rome, and of late years it has gained an additional claim on their attention. The present supreme pontiff Pius IX., whose affection for the Church in this country is one of the leading traits of his pontificate, has established in it a college for meeting the growing wants of England. The Collegio Pio provides a place and means of study for adults and for converts to enrol themselves among the secular clergy.

When a Catholic sovereign once more sat on the British throne, cardinal Howard hailed the event with the greatest delight and looked forward to bright days for the Church in his native land. But sorely was he dismayed when he found what headstrong courses James II. was pursuing, and his alarm was shared by Innocent XI. It was the aim of the pope and of the cardinal, not so much to raise the political powers of English Catholics in direct opposition to the fierce Protestant temper of the nation, as to give the Church internal strength and power, which in course of time must have won for Catholics their due position in the state. For fifty-six years there had not been any vicar-apostolic in England to govern the secular clergy, and English Catholics were indebted to Irish charity for those ministrations which belong to the office of bishop. Cardinal Howard set about repairing this evil as soon as possible. His great friend, secretary and auditor John Leyburn was consecrated bishop at Rome September 9th 1685 with the title of Adrumetum *in partibus infidelium*, and the spiritual charge of the Catholics of England was entrusted to him. He arrived in the following month; the king lodged him in Whitehall and gave him a pension of £1000. a year. With him came Ferdinand count of Adda as papal nuncio. Macaulay says that Dr. Leyburn, whom he mistakes for an English Dominican, "with some learning and a rich vein of natural humour, was the most cautious, dexterous, and taciturn of men;" and that "he seems to have behaved, on all occasions, like a wise and honest man." Adda was of mild temper and courtly manners. Innocent XI. sent these two to the English Court with the charge to inculcate moderation both by admonition and example; and had James listened to them and not to the hot-headed and wrong-hearted counsellors, who bolstered him up with grand ideas of his supremacy and urged him on to his extreme measures, he would have saved his crown and have done lasting good to the Church. Dr. Leyburn was kept at the court, but his advice had no weight. He boldly told the king that the fellows and students of Magdalen college were grievously wronged, and that restitution ought to be made to them on religious as well as on political grounds. James yielded only when he was forced to do so.

The pope saw clearly the fatal tendency of the royal policy. "Innocent was confirmed in his judgment," says Macaulay, "by the principal Englishmen who resided at his court. Of these the most illustrious was Philip Howard, sprung from the noblest houses of Britain, grandson, on one side, of an Earl of Arundel, on the other, of a Duke of Lennox. Philip had long been a member of the sacred college: he was commonly designated as the Cardinal of England; and he was the chief counsellor of the Holy See in matters relating to his country. He had been driven into exile by the outcry of Protestant bigots; and a member of his family, the unfortunate Stafford, had fallen a victim to their rage. But neither the Cardinal's own wrongs, nor those of his house, had so heated his mind as to make him a rash adviser. Every letter, therefore, which went from the Vatican to Whitehall recommended patience, moderation, and respect for the prejudices of the English people." Barnet visited Rome in August 1685 before James had entered on the most violent part of his career, and he was treated by the English cardinal "with great freedom." This bishop, in his *History of his own Times*, says, "Cardinal Howard showed me all his letters from England, by which I saw, that those who wrote to him reckoned, that their designs were so well laid, that they could not miscarry. They thought, they should certainly carry everything in the next session of parliament. There was a high strain of insolence in their letters: And they reckoned, they were so sure of the King, that they seemed to have no doubt left of their succeeding in the reduction of England. The Romans and Italians were much troubled at all this: For they were under such apprehensions of the growth of the French power, and had conceived such hopes of the King of England's putting a stop to it, that they were sorry to see the King engage himself so, in the design of changing the religion of his subjects, which they thought would create him so much trouble at home, that he would neither have leisure nor strength, to look after the common concerns of Europe. The Cardinal told me, that all the advices writ over from thence to England were for slow, calm and moderate courses. He said, he wished he was at liberty to show me the copies of them: But he saw violent courses were more acceptable, and would probably be followed. And he added, that these were the production of England, far different from the counsels of Rome.

"He also told me, that they had not instruments enough to work with: For, tho' they were sending over all that were capable of the Mission, yet he expected no great matters from them. Few of them spoke true English. They came over young, and retained all the English that they brought over with them, which was only the language of boys: But, their education being among strangers, they had formed themselves so upon that model, that really they preached as Frenchmen or Italians in English words; of which he was every day warning them, for he knew this could have no good effect in England. He also spoke with great sense of the proceedings in France, which he apprehended would have very ill consequences in England. I shall only add one other particular, which will show the soft temper of that good natured man.

"He used me in such a manner, that it was much observed by many others. So two French Gentlemen desired a note from me to introduce them to him. Their design was to be furnished with Reliques; for he was then the Cardinal that looked after that matter. One evening I came in to him as he was very busy in giving them some Reliques. So I was called in to see them: And I whispered to him in English, that it was somewhat odd, that a Priest of the Church of England should be at Rome, helping them off with the ware of Babylon. He was so pleased with this, that he repeated it to the others in French; and told the Frenchmen, that they should tell their countrymen, how bold the hereticks, and how mild the Cardinals were at Rome."

A single vicar-apostolic and mere titular bishop for the whole of England was far from contenting the king. James through his ambassador at Rome prayed the pope that F. Edward Petre vice-provincial of the Jesuits (who became one of the four Catholic privy councillors) might be made a bishop and cardinal, with the view it was bruited abroad of thrusting him into the vacant archbishopric of York. Innocent firmly refused though the matter was again and again strongly urged on him, as he thought the proposal most imprudent and rash. But he appointed another vicar-apostolic, and January 30th 1688 he divided England into four districts, and let James name the persons who would be fit to govern them. Bonaventure Giffard the king's chaplain was consecrated April 22nd (*o. s.*) 1687 at Whitehall by title of bishop of Madaura, Philip Michael Ellis O. S. B. May 6th (*o. s.*) 1688 at St. James's palace by title of bishop of Aureliopolis, and James Smith May 13th (*o. s.*) following at Somerset-house by title of bishop of Callipolis. The London district was given to Dr. Leyburn, the midland to Dr.

Giffard, the northern to Dr. Smith, and the western to Dr. Ellis. Each vicar had a salary of £1000 a-year out of the royal exchequer with £500 when he entered on his office.

During the reign of James II. there were several Dominican fathers in London and about the royal court. Many of them have been already named; only three now need to be particularly noticed.

F. Dominic Gwillim after F. Thomas Howard was made a cardinal governed the convent of Bornhem as vicar-in-capite, till early in 1676 he was elected prior. In 1679 he was reinstalled for another term of three years. When his second priorship was over he came to London, and was probably a chaplain in the army as he went by the title of *captain:* on the death of F. Vincent Torre in August 1687, the master-general appointed him provincial of England. In that office he died at London September 11th (*o. s.*) 1688 in the forty-sixth year of his age.

F. Ambrose Thomas Grymes returned from Rennes to Bornhem late in 1675, and taught philosophy. Then he had a professor's chair in Italy, but the place is not named; it was probably at the convent of SS. John and Paul in Rome. In England he became preacher-in-ordinary to the queen-dowager Catherine of Braganza. He was vicar-provincial for England while the provincial was abroad. The queen-dowager broke up her establishment at Somerset-house in March 1692-3 and returned into Portugal; and after some time, F. Ambrose recrossed the sea into Flanders. The master-general made him provincial of England in 1699 and again in 1704; and in this time he was confessor at the Spellekens. In 1708 he was appointed rector of the Dominican college of St. Thomas at Louvain, of which we shall hereafter speak; and in May 1711 was elected prior of Bornhem. In 1718 he was again at St. Thomas's college, where he was master of studies and professor of sacred Scripture. He closed his days at Louvain February 18th 1719 in the seventy-fourth year of his age. As the English fathers had no cemetery attached to their college he was buried among the Irish Friar-Preachers of the convent of Holy Cross.

F. Lewis Thursby was for thirty-nine years on the English mission, probably in London where we find him in 1709. In his old age he returned to Bornhem about 1720, and there died October 12th 1726 in the seventy-eighth year of his age.

It does not appear that the Dominicans* took any part in the political affairs of James II. In the archives of the English Dominican province is a record which gives a curious incident in the babyhood of James Francis Edward Prince of Wales, who afterwards became famous as the "Chevalier de St. George" or "the Old Pretender." It has escaped alike the political misrepresentations of Burnet and the malignant tattle of Macaulay. This son of king James and Maria Beatrice his consort, born June 10th (*o. s.*) 1688, was grievously afflicted with convulsions. As the hope of the kingdom and of the Catholic religion seemed to be centred in this prince, no human means were spared to save him from the disease, which had carried off all the other children of the queen. By the advice of the physicians the child was fed in place of milk on black-cherry water, which was thought best for guarding against or driving off the fits; but this remedy did no good. When medical skill failed the queen, who had long before heard of the merits of St. Macharius in curing such diseases, had some relics of the saint sent to London by

---

* In the Life of Dr. John Radcliffe physician to the princess Anne of Denmark and founder of the library which bears his name at Oxford, it is said that he "was sorely beset" "by the court chaplains Father Saunders and another Dominican, to change his religion, and turn papist." Though they had been sent to him by James he was deaf to their solicitations. Now F. Francis Saunders the king's confessor was a Jesuit and not a Dominican.

the reverend Marianus Irvin abbot of the Scotch Benedictine monastery of St. James of Wurzburg. One portion of the relics sewn in a cloth was placed upon the head of the royal baby, the other by order of the nuncio Adda was exposed in the royal chapel for the veneration of the faithful. The child was immediately freed from the convulsions and never had them again. All this was told to the fathers by the duke of Perth chancellor of Scotland, who at the queen's desire engaged one of their missionaries to write the life of St. Macharius in English, which was accordingly done. In memory of so great a benefit, much good was promised in honour of the saint to their monastery, but all was lost by the revolution.

The birth of this heir to the throne was a source of great joy at Rome. On the occasion cardinal Howard gave a feast in which an ox roasted whole stuffed with lambs and fowls and provisions of all kinds stirred up the wonder and gladdened the hearts of the common people of the city.

The flight of James was the signal for riots and general uprisings against *popery.* The chapels and convents, and the houses of the leading Catholics in London and throughout the country were sacked and destroyed. Three of the vicars-apostolic were cast into prison, Dr. Leyburn in the tower, Dr. Giffard and Dr. Ellis in Newgate; Dr. Smith withdrew into concealment in a gentleman's country-house. But their blameless conduct which even their enemies could not impeach, secured their liberty and leave for them still to dwell in England. Dr. Leyburn and Dr. Giffard lived privately in London and died, the one in 1703, the other at Hammersmith in 1733. Dr. Smith died in 1711. Dr. Ellis joined his exiled king at St. Germain; thence he went to Rome where he formed a close friendship with cardinal Howard; in 1710 he was made bishop of Segni, and closed his life in 1726.

CHAPTER XIV.

The sorrow of cardinal Howard for the renewed affliction of the Church in England was one of delayed and not of destroyed hopes. He did not live to witness every chance fail that James would win his throne again, as he died within six years after the revolution. His direct intercourse with England was cut off; and all he could do for the English mission was, to return to the old state of things, and aid it by bringing up priests in the college at Rome, by forwarding the interests of the English Dominican province, and by receiving and bounteously assisting the English Catholics in exile who flocked around him and sought his aid or friendship. Within the last three weeks of his life he saw his cherished province placed on a better footing with the rest of the Order. The province was now strong enough to return to a more normal form of government as soon as political affairs would allow, by means of provincial chapters. It is true that the fathers being brought up chiefly for the mission could not go through the long and deep studies needed for the honorary degrees of the Order, and there was only one religious house of men, so that the province had no regular masters of theology, preachers-general, and priors to form a canonical assemblage for electing a provincial. But the difficulty was met by the general chapter held May 30th 1694 at Rome, which ordained that those English fathers whose labours made them deserving of honour might be decorated with the titles of masters or preachers, and of priors of the ancient desolated convents in England, and enjoy the privileges and powers of graduates and real priors. And at the same time the length of the provincialship was fixed at the regular standard of four years. Under these arrangements it was attempted to form a chapter for 1712, and the provincial created several titular priors. But owing to the perils of the times the fathers were afraid to meet together in England; and the master-general continued to select and appoint a provincial till the fathers in 1718 had leave to nominate three of their body out of whom the choice should be made. In 1730 the provincial chapters were begun again; and they have been carried on to the present time in a regular order every four years, broken only in 1746 when the last desperate effort of the Stuarts for the British throne made it dangerous for any reputed Jacobites to assemble. This was the last act in favour of his Order promoted by cardinal Howard. Like the restoration of the hierarchy in respect to the English Church, it placed the province on the lasting and normal footing on which it still remains.

Cardinal Howard assisted in three conclaves for electing sovereign pontiffs, when Innocent XI. September 21st 1676, Alexander VIII. October 6th 1689, and Innocent XII. July 12th 1691 were chosen to fill the chair of St. Peter. He went through all the duties of his high post with an uprightness of intention, earnestness of mind, and simplicity of manner that did honour to the dignity which honoured him. He never forgot that he was a Religious nor allowed ambition to carry him away. Greatness had been thrust on him without his having sought it, and he accepted it only when he believed it would help him on in the great aim of his life. He refused all other dignities that would have drawn him from his purpose and allured him from the path he had so long trodden. His great idea was, to restore the Dominican province of England as a means of forwarding the spiritual welfare of his country. It unfolded itself in his mind from the moment when he became a member of the Order; he took it up as soon as he was freed from the trammels of the noviciate, and spite of all difficulties and dangers carried it on for forty-five years with a singleness of purpose and an energy which shows it was the great work Providence had given him to do. He lived just to see his province restored lastingly and as fully as the circumstances of the age would permit. Then his task was over and he was called away to his everlasting reward, though many years of after-labours for the good of the Church seemed to be still in store for him. He fell into weak health, which in the spring of 1694 rapidly failed. On March 11th of that year, he thus wrote his last will, by faculty which Clement VIII. had granted to him July 8th 1676 to dispose of his property. He recommended his soul to the infinite mercy of God and to the intercession of the most holy Virgin Mary, St. Dominic, St. Thomas of Canterbury, St. Thomas Aquinas, St. Peter Martyr, St. Catherine of Sienna, and all his other holy advocates. He desired to be buried with as little pomp and at as little expense as possible in the church of the Minerva, with a small and very common stone over him and only his name upon it: and that two thousand low masses of requiem should be said for his soul. But in case he did not die in Rome he desired to be buried in the commonest fashion where his executors pleased; and in the same place if possible the masses were to be said. He desired that the 8000 Roman crowns lent him by his brother Henry late duke of Norfolk (who had begged it might be paid back for the good of his children by his second wife) should be given over to his nephew lord George Howard of Norfolk, the duke's eldest son by the same wife, to be duly shared among those children. He bequeathed to all who were his servants at the time of his death and to his physician Guidarelli a whole year's wages; to found in the Flemish Dominican convent at Bussels two places for the confessor of the English Dominican sisters and for the priest or lay-brother his companion 2000 crowns, and he desired that Brother Henry Packe* should be the companion;

* Brother Henry Packe was companion and steward of F.

to the convent of the same English nuns at Brussels 2000 crowns; to the convent of Flemish Ursuline nuns in Rome 500 crowns; to found for ever a chaplaincy of one daily mass in their church, the mass being for the convenience of the nuns but applied to his own soul, 1000 crowns; to the same nuns for the good of their convent all the vestments and everything else he had left in their keeping; to the Chiesa Nuova in Rome his four great candlesticks with the cross also in his chapel; to the convent of the Minerva one of his best white vestments; to his chamberlain sig. Giovanni Battista Novelli's first-born daughter, whose god-father he was, two of his largest candlesticks standing upon his dressing-table; and to the English bishop Mons. Ellis 100 Roman crowns. He besought his holiness to accept a picture of our Lady with the Child Jesus and St. Joseph and St. John Baptist painted by Raffaello. He left to cardinal Paluzzio Altieri the best of his English clocks; to cardinal Nerli, cardinal Mareschotti, and cardinal Spada, each another clock which they pleased: and he besought their eminences to compassionate his poverty and his confidence if he begged them to be his executors in case he died in Italy. And all the residue of his goods he gave to buy and found the college of St. Thomas Aquinas, of the Walloon Dominicans of Douay, to form a college for the English Dominicans. And in case that college could not be bought, or some other convenient place for that purpose in Louvain, Brussels, Antwerp, or elsewhere in the Low Countries, where it should seem good to the provincial of England, he willed it to be given to the convent of Bornhem, being himself a son though a most

---

Thomas Howard when grand-almoner, went with him to Rome, and served him while cardinal in the same office. After the cardinal's death, he became provincial procurator in England, and at last went to be the confessor's companion at Brussels, where he died December 26th 1716 in his 89th year.

unworthy one of our holy patriarch St. Dominic. And therefore he begged their eminences that the provincial of England might also be one of the executors of his will.

The health of the cardinal became still worse, and while he lay sick in bed June 9th he sent for a notary, gave him his will, and dictated a codicil. He now bequeathed to Mr. Charles Hill, to Mr. Francis Clayton, to Mr. Stephen Wagman, and to Mr. Peter Smitt 100 crowns a-piece: to Mr. Charles and Mr. John Dryden 50 crowns a-piece; to George Kell his cupboard of provision; and to the venerable college...[stables]...for one [year's]* rent of the said palace. To all the residue of his goods he made his universal heir the venerable religion of St. Dominic, of the province of England, and for that F. Thomas Bianchi [White] provincial, and after his death the other provincials succeeding him. And lastly he left to the bishop mons. Philip Michael Ellis the coach which used to serve his lordship, with the horses and harness.

Full of his good designs for the English province cardinal Howard died at Rome June 17th 1694 in the 64th year of his age, the 48th of his religious profession, the 42nd of his priesthood, and the 20th of his cardinalship. His tombstone records that his death took place "14 kal Julii" June 18th, and some authors have given the 16th. But the Bornhem mortuary rolls and all the records of the fathers of Bornhem and of the sisters of Brussels agree in dating the fatal event on the 17th, in which Jonghe, Touron, Guarnacci, and other most trust-worthy writers agree. The loss of him was much deplored, and by none with deeper sorrow than by the

* Here the copy of the will, which is written in Italian, must have a line or two by oversight left out. It seems to have been a bequest to the English college and connected with the cardinal's own palace. A different hand has interlined the words "stalla" and "anno."

Religious of Bornhem, who reverenced him as their Father, Founder, and Friend, and as a most exemplary and zealous prince of the Church. The master-general F. Antoninus Cloche addressed an encyclical letter to the whole Order (June 19th) in which he lamented his death and praised his great virtues; and the suffrages of all his brethren throughout the world went up to heaven, that the soul of the Cardinal of Norfolk might rest in peace.

In Mudie's 'English medals' is engraved a splendid one having on the obverse the cardinal's likeness with the legend,

PH. T. HOWARD S. R. E. CARD.
DE NORFOLKE TIT. S. M. S. M.

on the reverse, Hercules destroying the Hydra, and above, an eagle about to crown the conqueror, with the legend,

NE VICTA RESVRGANT.

Bromley in his catalogue gives the names of six engravers of the cardinal's portrait. Several engravings have fallen under our notice. One by H. Noblin consists of a good likeness nearly full face within a medallion, around which is inscribed,

PHILIPPVS ✠ HOWARD ✠ CARDINALIS ✠ DE
NORFOLK.

At the base, are his armorial bearings containing the eight principal quarterings of the Howard family and escutcheon of pretence: all surmounted with the cardinal's hat. Motto, VIRTVTIS LAVS ACTIO. The subscription

Offerebant Alumni
Anglo- duacensi

seems to show that the engraving was brought out by the students of Douay to commemorate the cardinal's visit to their college in 1675. At Norfolk house is a very curious folio print by Vesterhout 1688, depicting 'Cardinal Ovard de Norfolcia' giving to the people of Rome the roasted ox, out of which the lambs and fowls are seen peeping. Another engraving from the collection of Sheffield Grace is of no value as a likeness. It is by some nameless artist, and must have been published soon after the death of the cardinal. At the top, on the right the arms of Howard, on the left

PHILIPPVS THOMAS HOWARDVS
TIT. S. $M^{Æ}$ S^{A} MINERVA PRESBYT.
CARDINALIS DE NORFOLCIA OB. 1694.

There is a good engraving in Guarnacci's 'Historiæ Pontificum Romanorum et S. R. E. Cardinalium.' An admirable portrait in oil-colours formerly at Bornhem belongs to the English province and consists of a third length full-sized figure. It is by an unknown artist. Another large portrait was painted at Rome in 1687 by H. Tilson, and in 1808, was in the possession of F. Eyre esq.: from it was taken the engraving in the Catholic Directory of 1809. The earl of Carlisle possesses at Castle Howard another fine painting, full length, by Carlo Maratti. There is a fourth at Arundel castle the chief seat of the duke of Norfolk; a fifth-half-length portrait, with scarlet berretta, is at Greystock castle; and a sixth may be seen at the Minerva in Rome. The portrait by Du Chatel was engraved by J. Van der Bruggen: a copy of this fine likeness adorns our present work.

The body of cardinal Howard was buried in the choir of his titular church Santa Maria sopra Minerva. His tombstone bears this epitaph.

D. O. M.

Fr. Philippo Thomæ Howardo
De Norfolcia & Arundella
S. R. E. Presbytero Cardinali
Tituli Sanctæ Mariæ super Minervam
Ex Sacra Familia Fratrum Prædicatorum
S. Mariæ Majoris Archipresbytero
Magnæ Britanniæ Protectori
Magno Angliæ Eleemosynario
Patriæ, & Pauperum Patri
Filio Provinciæ Anglicanæ ejusdem Ordinis
Parenti, & Restauratori optimo
Hæredes inscripti mœrentes posuere
Annuentibus S. R. E. Cardinalibus Eminentiss.
Palutio de Alteriis
Francesco Nerlio
Galeatio Marescotto,
Fabritio Spada,
Supremi Testamenti executoribus,
Obiit XIV Kalendas Jul. Anno sal. MDCXIV.
Ætatis suæ LXIV.

CHAPTER XV.

In spite of its poverty the convent of Bornhem went on successfully after cardinal Howard left it in 1675. The prior F. Dominic Gwillim had the church dedicated September 13th 1676, the high altar in honour of the Holy Cross and to the most blessed Virgin of the Rosary, the little altar on the right to St. Dominic and St. Thomas Aquinas, and the little altar on the left to St. Catherine of Sienna and St. Rose of Lima. As the see of Ghent was then void the vicars-general of the diocese gave leave for Dr. Nicholas French bishop of Fernes in Ireland* to perform the ceremony; and he also ratified the benediction of the cloister given in 1661 by F. William Collins. The anniversary of the dedication was fixed for the third Sunday of September.

All the difficulties of founding the convent were now overcome. The clash of opinions as to the manner of organizing the house shown in the case of F. Vincent Torre had long vanished. Discipline had by degrees taken its right course; religious observance was fully established, and went on with a harmony which was never again disturbed. The perpetual abstinence and the long fasts of the Order were strictly kept, and the choral services were carried on with a regularity and a devotion that made the house a point of great attraction for piety particularly on the feasts of the Holy Cross, of the Most Holy Rosary, and of St. Dominic. After a time pilgrims flocked to it not only from the neighbourhood

* Dr. French was then living in exile at Ghent. Being a Dominican he spent much of his time at Bornhem. He was at the convent for six months a few weeks before his death, which took place August 23rd 1678.

but also from all Flanders. These pilgrimages were made to the relics of St. Amantius. That great martyr of Christ who was highly venerated in the early ages of the Church suffered about the year 133 under the emperor Adrian. His Acts tell us that he was beaten, cast into prison, and condemned to the flames, and that when the fire failed to do its work he was despatched by the blows of a club on the head. His brother's wife buried him in the sandpits on her estate at the thirteenth milestone from Rome along the Salarian way. His tomb was found in the catacombs hidden within those sandpits, and Innocent XI. gave the relics of the martyr to cardinal Howard. The bones were whole but disjointed, and the skull was deeply broken in; there was also the *ampulla* filled with blood and sand. These holy relics were sent in 1697 from the convent of SS. John and Paul to the English Dominican nuns of Brussels who kept them for thirteen years. The fathers of Bornhem September 26th 1710 translated them to their own convent. A new altar in honour of St. Amantius given by the count of Bornhem was put up in April 1713 in place of St. Catherine's. In June 1714 the saint's bones were with great pains set together and each joint secured with the bishop's seal. The skeleton was then placed in a magnificent shrine with crystal sides above his altar, and on the 17th the exaltation of the body of the holy martyr was celebrated with very great solemnity. His festival richly indulgenced was kept June 14th every year, and drew the devotion of the faithful till the French revolution desolated religion in Belgium.

The bequest of cardinal Howard for a college in Flanders was very serviceable to the convent of Bornhem. The Walloon convent at Douay could not be had, so the fathers bought a house at Louvain in Kraeke street, fitted it up, and opened it in 1697 as the college of St. Thomas Aquinas. It was governed by a rector with a staff of professors; and being incorporated with the university of Louvain, and recognized by the Order in the general chapters of 1706, 1721, and 1725, became the regular house of studies for the English province. After all the costs had been paid there was left from the cardinal's property a capital of 8,100 florins towards endowing the foundation.*

---

* The following lists contain all the provincials of the restored province down to 1834; and the priors of Bornhem, rectors of Louvain, and prioresses of Vilvorde and Brussels down to the French revolution.

F. Thomas Howard. Appointed prior December 15th 1657, November 20th 1660; and vicar-general of the province July 24th 1661. Continued in both offices till 1675.

F. William Collins. Installed prior August 23rd 1685.

F. Vincent Torre. Appointed vicar-general of province 1675; provincial about April 1685, and died in office August 24th 1687.

F. Edward Bing. Appointed provincial March 8th 1695.

F. Dominic Gwillim. Elected prior 1676 and 1679. Appointed provincial September 1687; died in office September 11th (*o. s.*) 1688.

F. Ambrose Thomas Grymes. Appointed provincial 1699 and 1704; and rector 1708. Installed prior May 23rd 1711.

F. Thomas White. Appointed provincial 1688; died in office November 19th 1694.

F. George Thomas Gibson. Governed the convent as vicar from 1682 to 1685, the vicar-general being the superior of Bornhem till August 1683.

F. John Ovington. Governed Bornhem as vicar-in-capite from 1688 to 1691 and then elected prior.

F. Raymund Greene. Elected prior 1694 and 1697. Appointed provincial 1716. Instituted rector June 9th 1736; died in office July 28th 1741.

F. William Barry an Irish Dominican. Installed prior October 10th 1700.

F. Dominic Williams. Instituted rector 1697, 1711, and twice

But while the fathers gained another house in Flanders they lost the one in Rome. In 1697 Innocent XII. took back the convent of SS. John and Paul into his own hands. Certainly this was not done for the sake of any other reli-

---

again. Appointed provincial February 28th 1712. While rector for the last time, elected prior, and installed May 18th 1724. Appointed provincial July 25th 1725. By pontifical brief of December 22nd following made bishop of Tiberiopolis a desolated see in the archbishopric of Hieropolis in Phrygia Magna: consecrated December 30th by Pope Benedict XIII. himself in the chapel of the apostolic palace; and by brief of June 7th 1726 made vicar-apostolic of the northern district of England.

F. Thomas Gibson. Elected prior May 23rd, installed June 11th 1714.

F. Gilbert Parker. Installed prior October 21st 1703, resigned February 1705.

F. Thomas Worthington. Installed prior March 10th 1705; elected again March 12th and installed March 15th 1708. Appointed provincial April following, took office May 2nd. Installed prior January 25th 1718, March 14th 1721, and October 15th 1725, but February 15th 1726 appointed provincial. Elected provincial May 10th 1742: prior 1750, but excused on account of age: and provincial September 26th in the same year; died in office February 25th 1754.

F. Albert Lovett. Elected provincial April 24th 1738.

F. Alan Pennington. Installed prior May 13th 1708, and February 21st 1726, dying in office March 31st 1728.

F. Joseph Hansbie. Appointed provincial 1721. Installed prior September 2nd 1728 and October 13th 1731. Elected provincial May 4th 1734; and being appointed again about June 1747 died in office June 5th (*o. s.*) 1750.

F. Antoninus Thompson. Appointed rector 1754 and 1758; died in office November 7th 1760.

F. Ambrose Burgis. Rector from 1715 to 1720, and from 1724 to 1730. Elected provincial April 20th 1730. Installed prior

gious body, for it was very long before the house was inhabited again. No reason was given for it being taken away, and as the community was never charged with any fault the fathers of Bornhem always thought that the loss

---

April 4th 1741. Appointed vicar-general of the province in 1746; died in office April 27th 1747.

F. Andrew Wynter. Appointed rector March 1734. Installed prior January 3rd 1735 and March 7th 1738. Rector again about 1743. Appointed vicar-general of the province about May 1747.

F. Pius Bruce. Elected prior February 1757.

F. Dominic Darbyshire. Installed prior October 1st 1747, resigned May 11th 1750. Elected prior again but died January 7th 1757 before he started from England.

F. John Clarkson. Elected prior in 1753. Appointed vicar-general of the province about July 1750 and in March 1754, only for a few months each time. Elected provincial April 17th 1758.

F. Stephen Catterell. Elected provincial May 5th 1762, died in office December 25th 1765.

F. Antoninus Hatton. Elected provincial May 21st 1754 and May 7th 1770.

F. Vincent Teasdale. Installed prior October 28th 1750. Rector from about September 1757 to the following March. Elected prior in 1760 and in July 1763. Rector again from October 1780 to June 1782.

F. James Barbour. Installed prior April 20th 1744.

F. Benedict Short. Elected provincial April 25th 1766, May 12th 1778, May 10th 1786, and May 13th 1794.

F. Ambrose Gage. Elected prior December 18th 1770. Appointed rector December 1773, but resigned in a few months.

F. Joseph Edwards. Rector from about 1754 to April 25th 1774 when he was elected provincial. Elected prior in 1781, but died suddenly in England September 4th before he could take office.

F. John Kearton. Elected prior June 3rd 1778. Instituted rector June 1782, ceased June 1793.

was owing to the poverty of the foundation and the small number of the Religious. But there are good grounds for supposing that F. Dominic Williams who was at the convent in 1697 had the chief hand in the business. He was

---

F. Thomas Norton. Elected prior in 1767 and 1774. Appointed rector February 1775; resigned about September 1780.

F. Hyacinth Houghton. Installed prior February 1775.

F. Albert Underhill. Rector from 1771 to 1774.

F. Peter Robson. Elected provincial April 22nd 1782.

F. Lewis Brittain. Elected provincial May 3rd 1814.

F. Raymund Bullock. Elected prior 1781, and according to the imperial edict June 1782 for four years. Elected provincial April 26th 1790 and May 1st 1798.

F. Anthony Underhill. Elected prior July 1792: provincial May 11th 1802.

F. Charles Bullock. Elected prior June 1786. Appointed rector about June 1793, died in office June 12th 1794.

F. Francis Xavier Chappell. Elected provincial May 14th 1810.

F. Pius Potier. Elected provincial April 13th 1806 and April 13th 1808.

F. Ambrose Woods. Elected provincial April 30th 1822; appointed vicar-general of the province for four years May 17th 1826; elected provincial again May 4th 1830.

PRIORESSES.

Sister Lewisa de Hertoghe a Dutch Religious, appointed 1661. Sister Barbara Boyle, appointed 1667 and continued till 1697; elected 1700, 1706. Sister Dorothy Canning, elected 1703; Sister Mary Crofts, 1697; Sister Ann Busby, 1709; Sister Catherine Mildmay, 1715; Sister Letitia Barker, 1727; Sister Julia Browne an Irish Religious, 1730; Sister Agnes Atmore, 1712, 1718, 1724; Sister Mary Ann Chilton, August 1733, 1736; Sister Mary Rose Howard, June 21st 1721; Sister Mary Teresa Sarsfield, October 1739, died in office February 22nd 1740; Sister Margaret Joseph

appointed first rector of the college at Louvain, and might have thought it best to gather all the studies into one house. The fathers deeply lamented this loss and tried to repair it. When they sent a proctor to the Roman court in 1718 he was to petition that the convent might be restored or an equivalent given either to Bornhem or Louvain for what cardinal Howard had laid out in repairs, as there were more novices and students than the two houses in Belgium could well hold or provide for: or at least a yearly pension might be given as was often done for other missionaries in England. But the master-general did not think it was a fit time to make such an application. After a Dominican had been called to the chair of St. Peter as Benedict XIII. the fathers reckoned that the good time had come, and in August 1724 sent F. Dominic Williams to Rome directing him to explain their right to the convent, what cardinal Howard had done for it, and that out of the six Religious who had belonged to it, four were still alive and had to be supported by the English province. F. Dominic had an audience on the matter with the pope, who reminded him that he had been the cause of the surrender, and the application was unsuccessful.

The convent of Bornhem owed its great success mainly to the college which was begun November 12th 1703 in connection with it. The most talented of the fathers were chosen professors in every branch of humanities. This college became one of the most flourishing Catholic secular schools

---

Compton, March 21st 1743, 1752, 1764; Sister Mary Young, February 1740; Sister Ann Mary Short, March 24th 1746, 1749, April 13th 1755, April 1758, 1761, 1767; Sister Mary Agnes Short, 1770, 1773, 1776; Sister Mary Ann Calvert, 1786; Sister Ann Dominica Brooke, 1783, 1789; Sister Mary Hyacinth Wilkinson, 1780; Sister Mary Louisa Allgood, December 8th 1792.

on the continent, and was open both to English and Dutch youths. It was the great means of furnishing Religious to the province. In 1769 the old convent was pulled down and a much larger one built, for after the Netherlands had passed in 1714 from the thraldom of Spain to Austria the condition of the royal grant limiting the number of Religious was relaxed. In 1773 a new college was begun, the first stone of which was laid September 14th, to contain from 100 to 150 scholars. The new buildings formed the three sides of a square, the fourth side being formed by the old church which with the sacristy was not rebuilt, and so far the design was not carried out, though it would have been had it not been for the French revolution. So great was the fame of the college that when the Society of Jesus was put down, the Austrian government in 1773 chose the Dominican fathers to take the place of the Jesuits in the greater and lesser English colleges at Bruges, and September 30th the prime minister ordered the prior of Bornhem to confer with the secretary of state on the subject. But the fathers did not think it prudent to sacrifice their own for other establishments.

The community of the English Dominican sisters at Brussels flourished till the French revolution. In time the buildings of the Spellekens became very much decayed, and about 1777 were ready to fall, so the sisters built a handsome new house and church in the upper part of their garden. When the emperor Joseph II. set himself up for a church reformer, and by an imperial edict in 1782 threatened to put down all houses of nuns not given up to an active life the sisters fitted up a school and thus remained undisturbed. Notices of the very holy lives of some of them are still preserved, particularly of Sister Frances Peck who died July 14th 1680, and of Sister Christina Touchet only child of the Hon. James Touchet baron Audley and earl of Castlehaven by his second wife Catherine Stanford of the family of Stanford of Perry-hall near Birmingham. Susanna Touchet was born in

London August 16th 1655 and was professed February 28th 1677: the following epitaph for her was copied if not composed by F. Raymund Greene.

"Bene pinxit sed melius vixit æternitati
Divi Dominici Religiosa Filia,
Soror Christina Touchet de Castlehaven,
Sanguine, Forma, Sanctitate, clarissima Virgo.
Bruxellis Vivere et Pati desijt, non Amari,
Die 19 Novemb. 1694, Ætat: An: 39."

The missionary work of the fathers was carried on very zealously and successfully in England. At first they were chiefly chaplains in the households of the foreign ambassadors and in the families of some of the principal Catholic nobility and gentry of the country. Then they became pastors of small congregations and ministered in their humble houses to the chosen few,* whilst they were generally known only as agriculturists or retired officers or gentlemen. But as soon as the penal system became relaxed, when the American war forced the government to make friends with Ireland or risk its dismemberment, the fathers built small chapels and performed their ministry more openly. In London they served the Spanish, Portuguese, Austrian, Sardinian, Venetian, and

* Among the papers of the mission at Aston-Flamvile about 1748 is a small but interesting memorial of the persecution, which brought back into England the early ages of the church when it was dangerous to let an unknown person into the secret assemblies of the faithful lest he should be a spy and informer. It is the form for certifying that a person might be admitted safely to the sacraments and to the devotions of Catholics, and runs thus: "Ego Infrascriptus Fidem facio N. Catholicum esse, et tutò ad Sacramenta et cæteras Catholicorum devotiones admitti posse: in cujus rei fidem has manu propriâ subscriptas dedi, —— mensis ——, anni ——."

Neapolitan embassies. Connected with the Sardinian chapel they had a house in Duke street, which they made into a *quasi*-convent. One of the Dominicans there was F. Patrick Bradley who changed his affiliation from the Irish to the English province as was declared in the provincial chapter of 1750. Benedict XIV. made him bishop of Derry, and he was consecrated March 3rd 1751 in this chapel; but he found the bishopric too burdensome in those hard times, resigned in the following year, and taking up his old quarters in London closed his life March 22nd 1760 in his 56th year, a little more than three months after the chapel (December 1st) had been unfortunately destroyed by fire. Some of the families in which the fathers were chaplains founded and endowed regular missions, as Widdrington at Stonecroft in Northumberland; Martin at Long-Melford in Suffolk; Brandling at Middleton lodge near Leeds; Tourvile at Aston-Flamvile in Leicestershire; and Southcote at Woburn near Chertsey. Out of these many other missions soon sprang, and among them, Hexham, Leeds, Hinckley, Leicester, and Weybridge.

The devotion of the most Holy Rosary of our Lady was cultivated with peculiar care. By special orders of each provincial chapter the fathers on the mission were strictly bound to encourage and spread it by every means within their power, and one or two of them wrote popular works on the subject. The Arch-confraternity of the Rosary was spread all over England, the convent of Bornhem being the head-quarters, and the Perpetual Rosary formed a guard of honour which hour by hour watched around the throne of the blessed Virgin. It is interesting to find in the old lists of these associations the names of the noble and chief families of England still distinguished for their steadfastness in the faith.

The French revolution checked in the heyday of its success the work which cardinal Howard had so happily begun, and destroyed the houses he founded in Belgium. Towards the end of 1792 the French army extended the dominions of the Republic from the Alps to the Rhine and from Geneva to the mouth of the Scheldt. Early in November general Dumourier entered Austrian Flanders, and on the 6th his victory over the Austrians at Jemmapes secured the conquest of Belgium. The general entered Brussels on the 14th, Ghent and Antwerp soon yielded to him.

The success of France troubled and dismayed the fathers at Bornhem and the nuns of Brussels. When the enemy were advancing on Brussels the nuns at the repeated and urgent advice of their friends secreted all their most valuable goods in the house of a neighbour and used the commonest articles for the altar. Late one evening after the French had entered the city some soldiers were billeted on them for three or four days. While these rude guests were in the house an English gentleman named Martin kindly saw to the safety of the buildings and went round regularly every night to see that the soldiers' lights were properly put out.* On Wednesday March 6th 1793 about half past three o'clock in the afternoon, a band of soldiers demanded to be let into the convent. They applied first to the nuns' director F. Lewis Brittain, and when he refused they became so much enraged and pointed their bayonets at him so threateningly that he fled affrighted. They then went to the convent-door, rang the bell, and ordered the portress to open the enclosure-door. The poor lay-sister not understanding their language could only answer, "Oui, oui," and ran off to the prioress. While she was away the impatient soldiers broke down the staves of the turn and entered. An officer called for the prioress, but when in her great alarm she did not immediately make her appearance the men scattered themselves over the house in search of

* The account of the sufferings of the nuns has been given in the "Rambler" for 1851. Our narrative contains many additions and corrections.

plunder. They first ransacked the cells of the nuns but found no booty. In the church two or three of the officers entered the sanctuary. One of them opened the tabernacle and took out the Blessed Sacrament; and when the gardener who was also sacristan tried to rescue the ciborium from him, in order to carry it to two nuns who were waiting at the grate to receive it into a corporal, he ordered the man off, saying that he had no more right than himself to touch the sacred vessel. The officer then called for a purificatory, uncovered his head, poured out the Host into the corporal, and most carefully wiped out the ciborium, which he then struck with the key of the tabernacle, and crying out, "Now it is profaned," threw it down upon the ground. Thereupon the soldiers set up an infernal yell and seized the spoil. From the sacristy they took the church plate consisting only of a chalice, paten, pair of silver candlesticks, and silver cruets. From the refectory they pillaged the tea, sugar, chocolate, and such articles, which they partly eat on the spot and partly carried off in their pockets. F. Lewis Brittain's apartments enriched them with a single silver spoon, which one of them stuck in the front of his cap. From the choir they took the nuns' veils and mantles, to make as they said cravats and waistcoats. The behaviour of the soldiers towards the nuns personally was not wanting in respect. When they had gathered up their booty they met together and an officer read aloud a paper, which he said was the warrant for what they had done. All then decamped to the great relief of the nuns. Next day these soldiers hearing that the Austrians were close on Brussels nimbly beat the hoof leaving the plunder behind. The nuns claimed their property again; F. Lewis Brittain recovered all the church plate in a sadly battered condition.

The fathers of Bornhem too were for many weeks in constant alarm. On Sunday evening February 17th 1793 a commissaire of the French executive power at the head of twenty-five men entered the convent, and next day took an inventory of everything in the house and placed the French national seal on the procurator's office. They stayed for three or four days and lived at the cost of the community. Bornhem was saved from such another visit by its distance from any head-quarters of the French army. That part of the country fell into the charge of general Eustace an American. In a singular letter to the prior dated March 26th he boasted that he had protected the country, so that not one altar or family had been polluted or disturbed. But at the same time he owned that the conduct of the French troops had been truly infamous, and that the numberless vexations the people had received from his fellow-officers and soldiers *almost* justified their indiscriminate aversion for every individual who wore the French uniform.

A short success of Austria over France seemed to promise peace. The French were defeated March 18th in the battle of Neerwinden and were forced by degrees to withdraw. On the 25th F. Pius Potier broke the French seals and entered again on his office of procurator. In the general contributions for defending the country the fathers July 5th made a "free gift" of sixty-one florins and 13½ oz. of old silver to the emperor of Austria.

But an ebb in the tide of fortune spread another general alarm. In the spring of 1794 the conquering and angry armies of France again attacked the Netherlands. On Sunday May 4th they were at Rousselaere, six leagues from Bruges. This created great terror: two-thirds of those who had any property ran out of Bruges into Holland, into villages on the borders, or into Ghent, while in the confusion many from Ghent sought safety in Bruges. The week before, the English nuns of Bruges began their flight towards their native country and were speedily followed by other English communities. After besieging Ypres and Oudenarde, the Republicans passed within a few miles of Brussels to Charleroi. Brussels was panic-stricken. The Dominican nuns yielded unwillingly to the pressing entreaties of their friends to make ready to fly at any time. From Charleroi the French turned towards Brussels. On Saturday evening June 21st F. Lewis Brittain told the nuns that no time was to be lost for they must quit the city without delay. All the night was spent in packing up and securing their goods. F. Lewis Brittain was so agitated that on the following day he could not celebrate, and the nuns were indebted to a Dutch Dominican for their Sunday Mass at a very early hour. The rush of inhabitants out of the city made it almost impossible to find conveyances; two carts at last were hired at a very high price, and were given up to the sick and aged and for the goods. One of the Religious, Sister Mary Joseph Hunt lay in the last stage of pulmonary consumption, but she could not be left behind and was placed in a cart with all care. The food which had been got ready for the journey and a vast quantity of luggage could not be taken away and was lost.

The nuns determined to seek shelter at Bornhem till either they could return home or were forced to go on in their flight. At length the sorrowful moment of departing came. Several of the nuns had been hardly prevailed on to change their habits for secular clothing, some of them now refused to cross the threshold of their sanctuary and were forcibly carried out in the arms of others. All but the aged and sick had to walk, and a wearisome march they had with their unpractised feet for twenty miles under a burning sun and ankle-deep in hot sand. The two carts reached Bornhem in the afternoon, F. Lewis Brittain and his companions completely exhausted did not arrive before eleven o'clock at night. The nuns were Sisters Mary Ann Calvert, Ann Dominica Brooke, Louisa Allgood prioress, Mary Joseph Hunt, Margaret Joseph Smith, Mary Magdalen Bastow, Mary Rose Stowers, Catherine Teresa Dantan, Mary Teresa Leadbitter, and Rosalia Bourdon and Emilie Cloppes, two French Dominicanesses of Metz, who had taken refuge at Brussels, choir-sisters: Jerome Kitchen and Catherine Leroi, lay-sisters; and also Mary Stennet a choir-postulant.

Amidst the frequent alarms the fathers of Bornhem did not cease to hope that some good turn of fortune would once more favour the Austrian arms. But when the fugitive nuns arrived from Brussels and threw themselves on their protection, it was plain that no time must be lost, for the only chance of safety lay in following the example of the other English religious Orders in Belgium and seeking safety in England. It was thought best to leave some on the spot for the sake of watching events and guarding if possible the house and property. Those who were chosen for this dangerous duty were F. Dominic Fenwick an American, Brother Hyacinth Haime not then ordained, and three native lay-brothers. The Religious who had to leave were FF. Vincent Patient, Augustine Noel, Lewis Brittain, Anthony Underhill prior, Bernard Smith, Hyacinth Brown, Vincent Bowyer, Peter Potier, Benedict Atkinson, John Fenwick, Joseph Smith, Thomas Wilson, Antoninus Angier sub-prior, Ambrose Woods, and Raymund Tuite, and Brother Thomas Dias Santos: also two foreign Dominicans, FF. Benedict Caestryck and Hyacinth Lefebvre, and an English Carthusian who had lived in seclusion at Bornhem since 1783 when the emperor Joseph II. suppressed his convent at Nieuport.

On Monday, Tuesday, and Wednesday affairs were arranged as rapidly as possible, and the most valuable goods secured or packed to be carried away. The relics of St. Amantius were taken out of their costly shrine, placed in a box, and hidden in a neighbouring house: the ampulla of his blood was brought into England, and is now carefully kept, though it has been deprived of its sacred contents by the over-care of a sacristan whose ideas of cleanliness were greater than his antiquarian knowledge. The fathers carried with them their other holy relics, and particularly the venerable Cross which had so long hallowed their convent-home, and now became to them an earnest of their trials and a pledge of their success. The fathers had to provide themselves with what secular clothes they could get and with wigs to hide their tonsures; sorry figures most of them cut in their ill-assorted and ill-fitting attires. Two vessels were engaged for 634 florins to convey the whole party to Rotterdam, waggons also being hired for the nuns and baggage down to Scheldt. On Wednesday evening June 25th the flight began. F. Ambrose Woods mounted the first waggon armed with an old musket, and F. Pius Potier followed on the other with a double-barreled gun, all *in terrorem*, for the feat of firing would have been more perilous to the equilibrium of the trigger pullers than to the lives of the enemy. The other Religious hastened on foot to the vessels and all safely embarked, the fathers in one boat and the nuns in the other. They made their way down the Scheldt to Antwerp which they reached next day. There they were delayed some time, and the nuns had to undergo many privations, as the advantage was taken to make them pay exorbitantly for what they needed. For one night they had to sleep on bare mattresses laid on brick floors. Taking in a supply of food the fugitives continued their flight on the 27th in the evening, as it was thought safest to avoid the bustle of the day. The nuns had a happy escape. One night heavy clouds completely covered the heavens, and the intense darkness was made only more painful by frequent flashes of lightning. Two of the sisters more wakeful than the rest noticed an unusual motion in the boat and gave the alarm. It was found that a large leak had been sprung, which kept the sailors in constant labour at the pump till on the evening of Tuesday July 1st they reached Rotterdam.

At Rotterdam the fugitives met with many trials. They had much trouble and delay at the custom-house, and Sister Mary Joseph Hunt was so ill that it was very doubtful if she could reach England alive. The poor nuns knew not whither to turn, but after consulting together a long time they made up their minds to push on for England. No vessel could be found. At last the fathers fell in with an Americal captain who wanted ballast after discharging his cargo; and he agreed to carry the whole party to England for £100. This offer was gladly taken, though the wretchedly small vessel had no conveniences for passengers. On Wednesday July 9th the fathers and nuns embarked. Of his own will the captain gave up his cabin to Sister Mary Joseph, but at the end of the voyage he charged six guineas extra for it. They had to look about them well and sail not in the open sea for fear of ships of war, nor too close to the shore lest they should fall in with the press-gangs. They were fired on many times by vessels passing them to make them show colours, and once one of the nuns by hoisting the British flag stopped a regular attack, when the captain through carelessness or oversight did not answer the signal. On their passage F. Benedict Caestryck cheered the nuns with his clarionet and F. Pius Potier with his flute. As they drew nigh to England a most serious alarm was raised by the appearance of a French man-of-war. The captain made up his mind that if he was chased, rather than be taken he would run his ship aground and take to the boat. But by the goodness of Providence the French did not notice the little craft, which they might have looked on as a common fishing-smack. All the Religious arrived safely in the Thames on Wednesday July 16th after twenty-five days of peril, hardship, and fatigue. The provincial had heard of their flight and went three times from Woburn near Chertsey, to London to meet them, and at length all his fears for them were over when he welcomed them to England. He had already provided for their accommodation. The fathers were kindly received into the houses of several Catholics in London, and the nuns had lodgings at three guineas a-week in a house in Seymour-street Portman-square, where August 10th Sister Mary Joseph Hunt died,

Events showed how wisely the Religious had acted in

leaving Belgium. A furious battle took place June 26th at Fleurus between the French and the allied armies of Austria and England, which lasted from morning till late in the afternoon. The allies were defeated with a loss of twenty thousand men and retreated to Halle about thirty miles from the battle-field and nine from Brussels. The French pushed on and made their enemies decamp in all haste from Halle and leave Brussels to its fate, and thither the conquerors marched without delay.

The French entered Brussels July 10th and immediately levied contributions, two thousand livres being laid on the nuns' convent, which their agent paid. In August the building was seized and made into a washhouse for the hospitals, but as there was not enough water there in the winter it was changed into an *entre-pôt* for the foul linen of the soldiers. The gardener went on cultivating the ground for the directors of the hospital till they let the garden for six months. But in June 1795 the house was made into a magazine of clothing for the army, where shoemakers and tailors daily plied their trades. The goods of the nuns and the library of F. Lewis Brittain were nearly all lost, being partly sold to pay the contributions for the army and partly carried off by some of the nuns' servants, and so scattered that they could not be traced. The greater part of the large moveables was placed in the care of a tenant; and the misery which his family underwent in the first winter after the French seized Brussels in the words of the agent "les a fait oublier leur ancienne honnêteté." The nuns' capitals invested abroad amounting to £12,000 were seized by the government.

After Brussels the French began to take the other towns of Belgium. On July 17th they entered Louvain. There were in the college of St. Thomas only three fathers and one lay-brother. Two of the fathers fled into England, the others remained till the college was confiscated, and both within two or three years died there.

The five Religious and the scholars at Bornhem awaited the issue of events in the utmost anxiety, and their suspense was very short. The trumpet soon spread the alarm that the enemy was advancing on the village, and summoned the inhabitants to drive back the invaders. The French were met with a vigorous onset. The struggle too unequal to be kept up long only served to check for a moment and to enrage soldiers whom the prestige of success had worked up to enthusiasm. The fighting men of Bornhem were routed and driven from the field. The French general was wounded in the knee, and was so maddened by the stubborn and brave resistance that he gave up Bornhem to pillage and to the flames. His soldiers afterwards said that they got more booty out of the village than out of many a town. The general mistaking the convent for the chateau of count Marnix then baron of Bornhem commanded his men to set it on fire. Br. Hyacinth Haime saved it. While the soldiers were obeying their orders he hastily gathered together the scholars, went at their head to the general and told him that the house was a school. The general regretted his mistake, but feared it was too late to do anything, as the flames had already reached the roof of the building. Brother Hyacinth said he thought the fire might still be put out and begged leave to attempt it. The general was appeased by a few boyish words of hearty kindness from one of the scholars, who expressed great sympathy for him on account of the wound he had received. No time was lost and with immense exertions the fire was got under. But the convent was sacked and a great deal of the property destroyed. One of the lay-brothers was lucky in saving a little money by laying it on the top of a window-frame. F. Dominic Fenwick was led off a prisoner, the other Religious and scholars had to secure their safety by hiding themselves. The prudence of the fathers in leaving F. Dominic at Bornhem was now seen: he claimed the sympathy of the French as an American citizen, and was soon set free. Still he had some very narrow escapes of his life amid the brutal republican soldiery. Afterwards he and the English of the house found safety in England. The convent was now deserted. As all communication between England and Belgium was cut off it was many months before the fathers learned the fate of their continental houses.

After the French had established their government and peace was outwardly restored some of the fathers in 1795 returned to Bornhem, but durst not openly settle themselves again in the convent. In 1796 the possessions of all religious bodies in Belgium were declared national property and the sale of them was decreed. A commissaire sent to Bornhem valued the property at 24806 livres: it so happened that five pieces of the best land escaped the man's notice and were not sequestrated. As a compensation the directoire executif offered the fathers the amount in *bons*, and although those notes were available only for government purposes and their value was very precarious the fathers took them as they were better than nothing.

The property was brought to auction in April and August 1797, and the whole was sold to a perfumer of Antwerp for 13,894 livres more than the government valuation. This perfumer was the agent of the English fathers, and so the convent of Bornhem returned to the rightful owners. The government was paid with its own *bons* with an additional sum of about £700.

As soon as the fathers had the house back they formed a small community there and opened the college again. The constitutional oath was tendered to them which they refused, but a trifling bribe offered in the most barefaced manner got over the difficulty. The meanest scoundrels stood at the head of affairs; some whom the fathers had known in the lowest circumstances had thrust themselves by unscrupulous conduct into public notice and held great preferments. All the public functions of religion were stopped throughout the country and the churches closed; but the people assembled for their prayers in the churchyards. The college was for some time the only large house of Christian education left in that part of the country, so that the fathers might have had what number of scholars and what pensions they pleased.

The house at Bornhem never could be again revived as a convent. In 1804 and 1805 four fathers went to the United States and founded the Dominican province of St. Joseph, among whom was F. Dominic Fenwick, who was afterwards first bishop of Cincinnati. Other schools were opened in the country, and English youths could now have a good education without going abroad. The college became burdened with debts owing greatly to the heavy contributions levied by the government. The college dwindled, being at last occupied only by Dutch boys of no good rank in society and more famous for games and beer-drinking than for learning and obedience. Many great but ineffectual efforts were made to put it on a better footing.

The convent at Brussels was sold by the government. The college at Louvain was only leased out; and June 4th 1818 it was restored to the fathers. The house had fallen into a ruinous state; they almost rebuilt it and let it as a private dwelling.

At last the fathers resolved to get rid of all their Belgian property. In 1825 the college of Bornhem was sold. The unconfiscated lands were also disposed of for a low sum, on condition that the full value should be paid if the possession could be secured; but the government scented the matter, and the purchaser had to pay an *amende* to the wounded honour of the public purse. The convent of Bornhem happily passed to the monks of St. Bernard.

The house formerly the college in Louvain could not be sold on account of the title-deeds having been lost. The fathers determined to keep it in their own hands. Again the government pounced down on the property in 1827, and sold it. But with the price of it, two burses were founded in the university of Louvain, in favour of English students. The provincial in 1839 petitioned that English Dominicans might be preferred before others; and as the request was too just to be refused the English province now enjoys those burses.

Thus the houses which cardinal Howard founded in Belgium were destroyed. But the work which he set on foot, though for a long time it was grievously checked, did not fall with them. His spirit still lived in the English province. The nuns found generous friends in Catherine and Jane daughters of John Berkeley, Esq., of Hindlip, Worcestershire, who were afterwards married, one to Robert Canning, Esq., the other to Thomas Anthony third Viscount Southwell. These ladies established them in a house at Hartpury-court near Gloucester, whither they removed from London August 28th, 29th 1794 six weeks after they came into England. The nuns opened a ladies' school, which they gave up in 1832 so that they might keep still closer to their institute in lives of pure contemplation. They removed in September 1839 to Atherstone in Warwickshire; thence in June 1858 to Hurst-green near Whalley in Lancashire, and the brightest days are now dawning on them, in the Isle of Wight.

The fathers within three months after they left Bornhem in 1794 took a mansion at Carshalton near Croydon in Surrey. There they opened a large college, and in 1806 erected a noviciate. Both the school and the noviciate failed; financial difficulties arose from the loss of nearly £7000. on the foundation, the college was given up in 1810, and in the following year the fathers quitted the house altogether. This misfortune and the gloomy prospect of affairs so much disheartened them, that they would have broken up the province in the chapter of 1810, if one of them had not most strongly opposed it and awakened a faint hope for the future. Hinckley was made the head-quarters of the province in 1814 and the noviciate removed to it. A large house was built there in 1823, and a seminary for a limited number of scholars established which had the best success.

In 1832 there were only three of the fathers of Bornhem still alive, besides the two foreign Dominicans who in 1794 had fled into England. Since 1817 six had joined the province at Hinckley, but two of them had died. Thus the province consisted of nine members, five of whom were so aged that they were not equal to the toils of missionary duties. In order to keep up the province, it was needful to centre its remaining strength in the head-house at Hinckley, by giving up to the secular clergy the missions served by the fathers in distant parts of England. Hexham had been surrendered in 1830; Leeds followed in 1833, and Weybridge in 1834; so that the Dominicans kept only Hinckley, Leicester, and Hartpury or Atherstone. Between 1832 and 1851 four joined the order, but the loss of seven brought the whole number down to six. The province was in a state very like what it was in when F. Thomas Howard set about to found his first convent. And again came the words, "renovabitur ut aquilæ juventus tua."

Such was the life of Cardinal Howard, such were his works, and such have been the results of his works. "Omne opus electum justificabitur: et qui operatur illud, honorabitur in illo." *Ecclus.* xiv. 21.

Finis.

PRINTED BY RICHARDSON AND SON, DERBY.

www.ingramcontent.com/pod-product-compliance
Lightning Source LLC
Chambersburg PA
CBHW020356030726
47496CB00007B/2170
* 9 7 8 3 7 4 4 6 5 7 3 3 4 *